F.D. FAIR

Foundations Book Publishing
4209 Lakeland Drive, #398, Flowood, MS 39232
www.FoundationsBooks.net

A Hunter's Heart
Book 5
The Westwood Pack

ISBN: 978-1-64583-113-6

Book Formatting by Bella Roccaforte

Published in the United States of America

Chapter One

Drake

"Sorry to interrupt," I say walking toward Alaric, the alpha of the Westwood pack as he stands with his group.

"Drake. Good, you're here. We need to talk," he says, striding forward and clasping my hand in greeting.

"Actually, I came to ask for your help," I reply, unable to keep the anxiety off my face. This isn't exactly easy for me. But it needs to be done, for my coven.

"Help? What happened?" Phoebe, his phoenix mate, asks as she steps toward me, bringing along a woman who looks similar except for the contrasting features. I didn't know what brought the hunters back now, after so long, but if she is who I think she is, then I no longer need to wonder. The presence of a second phoenix would be like a beacon for them, wanting to capture her instead of being fearful like they should be.

"Well, we were looking into some strange newcomers over the past couple of days, trying to figure out what they want, when we stumbled across a group of mages and hunters just outside of town. They're a pretty large group. I'm assuming the mages, after seeing another phoenix, are here for you, Phoebe," I say, gesturing toward both Phoebe and the woman standing with her, "but the hunters have taken notice of our coven, as well. We've already had three disappearances in the last two nights."

Almost everyone looks completely shocked. Except for Phoebe, who just asks, "What's the big deal about the hunters?" A small growl slips through my lips, wondering how any supernatural wouldn't know what a hunter is.

Skarlyt, Alaric's best friend and High Priestess-in-waiting for the witches, shakes her head as she steps up. "I know what you're thinking, but not only was Phoebe not raised a supernatural—thus not knowing anything about hunters or what they do, but these hunters are different," she says looking directly at me before turning to Phoebe. "Hunters are a group of humans who have made it their mission to get rid of anyone who is supernatural. Most are simply brainwashed into thinking that we are all evil, but there are some that know what they are doing is misguided yet do it anyway."

"What? How can they do that?" Phoebe asks.

"Like Skarlyt said, most of them are brainwashed or conditioned from birth to believe that any race other than humans is evil. They believe that we go around killing humans, and from their skewed perception, they're protecting humans by getting rid of us," Trevan, a high-born Fae who lives in this world, answers, receiving a round of nods in agreement. At noticing his presence, it makes me wonder why he's here with this group. I know they're all friends, but I didn't expect to see him here; he normally stays clear of any issues, preferring to remain neutral. I don't have to wonder for long as he pulls a beautiful dark-skinned woman to his side. Her eyes flash a little gold telling me exactly what she is: Mountain Lion. And if I had to guess, an extremely strong one.

"So, what were you hoping for our help with? Obviously, with the mages here for us, we won't be able to do much," Alaric says, going back to the issue at hand. That's one of the reasons I respect him so much: he doesn't beat around the bush, never scared to be direct.

"I was hoping our women and children could stay in your bunker until this blows over. We've been fortunate that the only ones who have gone missing are fully grown adults, but we're all terrified that one of our young could be taken and killed, or worse, experimented on. We can't let that happen." Looks of sympathy cross his face as he's obviously thinking of my sister, Drusilla. I clear my throat and continue, "I know it's not the best time right now with this newest threat you're facing, but we have no one else to turn to, short of fleeing the area." I'm trying not to beg, but at this point, I would like to have a plan in place before I have to tell my sister about everything that's been happening.

Alaric and Phoebe share a look. "Of course, they can. There should be more than enough room down there for all of you." I let out a relieved exhale at his words.

"We're already packed up. We have a refrigerated trailer loaded with enough blood to last us a week, so we don't need to leave. While we're here, we'll help you with the mages if we can," I tell him. I'm extremely thankful that I corrected my mistake siding with those mages last time. Given the chance, they would have left us to be picked off one by one before they turned on us themselves. Sure, we would've taken down a few, but not one of the men in my coven are comfortable leaving their families unprotected while they fight. Me included.

"What were you going to do if we said *no*?" Phoebe asks.

"We didn't get that far. We had hope that you would say *yes*." I answer. The truth is: this was our only option. It's impossible to control teenagers. Even if I put the entire coven on lock down in our compound, they would find a way to sneak out. I know... that was once me.

I turn to leave when Skarlyt pipes up. "Oh Drake..." she begins, and I groan.

I was hoping I'd get away just once without her curiosity getting the better of her. Normally, I find it interesting and don't hate it as much as I make her think. But now is not a good time. "No, Skarlyt, I will not tell you if I get aroused while feeding, and I've already told you why we prefer to drink from the neck."

Everyone laughs, well, everyone except Skarlyt. "Fine. Be that way," she says with a pout.

"Wait, is that a thing? Do vampires get aroused when they are feeding?" The woman I'm assuming to be Phoebe's sister asks, looking around. I roll my eyes and notice that Alaric does the same, knowing exactly where this is going. And just as I expected, Skarlyt gets a super excited look on her face.

"From every vampire that has actually answered me when I ask that question, which is a lot, by the way," she says the last part with a pointed look in my direction before continuing, "they all confirmed that, when they drink directly from the 'source,' they get aroused, which is apparently why they enjoy feeding while in the bedroom, if you know what I mean." She adds an eyebrow wiggle on the end for emphasis.

I interrupt once again before Skarlyt starts explaining her weirdly accurate knowledge to the newcomer. "Okay, now we're done with that. I'm going to go collect my coven, the most vulnerable are already outside pack lands waiting and the rest will be here in the next hour or so. Thank you again, Alaric. Oh, and Skarlyt," I add, turning to look at her pointedly, "try and keep the questions to a minimum in front of the children."

"I'm curious, not stupid. I know better than to ask those types of questions in front of children," she says with a huff, crossing her arms over her chest. I raise my eyebrow, knowing that she can let her curiosity get the better of her a lot of the time, and turn to leave. A conversation with Drusilla is in order. I'm sure she's already noticed over half the coven leave and is probably wondering why; although, if she's still shut in her room, maybe she didn't.

I run back to the bus loaded with my people and walk up the steps. "Okay, everyone. We are cleared to stay in the pack bunker until this blows over. The mages are here for another phoenix who seems to be related to Phoebe, Alaric's mate. There will be a fight and in exchange for their protection from the hunters, I've offered our assistance." Murmurs and hushed whispers go through the bus with mothers clinging even tighter to their children. I raise my hand to quiet them down. "With two phoenixes and the strength of both the Westwood pack and the Coven of the Moon allied with us, we can win this. I will go gather the rest of our coven and meet you at the bunker. If the battle will be fought on pack land, it's better if all of us are there." I don't wait for anyone to say anything before simply nodding at the driver and stepping off the bus. I wait until it's driven far enough down the road that no one can see me before I lower my shoulders. I need to appear strong for them even when I feel anything but.

I allow myself a moment of self-doubt and pray to whatever gods are listening that they help us. After the fight with Alaric, some of my coven lost faith in me. They knew attacking the pack was wrong, even voiced their grievances with me, but rather than listening like a good leader should, I waved them off, ignoring them.

As I walk through the trees, back to our home, I allow my mind to wander. Though I've never been one to ask for help, going to Alaric to seek asylum for my people wasn't as hard as I thought it would be. When the hunters took two of our members the other day, with a third only getting free because she hid, I saw red. I have only ever felt rage like that one time in the past. No, that's not right. Twice. First when I found out my sister was taken and again when she escaped and told me her story.

If I was a stronger man, a stronger brother, I would've fought her on going alone to meet that boy. But she gave me those big blue puppy dog eyes of hers, and I caved like I have always done with Drusilla. She's had me wrapped around her little finger since the day my parents put the little baby wrapped in a pink blanket in my arms. I vowed then and there to be anything she needed—her brother, her protector, her best friend—and I failed at all three.

Now these monsters are back, and it's taking everything in me to wait to fight with everyone else. I'd rather begin picking them off one by one like they do with us, but I know that's a suicide mission —one that I won't come back from—and I can't leave her alone and unprotected. Not again.

I step into the building and see Colin, my second in command, assigning tasks to the men who stayed behind.

"Colin?" I gesture for him to follow, and we both walk into my office.

"What did they say?" He asks, not able to hide his anxiety. His mother and baby sister are both on that bus.

"They agreed." His body relaxes in relief. "But I offered our help in exchange."

"Help? We don't have the manpower to help while trying to protect ourselves," He exclaims, beginning to pace.

"Sit down," I command. Once he's settled in a chair, I continue, "Listen, it looks like the hunters and mages are working together. They're here for a new phoenix who seems to be related to Phoebe in some way. If I have to guess, they're sisters."

His brows fly into his hairline. "Two phoenixes?"

"Yes. It seems that the gods are breaking the mold. The Westwood Pack was already a powerhouse; now with two phoenixes, they'll be unstoppable."

"It's a good thing we're allies then, eh?" He says with a chuckle, and I agree before going back to the original discussion.

"In exchange for asylum, I've agreed to fight with Alaric and his people when the time comes. I will need a few to stay and scout for information, but the rest will need to come with me to pack land to prepare."

"Are you sure?" He asks, unable to hide his fear.

"I am. Now, I need to go talk to Drusilla to convince her to go stay at the pack."

"Good luck with that," Colin says, his eyes softening. He knows how difficult it will be to convince Drusilla to leave.

"Thanks," I say, heading straight for her apartment.

The door swings open before I even get a chance to knock. "I wondered when you were going to come tell me what's going on," she says, her bright blue eyes narrowing in on me.

I rub the back of my neck, unsure of how to start. She holds the door open wider and I step inside, sitting on the sofa as she closes the door and joins me.

"I know the hunters are back. I'm a loner, not deaf. You think I haven't heard everything going on the last couple of days?" She taps her ears for emphasis.

I sigh. "I just didn't know what to tell you. You've come so far; the last thing I want is for you to..."

"For me to break?" She supplies, and I pause, knowing there is no right answer here. If I say *yes*, she's going to be pissed, but if I say *no*, she's going to question why I didn't tell her earlier.

I lower my head in a slight nod. "Drake Dunkan!" She says my full name, and now I know I'm in trouble. "Just because you think I will break doesn't mean I will. I've been through more than you can ever imagine, and I didn't break then."

"I know you haven't. But you can't blame me for trying to protect you." Her eyes soften, and she comes to sit beside me, holding my hands in hers. "I need you to go to Alaric's. Stay in the bunker. It's warded and safe. There are two phoenixes protecting the pack now," I plead with her, but she releases my hand with a hiss.

"No." She gets up and walks to the kitchen to get away from me, but I follow.

"Drusilla, it's the safest place. There will only be a few people staying behind in case anyone escapes and tries to come home."

"I'm staying, Drake," she says with a growl before her words soften, "I'm not ready." When she finally raises her eyes to meet mine, I see the tears shining in them, and it breaks my heart.

I wrap my arms around her as her body is wracked with sobs. Like me, she tries to put on a brave face even when she is terrified. "Okay. But you need to lock yourself in here. Do not open the door for anyone except me or Colin. Okay?" I'm probably going to regret this, but when her tear-filled eyes look up at me in relief, I can't find it in myself to care at the moment. I was planning on going to the bunker, too, to help coordinate, but with Drusilla here, I guess I'll be staying, as well.

After ensuring that she has enough blood to last a week, I step outside the door, waiting to hear the multiple locks click to show they're engaged before I walk away.

There's a flurry of activity as I reach the common room. I seek out Colin. "What's going on?"

"Blake escaped," he says excitedly.

I snort, "More like they let him go." Colin nods, obviously not caring either way, while leading me to Blake.

"Drake!" Blake exclaims. "I heard them talking. They're going to attack the pack. They're giving the alpha twenty-four hours to trade the girl for his brother." I let out a hiss. Shit.

"Fuck!" I scream. I didn't realize they had Darren. This changes everything. It puts so much more on the line. Why didn't he tell me?

As I turn to leave, Blake calls out, "Wait there's more." I turn back around with a nod. "It seems that the hunters are teamed up with the mages. It's like the hunters are worshiping them, doing whatever they say. It's strange."

Without replying, I rush over to Alaric's and Phoebe's. All the lights are off, so I jump up onto the balcony of their room and knock on the window.

A very disheveled Alaric comes to meet me. "What the fuck, man?" he says, gesturing to the fact that he and his mate were clearly pre-occupied.

"This couldn't wait, and I didn't want to wake up the rest of your household by going through the front," I reply. Their private time isn't nearly as important as what Blake had to say.

"What couldn't wait?" Phoebe asks, covering herself as she approaches the balcony. I can tell that Alaric is still seething about being interrupted, but I shake it off.

"One of our missing members escaped. Well, I think they more than likely were released after overhearing a conversation between the mages and hunters."

"What kind of conversation?" Okay, now Alaric has caught up.

"Well, they said they overheard the mages tell the hunters that they were giving you twenty-four hours to trade the girl for your brother before they kill him and attack. The hunters apparently seem to think that the mages are some sort of saviors, and that the girl is an innocent hostage," I tell them.

"Twenty-four hours?" Phoebe whispers, looking briefly at Alaric before rushing inside. He goes to follow, but I snag his arm.

"Why didn't you tell me they have Darren?" I challenge, a little hurt that he didn't. I know we're not the best of friends or anything, but I thought we were closer than this or, at least, on the way to being that way.

He sighs, "You left before I could, and if I'm being honest, I didn't really want to voice it out loud." I nod, knowing what he's trying to say. It was the same when Dru was taken: the more I told people, the more real it was. But I learned that just because you don't say it doesn't mean it's not real.

"Listen, I know all too well how you're feeling. We will fight with you. Now, go get your mate before she does something stupid," I say as I clasp him on the shoulder.

"Thank you," he says before rushing inside to his mate.

Time to go get my coven ready for a battle. There's more on the line than just us this time: if Alaric loses Darren, I don't know if he'll be able to come back from that.

* * *

After leading my coven through the woods behind Alaric and his pack, we spread out in the trees, waiting. I take my spot at the very back of the group, hoping to stop anyone from sneaking up behind us.

Soon after, there's a big commotion at the front, and Phoebe's phoenix is flying high with a screech that has me covering my ears. Things must not be going the way they want it to. I rush toward the sound. From the looks of it, with all the mountain lions, bears, wolves, witches and my coven, we're winning. I don't pause, instead quickly jumping into the fray. I don't give two shits about the mages; there are others here that have more beef with them than I do so I leave them to be picked off. But the hunters? That's another story...

I'm leaping from tree to tree, focusing only on the hunters. I don't know if these are the same assholes that took my sister years ago, but it doesn't matter. They're all entitled pricks who think that they're better than everyone simply because they are 'normal'. They think there's nothing special about them, and to them that's a good thing—not to me. I know that the pure hunter bloodlines are descended from the Norse gods and are, in fact, more supernatural than human. But you can never tell any of them that. In reality, they're not much different from us. Yet they call us 'monsters.' Yes, we drink blood, but vampires, as a species, haven't practiced source feeding in years—other than from willing donors, of course.

I wish Dru were here to tell me if these fuckers are the ones that took her, but then we've made so much progress with her mentally that I don't know if this would set her back again. She escaped ten years ago, but she still frequently wakes up with nightmares and hasn't left our compound since.

As I'm thrusting my hand into the most recent hunter's chest and grasping his heart in my hand, I catch a whiff of the most amazing scent. Whoever's blood that is makes my mouth water. Saliva actually drips onto my lips. I haven't felt true bloodlust like this in...I try to think back to a time where I have felt like this and come up blank. Even in my teenage years when I had trouble controlling my thirst, I've never felt desire this strong for someone's blood. Never. I finish my task quickly and go in search of that arousing aroma.

I search for hours after the battle but never find the source. The only explanation is that the scent is coming from the one person I wasn't in a hurry to find. I was never too worried about finding my mate, but after tonight, one thought consumes me: I need to find her.

Chapter Two

Rayne

Ever since I was a little girl, I've had two things drilled into my brain: the first is that supernaturals exist, and the second is that they're all evil, existing only to destroy the human race. My family comes from a long line of hunters, and since I'm the only child lucky enough—or unlucky, if you ask me—to be born in this generation, my dad has made it his mission to make me his prodigy. He has force fed it to me that all these creatures need to be eradicated by any means necessary.

Sitting in the car now, driving away from the battle, I am forced to remember a time in my younger years when I first began questioning his ideology. It now seems like a nightmare:

I am just about to turn sixteen years old, training at six am when the rest of my friends are still sleeping. Running laps, doing push-ups, and jumping hurdles until it is time to get ready for school. I've been doing the same routine for as long as I can remember, but for whatever reason, today is different. He seems to push me harder, wanting me to move faster and jump higher.

Finally, not being able to take it anymore, I turn to my dad. "Why do we have to train like this? Surely not all supernaturals can be evil," I tell him. His face goes from serious to furious in a blink.

"Of course, they are! How could you question it?" he yells at me.

"It's just I've never even seen a supernatural. How do I even know what you're telling me is true?" I question him. I shouldn't have. I should've kept my mouth shut.

"You don't believe me, Rayne? Think that I'm putting you through all this training because I just want to be cruel? Me telling you that a vampire killed your mother wasn't enough?" he asks with a smirk on his face.

I look down at my hands, not knowing what to say. He's always told me that a vampire killed my mother, and I have been terrified of the thought. But after learning about myths and legends in school, it has me questioning whether it truly was a vampire or just an evil human pretending to be one. Even the legitimate news has me questioning. There is no doubt that there is evil in the world, but I just don't know if I believe it's caused by things that go bump in the night.

"Come with me," he says, turning and walking towards the shed on our property. I've never been allowed to go in here, and I'm now scared of what he's about to show me.

He slowly places a key in each of the locks that are securing the door. It opens, and he gestures for me to walk in first. As I walk in, he closes the door quickly, to prevent allowing any light in, and flicks a switch. The shed is lined with weapons, all the weapons that he is training me to use: stakes, guns, vials of something that looks like water. I look around in shock. Either my dad is super-prepared for the zombie apocalypse, or he really fights supernaturals. Either way, it seems a little excessive. He rushes past me, going to the back of the room, where I can see a large cage.

"This is what we fight," he says, sliding a knife through his palm and banging on the cage. I jump back as what looks like a small child rushes at the bars, hissing. I can see her fangs and red irises

from here. At that moment, I know my dad is telling the truth. He grabs a bag of what looks like blood from a blood bank and tosses it in the cage. The little girl, or what I think is a girl based on her long hair and dress, scoops it up, rips the top off, and guzzles it down like she's starving.

"See how she drinks blood? She's a monster. The only thing she knows is how to kill," my father says, looking at me, but I'm still looking at the girl. She turns toward me, and, in her eyes, I don't see a monster. I see fear and shame. I get a pang in my chest. My dad says they are the monsters, but right now, as I turn to look my dad in the eyes, I can't help but question if we are the monsters instead.

I'm pulled out of the memory by my dad. "Rayne, are you even listening to me?"

"Sorry, what were you saying?" I ask, giving my head a shake to clear the thoughts.

"I swear your head is always in the clouds," my father says, giving me a pointed look from the rear-view mirror. "I was just saying that the infestation is worse than we could have ever possibly imagined. The amount of vermin in those woods tonight shows just how important our work is," he finishes and everyone else in the car murmurs in agreement.

"But that fire chick saved us. Those mages, or whatever, who were supposed to be on our side, turned on us. If it weren't for her, we'd all be dead. Surely that shows that they aren't all evil!" I exclaim. Suddenly, I'm thrown forward as my father slams on the brakes, pulling to the side of the road.

"She just wanted the kill for herself. They're all evil. Surely, after tonight, you must *finally* see," he says, turning in his seat to look at me.

"I'm not so sure, Dad," I tell him honestly, I probably shouldn't have because now it's not only him looking at me, but the rest of the hunters in the car, as well.

"What more proof do you need? Do you need one of them to kill one of us in front of you? Would that be enough?" He spits at me. "Or do you want to save them all just like that monster you set free when you were younger?" I lower my head in what he perceives as shame. But in reality, I'm proud of what I did. I don't care what he says; keeping that girl in the cage made us the monsters instead.

I allow my mind to wander back to that memory as he resumes driving.

After that first day in the shed, when he showed me exactly what we do, they gave me the duty of feeding the 'monster'—as he called her—every other day.

Each time, I'd go in and say, "Hi, I'm Rayne. What's your name?" And every day, she would simply sit there and stare at me with her sad eyes, never saying a word as I laid her blood pack on a tray and slid it to her under the bars. One day, my father was being particularly hard on me during training, telling me how weak and slow I was, that I could never live up to his expectations. I know now, it was his type of motivation, hoping that it would make me kick my training up a notch, but at the time, it crushed me. It made me feel hopeless. I put my all into training every day, passing on hanging out with my friends or having a real childhood to train for him, and nothing was ever good enough.

I walk into the shed, grab her bag of blood, place it on the tray just outside the cage and sit on the stool and cry. "I don't understand. I do everything he wants. I do my very best. I basically kill myself every morning for him and what do I get? Told it's not enough. That my best isn't good enough for him. I don't know what more I can do. You know?" I peek through my tear-soaked lashes. "I know my problems are nowhere near as bad as yours, and if there was something I could do to help you, believe me I would, but I'm scared," I tell her, and it's the truth. If I could release her right now, I would.

Instead, I sit there and cry some more. I cry until no more tears are falling. And it is then that I hear her speak for the first time.

"It will be okay," she says to me, consoling me as if she isn't being kept prisoner and in need of consoling herself.

My head snaps up to the bars at the musical sound. "How can you say that when you're locked in there?" I ask.

"Because I have faith that the goddess has a reason for every plan put in motion, and maybe part of my plan was to be stuck in here to meet you in your time of need." Again, she reassures me. Her voice is soothing, caressing me like a mother's love.

"How can you have so much faith when you've been trapped in here and treated like a monster?" I turn my stool now so that we are facing each other. In the past weeks, I had hoped she'd speak to me, but I had just about given up. But as I am able to look closely at her now, she's not a child like I originally thought. She's a grown woman. The dirt and grime covering her, along with her petite size, are good at hiding her age, as does the innocence staring back at me.

"Since you've taken over my feedings, I've found my faith once more. You treat me like I'm a person. You don't taunt me and throw my blood on the floor. Those things may seem small to you, but for me, I've been locked in here for longer than I care to think about, and those simple gestures are enough to restore my faith." I'm taken back by her words. She's right, those things are small and to me, should mean nothing. Surely, they're not as significant as granting her freedom or giving her enough food to get strong, but I suppose, looking at it through her perspective, I could see how they could give her a little faith.

"I'm sorry," I tell her, hanging my head. And I am. I'm sorry for the way my father is treating her, for her current conditions.

"What are you sorry for? Improving my living conditions? Coming in and talking to me like a person, even when I don't answer you back? Trust me, though I haven't responded, I've listened and enjoyed hearing about your day or your worries. It has given me

something to think about rather than my own predicament." When she puts it like that, I guess I should probably clarify.

"No, I suppose not. But I am sorry that you're here, and for the way my father treats you." She nods as she opens her blood packet and sips slowly, savoring the taste.

"What's your name?" I must've asked this question a hundred times and never received an answer, but I feel like today is going to be different.

"My name is Drusilla, but my friends call me Dru," she responds between sips.

"Drusilla. That's a beautiful name. How did you get here? That is, if you don't mind me asking." I've asked my father numerous times over the past two weeks, but he just keeps telling me that it doesn't matter, that she's a monster and is where she should be. I've even asked why he's keeping her rather than killing her like he's training me to do. Again, he says it doesn't matter, just that she's a monster. Drusilla blows out a small breath and places the now empty blood packet on the tray, readying herself for her tale. "My father is the leader of a large coven in Northern Ontario and, like most children, once I hit sixteen, I started to rebel. I thought his stories about hunters were myths and stories told to all the children to keep us scared and in our beds." My mouth drops open in shock. Wow. So we *are their things that go bump in the night, told to children to get them to behave, just as they are ours. I wish there was some way to change that; I don't like the thought that there are people out there terrified of me.*

"Well, one night, my friend and I decided to crash a human party," I suck in a breath, and she lets out a small laugh. "Not to feed. Simply to interact with others our age. You see, there are not very many children in our coven, and we wanted to let loose and have a little fun for a night.

"It was all my idea. I thought that if we went out and nothing bad happened, then we could prove to our parents that we were old

enough to be trusted on our own. But I was wrong. That night, there was a boy there. I thought he was just a handsome, charming human *boy. He seemed so interested in me, like he wanted to be more than friends, if you know what I mean?" and I do, I know the type.*

"We talked for hours, almost until dawn. He begged me to stay with him, but I told him I had snuck out and needed to get back before my parents woke and found me missing. I promised to meet him the next night in the same spot. We shared a soft passionate kiss that I still remember to this day, and I returned home, my parents none the wiser. I told my brother Drake that I wanted to go again the next night, and he warned me not to go back, but after using my best puppy dog eyes, he relented as he always does, and I promised that I would be safe. He wanted to go with me, but I convinced him that no boy would be happy if a big brother tagged along, and I promised to take my friend Breanne with me," she stops for a minute as a tear slides out of her eye and she wipes it away.

"Breanne did come with me, but when we got there, hunters surrounded us. You see, the boy we had met was the son of a hunter, sent to human parties to try to sniff out supernaturals, and I was the stupid one to fall for the bait. Not only that, but I brought a second along with me." I suck in a breath at her words, fury simmering beneath my skin at the thought of anyone preying on young girls, supernatural or not.

"Once they had us both trapped, they separated us, and to this day, I don't know what happened to her. I hope that she is just being kept prisoner, too, though I don't know why they would do that. But, then again, I also think that maybe it would've been a mercy just to kill me and not have to go through this torture." She once again raises her head to look into my eyes. "To answer your question: I have been here for six years. Your father? He is not a nice man. You need to be careful. He says that I'm the monster, but the things he enjoys

doing shows a very different story," she finishes with a pleading look.

I wipe my own eyes of the tears flowing out. "I don't even know what to say, Dru, other than I promise that I will free you. Somehow, I will find a way."

From that day on, I look forward to my time in the shed, swiping extra blood packets from the deliveries on Wednesdays to help Dru build up her strength.

A month later, I enter the shed and find Dru laying on the floor of her cell, clothes torn and obvious lash marks covering her body.

"Oh my God, Dru! What happened?" I say as I rush over to her, quickly unlocking the cage and pulling her into my lap.

"Your dad found out about the extra blood but doesn't know it was you who was giving it to me. He thinks I compelled someone to get it for me, one of the other hunters that comes in on the days you don't to give me my 'punishments'," she whispers weakly.

"What punishments? Why didn't you tell me?" I ask, brushing her hair off her face. I rip open the first blood bag I brought and feed it to her gently. I watch in awe as her cuts begin disappearing and, by the time she finishes the second blood pack, they are all but gone

"You need to leave," I whisper to her.

"I can't. Think about it. What do you think they will do to you if I leave?"

"But I can't watch my friend go through this anymore," I tell her, and she sits up quickly, looking into my eyes.

"Friend?" She looks genuinely shocked.

I nod. "Yes. I consider you my friend, my only friend, and I hope you consider me yours. You need to leave. It's still dark enough outside that if you run fast enough, you should be able to gain some distance. We're in Orillia, Ontario, if that helps you figure out where to go," she stands and starts to pace, looking between me and the door.

"What about you?" she asks again, concern lining her features.

I think for a few minutes. "Knock me out. Hit me over the head hard enough to make me unconscious and run." She looks at me like I've grown two heads, but I continue, "It's the only way they'll believe I had nothing to do with it and for you to get away. Just don't do any permanent damage." I give a chuckle.

Once again, she looks between me and the door. "Come with me," she pleads, but I shake my head.

"I can't. That will only bring the entire force of hunters down on you and your family. They will believe you took me against my will, and my father will destroy the world to find me." I tell her, tears brimming in my eyes.

"Will you come find me when you are free, as well?" she asks, and I nod even though I know that I'll never be free.

"Okay," she says, wrapping her arms around me. "Thank you, Rayne. I'll never forget you," she whispers, and I snake my arms around her, returning the embrace. We stay like that for a minute before I feel a heavy thud on the back of my head and darkness consumes me.

When I wake up, my father is standing over me in the cell, with no Dru in sight. Thank God... or more accurately, the gods it worked.

We pull into our driveway, and I realize I haven't allowed myself to think about Dru in a long time. I'm sure that she would be very disappointed with my life now. Although I haven't personally killed or captured any supernaturals, I've been witness to it enough times to make me an accomplice.

After tonight, though, the way that fire woman saved us, even though we are the very people there to harm her and her family and friends...I'm not sure I can keep doing this. I think I need to leave, but where can I go so that they won't find me? Or that I won't be captured and tortured for revenge by the supernaturals? They would be justified, of course. After all the things my family and dad's group of hunters have done to them or their relations, I can't say I would blame them for wanting to take a little vengeance on the people that have killed, tortured, or held captive their kind for centuries.

Maybe that fire woman will help me. She looked like she might. I mean, she saved us and didn't attack even though I stood there staring at her. Is it worth a shot?

Chapter Three

Rayne

I bide my time over the next week, making my father think everything is fine and I'm not appalled by the actions our group committed last week. Not only did we help a group of mages capture shifters and vampires, but we helped them capture teenagers. How is it their fault that they were simply born supernatural? They can't help it any more than I can help the fact that I was born a female.

But I've finally come up with an escape plan. I'm going out tonight on my scheduled patrol, picking up the bag of all my necessities that I've stashed, and heading to Parry Sound. Hopefully, I'll already be checked into a crappy motel using a fake name by the time my dad even realizes I'm missing. I even went a step further by calling my boss and putting in my notice of resignation. He wasn't happy and tried to convince me to take a leave of absence instead. Of course, I couldn't tell him the real reasoning behind it, but after explaining that my family responsibilities are more important than my career, he gave up trying to convince me and accepted it.

That was probably the hardest part of my plan: to leave the job

I love in order to do the right thing. I've loved every second of being a police officer. Even the paperwork isn't as bad as some of my coworkers make it out to be. I'd love to believe that one day I can start fresh with a new police force, but I know that would be a lie. To become a police officer, there needs to be a very in-depth background check and personnel files. Both things that would flag my dad as to my whereabouts.

"Okay, Dad, I'm heading out. See you in the morning," I say to him as I make my way through the living room toward the front door. I'm dressed in my hunting leathers, as usual.

"Rayne?" he calls out to me, and I freeze, anxiety pooling in my stomach. Does he know what I'm planning? I shake my head and school my features. No, he can't. I've been very careful to keep all the plans to myself.

I turn around, "Yeah, Dad?" I try to keep the shakiness out of my voice.

"Be safe out there. Ever since the battle last week, there have been increased reports coming in." I feel a pang of guilt momentarily at the concern coming through in his voice. "Maybe someone should go with you?" I scoff away the guilt; he has been saying the same thing all week, that I should take one of the guys with me for protection.

"Dad. You know I could wipe the floor with every single one of the guys you would want to send with me. I'll be fine. Besides, the only thing I'd end up killing is whoever was with me. They annoy the crap out of me," I tell him and wrap my arms around his shoulders in a hug. "I'll be fine, I promise," I whisper into his ear. I will be fine, better than fine actually, but he doesn't know that, and I have been avoiding thinking about how he is going to react when he realizes I'm gone. I doubt it's going to be good. I just hope I don't bring a group of hunters down on the people that I'm asking for help.

"Okay, see you in the morning," my dad says, straightening up and placing his serious mask back on his face. God forbid he show any emotion to anyone, especially his daughter. That he hugged me back is a huge deal, but I had to at least try to get one last hug because I don't plan on ever coming home.

After hopping in my car and stopping to grab my go bag, I pull onto Highway 400 Southbound towards Toronto. I know I'm going the wrong way, but I need to make it seem like I'm heading in the opposite direction for when they come looking for me.

Pulling into the rest stop, I quickly grab my stuff out of the car and head over to the trucks in the lot. After questioning a few drivers, I finally find one heading to Parry Sound, and with an offer of one hundred dollars cash, he agrees to take me there once he finishes eating.

A short two-hour drive later and I'm standing outside the motel where I chose to lay low for the week. I wrinkle my nose. I'm not sure this was the best idea. This place is a dump, and that's putting it nicely. "Maybe it's nicer inside," I say to myself, shrugging my shoulders and walking into the office.

The young girl working looks up from her phone, seeming surprised to see someone walking in. "Can I help you?" she asks.

"Yeah. I need a room for the week, please," I respond, pulling the cash out of my pocket.

"Here?" she asks, and once again a shocked look crosses her face at my nod. "Well, you're in luck. You have the pick of the rooms," she says with sarcasm, gesturing to the row of keys hanging on the wall.

I let a chuckle slip past my lips. "I'll take one at the end. Doesn't matter which."

She grabs the key with number seven on it, placing it on the counter in front of me. "It's fifty per night." And that there is the other reason I picked this motel.

I count out three hundred and fifty dollars, hand it over to her, and pick up the key. "Thanks," I say as I walk out the door and head to the room. That was the other thing I did during this last week: I emptied my bank account, pulled everything out of my retirement savings, and stashed it in my go bag. I have just under fifty thousand dollars to get me through until I begin my new life. I hope it's enough.

A musty smell slaps me in the face as soon as I open the door. "Ugh. Nope, not better inside." I prop the door open and drop my bag on the bed before turning on the bathroom fan in hopes of ridding the room of the smell. It doesn't work, but I get used to it after a little while and settle into my new routine: workout in the room, watch TV in the room, order food to the room. Leaving would be a risk and one I'm not willing to take. Not yet...

* * *

After five days of this room, and nothing but this room, I am going stir crazy. Other than opening the door to get my food or sneaking a quick walk in the woods surrounding the motel, I haven't left. There have been no sign of other hunters looking for me, so I decide it's finally safe for me to try to reach out to the fire woman. I really wish I knew her name. Calling her "the fire woman" doesn't seem very nice, but I have nothing else to call her. I don't even know what type of supernatural she is, only that she looks like a woman with large wings behind her, completely covered in flames.

Tonight, I'm going to try and get past whatever magic is surrounding Supernatural—the bar in town that I know specifically caters to supernaturals—to get in and make contact. I've heard other hunters speak about how there's always a strange feeling coming over them when they get close, like their skin is crawling and they can't get away fast enough. I need to get in there, though. Short of showing back up on their land, which I'm sure I wouldn't survive doing, I don't have any other ideas.

I pull the only dress I own out of my bag and shake it out. It's not exactly a bar outfit, but it's the best option I had when packing. I really don't think showing up in my hunting leathers will do me any favors.

I shower quickly, then brush out my thick brown hair so it falls over my neck—to conceal my hunter's tattoo at the base—and slip into my black dress. It doesn't look too bad: form fitting on top with thin straps, flaring out at my hips, and landing just above my knees. It is supposed to have tulle underneath to keep it puffed out, but I didn't have room in my bag for that. I throw on a touch of makeup, shove my money and ID into the built-in bra of the dress, and walk out the door.

I slip into the office quickly before I leave, catching the young girl off guard. "Hey, any chance you can call me a cab?" I ask, and she nods, picking up the phone.

"They'll be here in five," she replies after hanging up the phone.

"Thanks," I say to her with a small wave before walking out the door.

It's almost exactly five minutes later when the cab pulls up and I get in. "Where to, sweetheart?" the older man, who smells of cigarettes, asks from the front seat.

"To Supernatural, please," I state, and he turns to look at me.

"You sure a pretty thing like you should be going to a place like that? I know a nice little bar just down the road where I think you'd be more comfortable," he tries to sway me.

I let out a little laugh and shake my head. "No, thanks. I'll be fine. Trust me." What's with men taking one look at my five foot three, petite frame and thinking that I can't take care of myself? I could probably take this guy out with one arm tied behind my back and blindfolded.

"If you're sure," he says, turning back around.

Ten minutes later, we're pulling up in front of a large brick building, and immediately I can tell what the other hunters were talking about. It feels like every cell in my body is urging me to leave, to turn around and never return. Well, almost. There's a small part that is pulling me toward it, like a magnet.

I reach into my bra once again, but the driver shakes his head. "It's on me. You just stay safe," he says with a concerned look.

"Thank you," I tell him and slip a twenty-dollar bill into the seat for him to find later. I don't want him to have to take the fare out of his earnings, especially when he was so concerned with my safety. Although, I'm pretty sure it's just a by-product of the barrier they have surrounding it; he probably doesn't even know why he wouldn't want to go in there.

I glance around as I slip out of the car. Growing up, I was taught how to recognize all supernaturals: shifters by their bulky frames, vampires by the way they carry themselves, Fae by the almost other-worldly glow that surrounds them, and witches by their mannerisms, though that one is a lot harder. Because of this training, I look around and see a couple shifters, Fae, and even a few vampires walking around the outside of the building. Two of the largest shifters I've ever seen are standing at the door. Well, shit. I hope I can get in.

I give myself a mental pep talk, pushing the urge to run deep down and focusing on the pull inside the building instead. "Hey, guys. Beautiful night, isn't it?" I ask the shifters at the door. They look quizzically at me, then at each other, before nodding and stepping aside for me to enter.

"Thanks, boys," I say with a wink.

There's a moment of resistance, where I'm not sure if my body will actually be able to push through the doorway, but eventually it gives away. As I step through, my jaw hits the floor. I've just stepped into another world. It's amazing here. Branches cover the ceiling with elderberries hanging from it. All the books I've read about the berries haven't done their beauty justice. I make my feet move, stepping further inside towards the bar.

Years of training have my eyes scanning the occupants, mentally noting their species and locations so I'm not snuck up on, all the while hoping none were at the battle and recognize me.

I slide up to the bar, find a corner where I can put my back against the wall, and wait for the blue-haired bartender to come get my drink order. I still feel the magnetic pull, wanting me to go into the bar, toward the booths in the back. Unfortunately, through the throngs of people out on the dance floor, I can't see who or what it is.

"What can I get you?" the bartender asks, breaking me from my scanning.

"I'll take an amaretto and coke, please," I say to him, noticing the awesome drink names on the board behind him. I seriously want to try the witches' brew. The picture on the sign shows a blue drink with what looks like smoke from it. But, without knowing what's in it, I don't feel comfortable ordering it, or any of the other drinks on the menu.

He dips his head in acknowledgement, making fast work of pouring my drink. I slide a fifty-dollar bill toward him and tell him, "Keep 'em coming," with a wink.

I go back to my scanning and, after downing my drink and picking up my second, decide that I should make my way to the back to figure out the source of the pull. I've always trusted my instincts; they've never steered me wrong. Plus, I should probably mingle for a bit before I start asking questions. The force that's pulling me gets stronger the closer I get, and soon I'm standing at the edge of the dance floor, my body swaying in time with the music.

I turn in a slow circle and stop dead when I recognize the force that's driving me. He's the most gorgeous man I've ever seen. Well, more accurately, vampire. He has shaggy blonde hair and angular features with a strong jawline and chin. I can't see his eyes, but I just know they're going to be pools that I will be able to get lost in.

Wait. What? Where did that come from? I've never thought of a man that way. Don't get me wrong, I've had my fair share of encounters with the opposite sex, but I always have "hit 'em and quit 'em" encounters. I've never had any thoughts of getting "lost in their eyes." What is wrong with you, Rayne?

As if sensing me, the man in question snaps his head up, scanning the area until his eyes land on me. He doesn't say a word to the others at the booth with him, just stands and walks straight to me. Now that he's getting close, I see his bright blue eyes looking back at me, and I realize I was right. I could get lost staring into them.

"I haven't seen you here before," he says once he's close enough. Oh goddess, that voice. It sends sparks straight down to my pussy, making it quiver with need. I have to squeeze my thighs together to keep the juices from soaking through my panties and dripping onto the floor.

He's looking at me with a puzzled look, and I realize I have just been standing here staring at him.

"Nope, it's my first time," I say in a sultry bedroom voice. When did I start talking like that?

He smiles at me, showing off his pearly white teeth, making my pussy gush more. That smile. For some reason, I feel like I would do anything to get him to smile at me like that forever. What the fuck? Where is this coming from? I try to mentally shake off whatever spell he's put on me when he speaks again.

"Want to go somewhere quiet to talk?" he asks. My mind is screaming, no, don't go. 'Danger, Will Robinson!' But my traitorous body is already moving toward him.

He takes my hand and leads me to a room at the back. Walking inside, my mind once again starts screaming at me. The walls are painted a deep red with black couches lining two of the walls, but the most notable thing is the big king-size bed in the back.

I'm snapped out of my perusing of the room by the lock clicking on the door and turn toward him. My body, once again acting on its own, moves closer to him, and I raise up onto my toes, placing my mouth on his, taking us both by surprise. But to his credit, he recovers quickly, snaking his arms around my body, lifting me up. I drop my drink onto the floor, not caring about the mess, as I wrap my arms and legs around him, my hands tangling in his hair.

He walks us back to the bed, lowering us both down. He moves his mouth to my neck, licking and sucking along the way.

"Wait," I say, as my mind finally breaks through some of the lust-filled fog and he jerks back, looking concerned.

That's weird and not at all what I expected. As a hunter, I was taught that he would've already drained me and disposed of my body, rather than being concerned about my reluctance to fuck. But at this point, if I focused on what I was taught, I wouldn't be here right now.

"No biting, okay?" I say, and as he nods, I pull him back down on top of me.

His hands roam my body as his mouth moves from my lips to neck and back again. His hands brush the inside of my thighs before quickly roaming away, and I groan in frustration. Grabbing his hand, I move it inside my panties, urging him to rub my pussy. "I need you to make me cum," I tell him breathlessly. To my utter delight, he begins moving his fingers in expert fashion, gathering my juices before rubbing on my clit.

"Oh, yes. Just like that," I say, and he stops. "What?" I ask, pulling back to look at his face. He simply gives me a smirk before lowering his head until it disappears under my dress. I wait with bated breath as he pulls my panties to the side and gives my pussy a tentative lick with a groan, then dives in.

He moves his tongue over my clit with a speed that rivals a vibrator until I feel my release beginning to crest. He moves his fingers up, replacing his tongue as he separates my legs more and begins fucking me with his tongue.

"Oh, my gods. Yes! I'm so close!" I half yell, half scream, seconds before my orgasm overtakes me, and I start shaking. He doesn't stop, though. He continues moving his fingers and tongue in time until my body stops spasming. I'm disappointed for a second before he flips me over, undoes his pants and slips into me.

Oh my, I can't see it, but he has to be huge. I've never felt this full. He pauses once he's fully seated inside of me, but I start wiggling, hoping to urge him to move.

A moan slips past both our lips at his first thrust. "Faster...Please," I beg, and he complies. Thank fuck. I don't think I would've survived another minute of his slowness.

His movements become frantic as he slams into me over and over. Each thrust extracting another moan from me until my pussy is detonating and pulsing onto his cock, milking him of his own release.

Once he finishes pulsing inside me, he places a kiss on my bare upper back, swiping my hair to the side to get access to my neck, but pauses and slips back from me hastily.

"You're a hunter?" he growls out. Oh, shit, he saw my mark. I feel a moment of panic before I decide fuck it, he just fucked me, so it's his bad too.

"Yup, and you're a vampire," I say, popping my p's for emphasis while straightening up my outfit. I wish I had something to clean myself with. He's still standing there in shock when I'm done. I pat him on the chest. "Let's just keep this our little secret. K?" and I walk out the door, pretending that my entire body is not protesting every step that I'm taking away from him. What. The. Actual. Fuck.

I quickly make my way back to the bar and get the attention of the bartender, gesturing for him to join me in the secluded corner.

"Everything okay, miss?" he asks, probably concerned by my very just fucked hair.

"Oh, yeah. Well...no. Actually, I'm hoping you can help me," I spit out. Trying to think how to put this so that it doesn't get me killed and needing this conversation over before the very sexy, very well-endowed vampire spreads the word that I'm a hunter.

He gestures with his head, "This way," and leads me into an office behind the bar.

"What exactly do you think I can help a hunter with?" he asks as he sits in the chair behind the desk, and I stop dead, with my mouth hanging open.

"How did you know?" I question.

"I could tell the second you walked in. Though I must say I never imagined a hunter would willingly go into a room with a vampire unless only one walked out. But since Drake is still alive, I assume you're not here on business."

Holy fuck. This guy is crazy perceptive. "No, not here on business. Actually, that's what I want help with," I say as I take a seat across from him. At his nod, I continue.

"I was at the battle two weeks ago," he lets out a growl, so I keep going quickly. "I didn't hurt anyone. But anyway, some mages that we were supposed to be helping cornered my family and me, and I thought for sure they were going to kill us, but then this fire woman stepped in and saved us.

"At that moment, I knew that everything they had ever taught me was wrong. I mean, I have always questioned it and was never really committed to the cause. But after that, how could anyone believe that a woman who would risk her life for the people there to kill her was evil?

"I left my family and have been hiding in a shitty hotel for a week. I'm hoping that you can put me in touch with her and maybe she can help me stay hidden." I watch his face throughout my speech, and although he does an outstanding job at staying neutral, I notice the intrigued look that passes over him.

"Say I could. Where would she get in touch with you?" He asks. Yes. He's going to help me.

"I'm staying at the Sunset Motel in room seven. I'll be there for the next two days before I move on. Thank you," I tell him.

"I'm not making any promises, but I'll pass on the message."

"That's all I'm asking for. Thank you, again," I say. I quickly make my way out of the bar and hop into a waiting cab.

Once I'm back in my room, I undress. I should probably have a shower, but I'm reluctant to remove the evidence of my time with Drake. "Drake," I whisper, touching my lips. I didn't realize until the Fae bartender told me his name that we hadn't introduced ourselves. Now that I know it, though, I can envision crying it out whenever I'm taking care of my needs. "What the fuck is wrong with me?" I growl to myself. Seriously. This is all kinds of fucked up.

Chapter Four

Drake

What the fuck did I just do? And worse...Why do I want to do it again? I'm frozen in my spot, reeling from the revelation that I just fucked one of my enemies. On top of that, I'm pretty fucking sure she's the source of the amazing aroma I smelled that night at the battle. Well, fuck.

I take my time getting dressed in order to get my mind right. I can't let the guys know. The battle is still so fresh that either Darren or Alaric will kill her on sight, especially after the mages had Darren captive. Why I care what happens to her, I have no idea, but the thought of her being hurt in any way fills me with anxiety. If I didn't know any better, I'd say she was a witch and put some sort of spell on me. But that mark on the back of her neck told me exactly what she is, so I know that's not the case.

I place my neutral mask back on before making my way back to the booth. "Where did you go?" Alaric asks, inciting a chuckle out of Darren and Sebastyn.

"He was getting some," Darren says with a wink in my direction. I just scowl at him and take my seat.

"Where were we? Oh, yes, that's right, we were talking about you keeping your nose out of my business," I tell him. Perhaps that's too harsh, but after all that just happened, I can't help it. He raises his hands in surrender while Alaric raises an eyebrow at me in question. I simply shrug my shoulders and grab my glass.

They talk for a bit, going back and forth about something or other. I'm not paying attention, though I nod every so often to seem like I'm listening. I'm just too caught up in the events of this evening. How can I be so stupid as to have fucked my mortal enemy? Even if hunters hadn't kidnapped my sister and kept her captive for years, they have still killed more than their fair share of my kind.

My sister, oh shit. If she finds out about this, she's going to kill me herself. I scrub my hand over my face, thinking about it. What's worse is the fact that just thinking about the sexy hunter has my cock standing at attention. I'm royally screwed.

"Earth to Drake," Alaric says, snapping me out of my thoughts.

"Huh?" I ask, raising my eyes to meet him.

"We were asking if you wanted to get another round or if you were ready to call it a night?"

"Oh. Whatever Darren wants to do, it's his night. You only have your mating ceremony once," I tell them, praying to the goddess that he wants to call it a night. I'm ready to go home and lock myself away until my mind stops swirling back to a petite brunette with strong thighs that are begging to be wrapped around my head. There I go again, thinking of her. I'm so fucked.

"I think we're going to call it a night. I want to get home to Sophia," Darren tells us. Thank fuck. Though I can't imagine ever wanting to go home to one woman for the rest of my life. At least not yet.

"At least she's letting you two spend the night before your mating ceremony together. Phoebe said it was bad luck," Alaric says with a little growl.

"Phoebe tried to convince her. But Sophia said we are true mates, so it doesn't matter," Darren replies with a chuckle, making Alaric shake his head.

We head over to the bar to pay Trevan for our tab. "Did you guys have a good night?" he asks.

"Some more than others," Darren says with a wink in my direction. I send him another scowl.

"Good. Glad to hear it," Trev says, with a knowing look on his face. Damn that Fae. Nothing gets past him. "Oh, Alaric, mind if I borrow you, Darren and Sebastyn for a minute before you head home?" I take that as my cue.

"You guys go ahead. I'm going to head home and see you tomorrow at the ceremony," I tell them and head for the door. I do wonder what that was about, though. Probably something to do with the mating ceremony tomorrow since it's a joint ceremony for him and his newly found mate as well.

The walk home is refreshing. There's a chill to the wind now, but it's never bothered me. Being a vampire means that no matter the weather, my body stays the same temperature. It's definitely a bonus in the freezing cold months, not that I would know. I'm just repeating what I've heard the humans say.

As I walk, I again allow my thoughts to stray back to the vixen. She was absolutely drop dead gorgeous: long brown hair, big brown eyes, and a toned body that I would love to have the time to explore. If only she weren't a hunter. With the way her scent makes my mouth water, I thought for a minute that it was possible she could be my mate, but there is no way the goddess is that cruel.

No, she's just a woman that I fucked. That's it. Though my traitorous body is craving her, I must find a way to get her out of my system.

When I reach the tree line, I pick up my pace, using my vampiric speed to run to the new bunker we're building just outside of pack land. After the battle with the mages, and when the hunters found our current compound, Alaric and I thought it would be best if we built a new underground compound closer to our allies.

My father thought it was a fantastic idea when I told him about it on video chat. He and my mother have been traveling for the past year or so after handing the coven over to me. I didn't think I was ready, and after my fuck up with the mages, I still don't think I am, but I have to admit that, without that shit show, I wouldn't have the friendship I now have with Alaric.

I've always been somewhat of a loner, at least since my sister was kidnapped when we were younger, anyway. Before that, I was outgoing, always going out—only with vampires, of course, or the humans during the summer to network for future willing donors. Back then, I didn't think it was right that the different supernatural factions mingled together like the shifters and witches do. After that night, though, not so much. It was my fault she was taken. I told her about the party the first night, thinking that I'd be the cool big brother, and then I let her talk me into not going with her. Sure, they didn't take her from that party, but that's where she met the fucktard who did. I've searched high and low the past sixteen years for him. If I would've had shifter allies, maybe they could've picked up on a scent, or if I was friends with some witches, maybe they could've done a locator spell right away rather than days later when the trail had already gone cold. The only reason we even knew it was the hunters was because of the crossbow they drew in the sand from where they took her. But even though Drusilla is back, I will continue to search for the ones responsible as long as I live, which is an extremely long time considering my father just celebrated his two-hundredth year on this earth. I'm about to celebrate thirty-four yet I still look to be in my early twenties. It's both a blessing and a curse.

Dru, though, hasn't been the same since she escaped. Sure, one of the hunters let her go, but that doesn't excuse their treatment of her before that. When she finally confided in me about her time in captivity, it took everything I had not to rush out and slaughter each and every one of them. The only thing that stopped me was the need to comfort her. That need outweighed my thirst for hunter blood. For the time being, at least.

As I walk into the house situated on top of the bunker, I'm hit with a wave of loneliness. I've never felt this hollow before, probably because I had no desire to find my mate. I have been completely satisfied with my life and string of one-night stands. Along with my agreement with Colleen, who's been able to satisfy me for years. What changed? Why, all of a sudden, do I feel like I'm missing something in my life?

I run my hand through my hair and blow out a breath. I'm not even sure why I approached her. I was enjoying myself in the company of Alaric, Darren, and Sebastyn just fine before she walked in. It was as if she put some kind of spell on me. As soon as she walked onto the dance floor, my eyes were drawn to her, and my body moved on its own until the next thing I knew, I was looking down at her swaying body, thinking of nothing but sinking my fangs into her pussy. What the fuck is wrong with me?

I walk into my barely finished office and glance around. There is so much to do before this place is finished. We need to finish building the apartments, the rec rooms, and the bunker in the basement so that we don't need to keep bothering Alaric or the pack.

I pull off my jacket, setting it on the back of the folding chair and get to work. I spend the next couple hours mudding and sanding the drywall in here, before making my way to what will be my apartment and collapsing on the futon I bought for this purpose. I can't go back to the coven tonight. There is no way I can face Drusilla after what I just did. She's going to hate me.

I groan, swiping a hand down my face. How do I fix this? Maybe it can be a secret just like the hunter said. But even as I think that, there is something about the statement that doesn't ring true. Not when my body buzzes with need just from the mere thought of her.

I wake up multiple times throughout the day, startling myself with dreams of the forbidden fruit I yearn for. There must be something I can do to get her off my mind.

As dusk settles in, Colleen makes her appearance, like clockwork. She shows up nightly at dusk to help take care of my needs. Since the battle, though, it's more like her needs are the ones being tended to as I've honestly had very little interest in her.

"There you are," she coos, coming straight up to me and sliding her perfectly manicured hand down my throat.

"Not tonight, Colleen." I say gruffly, batting her hand away. "Go find someone else to be your conquest for the night.

"Oh, come on, Drake. You know you're the only conquest I want."

I snort. "Sure, and I'm the fucking pope."

"It's been over a week since we were together, Drake. Surely, you need a release as badly as I do," she pouts. Normally, she would be right. Vampires are highly sexual creatures, and loathe as I am to admit it, Skarlyt was right about us getting highly aroused when feeding, which we need to do daily.

"I don't have time to play games with you right now. I have too much to do." I brush past her, heading down to the lower levels where the workers are.

I quickly find the foreman and offer my services. He hands me a list with all the apartments that are ready for the tapping and mudding, and I get to work, hoping and praying that it can keep my mind off that hunter and all the things I want to do to her.

Despite my best efforts, the night doesn't go as I planned. Each time I have a moment to think—which is all the time because my task doesn't require much use of my brain—I slip back into memories or fantasies of *her*. The hunter. I try and fail to paint her in a bad light by envisioning her perfect nose much larger than it truly is, making her chocolate brown eyes seem less bright, pretending that her perfectly perky tits are hanging down to her waist. And each time, the vision reverts to normal.

"What's going on with you?" Colin says, snapping me out of my thoughts. I didn't even hear him come into the room.

"Nothing. Just trying to get this place ready," I tell him, getting a glob of mud on my trowel before spreading it on the wall.

"That's not what I mean, and you know it. First, you don't come back to the coven this morning, and then I just walked passed a very pissed off Colleen on my way down here. What gives?" I turn to look at him. I should be annoyed at all his questions, but the concern on his face has me pausing.

I sigh, "I just have a lot to think about right now. There's a lot riding on my shoulders."

He dips his head, "I know. But that's why you have me. I'm supposed to be your second in command. I can't help you if you don't let me or answer your damn phone."

I reach into my pockets and pull out my phone, noting the dozens of missed calls and texts from him and Drusilla. "Sorry, man. I forgot I turned the ringer on silent."

"Yeah, well, you should be. We thought the worst. I called Alaric, and he said you left the bar before them and then you didn't come home. Dru's been awake half the day pacing. She was even considering leaving to make sure you were okay."

Shit. I really didn't mean to make them worry, though I should have thought about that possibility. Since the hunters returned, Dru's been hounding me constantly, asking me where I am, what I'm doing, worried that I'm going to be taken. "I need to call her," I say, pulling up her contact on the phone.

"You really do," Colin says as he leaves the room, obviously still pissed at me.

"Drake?" A very concerned Drusilla calls through the speaker.

"Yes. I'm sorry for not calling. I'm safe at the new building, trying to get things ready," I tell her, and she lets out an audible sigh.

"I thought..." She begins. I hear the shakiness in her voice and a pang goes through my heart.

"I really didn't mean to worry you. I just want this place ready sooner rather than later."

"I know, but a phone call or text only takes a second, Drake," she scolds.

"I really am sorry, Dru. My phone was on silent from when I went to the bar with the guys, then I got straight to work when I got here and forgot to turn the ringer on. Please forgive me," I plead.

"Just don't do it again," she says.

"I promise," I agree.

"I'm going to sleep now since I've been up half the day worried about you."

"I'll come home before dawn. If I don't, I'll send you a text."

"You better," she growls, hanging up the phone and leaving me standing in the middle of the half-finished apartment, feeling guiltier than ever. Not only am I lying to her by not telling her about the hunter, but now I'm worrying her about my safety. It really feels like I'm losing control of myself.

Chapter Five

Rayne

I wait at the motel for two days, hearing absolutely nothing from the pack or the blue-haired bartender, all the while dreaming of a certain sexy vampire. Each morning I've woken up horny as fuck, and no matter what I do, I can't cum. I've tried everything I can think of, going as far as to run out and grab a toy from a sex shop down the road. I get close but can't seem to take the final plunge over the edge into orgasm land. It's driving me insane. I thought I knew what being sexually frustrated was like, but all those times in the past have nothing on this.

After trying for twenty minutes today, I finally decided that I'm returning to Supernatural tonight to find someone who will let me ride them into oblivion. I don't care if I have to pay someone. I'm going to fucking cum before I go to bed tonight.

Just as soon as I convince myself that I am not going to hear anything again today and get ready to go out, there's a knock at the door. I quickly grab my knives from under my pillow and peek out of the peephole in the door. I breathe a small sigh of relief that it's not one of the hunters from my dad's group, but anxiety still pools in my gut at the extremely large man—who can only be a shifter—waiting outside my door.

I crack the door open without removing the chain. Not that any chain would be able to stop him if he really wanted to get in here, but it might give me time to gather more weapons. "Can I help you?" I ask.

"My friend Trevan said you wished to speak to me," the large man with the bluest eyes I've ever seen says to me.

"Trevan?" I ask. I don't know any Trevan.

"The Fae who runs Supernatural," he replies.

"The blue-haired bartender?" I ask.

"That would be the one."

"I asked to speak to the fire woman, not a shifter," I state to him. He quirks an eyebrow at me.

"Fire woman?" he chuckles. "She'll get a kick out of that. But you won't be speaking to my mate without convincing me you don't mean her any harm," he tells me. As annoyed as I am at the fact that I have to wait to talk to her, I understand his wanting to protect her. I've learned about mates, though probably from an alternate perspective from his. Where he cherishes and obviously protects his mate, I learned that it was a weakness to exploit. Supernaturals, especially shifters, will do whatever you want if it means the safety of their mates.

"Okay," I say.

"Do you mind if I come in?" he asks. I hesitate for a moment, wondering if that's a good idea but then think better of it. If I want them to trust me, I need to show them a little trust too and hope and pray he's not here to kill me.

"Oh, shit. Yeah. One minute," I say, closing the door quickly and removing the chain. I open it back up and gesture for him to enter the room.

His nose wrinkles up at the smell. "Maybe we should talk outside?" he stops just inside the door. I feel like maybe I should be insulted by that, but I know it's not me, it's just this room. It's gross.

I grab my coat off the back of the chair and follow him back outside. He leads me over to a picnic table at the edge of the forest and takes a seat. We sit there in silence for a few minutes before he speaks. "You wanted to talk to Phoebe about something?"

"That's her name? The fire woman?" I ask, causing him to chuckle again.

"Yes."

I blow out a breath. It was one thing to think about doing this, but another thing entirely to actually sit in front of a shifter as a hunter and ask for help. "I want her help."

He looks at me, shocked. "Help?"

I nod. "Yeah. I left my family behind because I can't stand by and condone what they do anymore. I need help to hide or disappear or something without being hunted down by other supernaturals. I don't even know what I'm doing anymore."

"And why did you think she could or would help you?" he asks.

"Because she saved me," I respond.

"Saved you?"

"Yes. The night of the battle, those mages who convinced my father to help them cornered us, and I'm sure that they were going to kill us. But the fire woman came and saved us. It was at that exact moment, when she was standing there—all on fire and shit—having just stopped the mages, when the group I was with started firing on her rather than thanking her, that I decided I couldn't stay. My father always said that we are descended from Ullr, the Norse god of the Hunt, and for a time I believed him and was committed to his mission, but that changed when I was a teenager." Maybe I gave him a little more information than I needed to, but once I started talking, I just couldn't seem to stop.

"Of course, she did that," he says, seemingly annoyed, and

scrubs his hand down his face. "Let me get this straight. You were born and raised as a hunter. But not just any hunter, one of the Chasen bloodline?" As he says my last name, I let my jaw drop open.

"How the fuck?" I can't even finish my sentence. I'm in so much shock.

"What?" he asks.

"How did you know my last name?" I question.

"All supernaturals are told stories of the Chasen Hunters. Your bloodline is basically the bogeyman to us. Where you were probably told stories of the evil supernaturals, they warned us of your family since the day of our birth. I honestly thought that my parents made it up until you just told me you were a descendant of Ullr," he tells me.

"I.... wait. You're saying that my dad was telling the truth? We really are descendants of the gods?" I ask.

"I can't say for sure because I don't know your exact lineage, but if you are a Chasen, chances are that he was, yes. But it's also for that reason that you will not be talking to Phoebe. I can't trust that you aren't just talking out of your ass to get to her. No offense," he says.

"Well, I do take offense to that. I'm not just talking out of my ass. Do you think that I would be staying in that dump if I were just here to trick you?" I say, gesturing to the motel behind me. He just shrugs his shoulders, and I begin to get more than a little pissed, jabbing my finger in his face. "Listen here. I've left my entire life behind because what they're doing is wrong. I quit my job as a cop, which I was pretty fucking amazing at, by the way, all because I don't want to hunt supernaturals anymore. I drove my car in the opposite direction to throw them off my trail. I have been staying in this fucking dump for a week, hoping to just get an audience with her. I know she would help me if she were here." I am about to go on to tell him what an ass he is, but I'm interrupted.

"Yes, she would," a feminine voice calls out, walking up to us. Oh, my goddess, it's the fire woman. Even without the flames, I can tell. "Hi. I'm Phoebe," she tells me, reaching out her hand.

"Rayne," I respond, grasping her hand and shaking it.

As soon as our hands touch, my mind is thrown back to the battle.

My family and I are at the edge of the forest, fighting for our lives against a group of mages, the same people we were here to help. Suddenly, a woman on fire lands in between us, facing off against the mages with a loud screech, and I watch them cower in fear. A couple teleport away quickly, but there are a brave few who think that their magic can withstand the heat. One by one they throw energy at her, which her flames melt before any of it can get close. I watch in awe as she lets loose a steady stream of flames towards them, turning them to ash within seconds.

She turns to us, cocking her head from side to side. For some reason, I trust that she's not going to hurt us, that only if we provoke her will she attack. I stand rooted to my spot as the rest of my group open fire on her.

Once again, she lets loose a stream of fire, although this time I don't think its intended to hurt us. Only a warm breeze caresses my hair, sending it flying behind me. I hear the others turn and run away, but I can't.

"Thank you," I say, and she gives a slight nod, leaving me reeling. That interaction was the complete opposite of what my father taught me to expect.

"Rayne, come on," Price yells for me, and I share one last look of thanks with the fire woman before turning and running to catch up.

"Love," the male shifter says, snapping me out of my flashback.

She rounds on him, putting her hands on her hips. "Alaric." To his credit, he shrinks down under the stare of this woman. Smart man. Well, a smart man wouldn't have pissed her off to begin with. Doesn't he know she can go on fire?

"I..." he starts, but she holds up her hand.

"Don't. Just don't. We will talk about this later when we're alone," she growls out before sitting down next to him. "I remember you," she cocks her head to the side to look at me.

I dip my head at her in response, hoping that she only remembers me from when she saved me and not from when I was fighting alongside the hunters in the battle.

"You were the one who thanked me," she states again.

"Yeah. That was me," I admit.

"So, why did you come looking for me?" she asks.

"Well, after what you did, I realized that the way I was raised was wrong." I pause. "No, that's not right. I've known for quite a while that it is wrong, but it was your actions that night that cemented the fact that I can't stand by anymore and let them hurt more innocent supernaturals. It's not anyone's fault how they were born. You can't help being a fire woman any more than he can being a shifter, or I can being a hunter, but what I can help is how I choose to live my life. And I refuse to stand by and watch as families are torn apart, all in the name of some misguided idea that just because you are different means they should eradicate you. Except maybe guys like this asshole, who judged me for being a hunter just as they judge you for being a supe. Pot calling the kettle black much?" As I speak, I watch her face go from shocked to compassionate, and finally she bursts out laughing. I wasn't really expecting her to laugh at my calling her mate an asshole, but after the way he just acted, it's justified.

"Well, I agree with almost everything you just said, but perhaps you and Alaric got off on the wrong foot. He's really not so bad when you get to know him," she says, placing her hand on his. "But I still don't understand what you want from me?"

"I want your help, or to help you, or for us to help each other," I stammer over my words as nervousness blooms in my chest. "Since the battle, my father is now more obsessed than ever about the mission. He has already contacted other groups of hunters, calling them here to help. He's planning on returning and attacking here. I thought if I gave you some inside information, maybe you would be willing to help me hide or disappear or something," I tell her.

"When is this attack supposed to happen?" Asshole Numero Uno asks.

I shoot him a quick glare before turning back to Phoebe. "Did you hear something?" I ask her.

She starts laughing so hard that tears flow from her eyes. She has to wipe them away while Alaric growls. "Oh, my goddess. Alaric, I love this girl. Can we keep her? Pretty please?" She looks at him with big puppy dog eyes that even I would have trouble saying *no* to.

After a moment, her laughter dies out, and she turns back to me. "But in all seriousness, when is the attack supposed to happen?" she asks.

"A month from now. My dad wanted to ensure that he had the numbers and information he required to win. He's been sending scouts to watch you. Although I'm sure if they actually were, you'd know it. They aren't very good at keeping a low profile. Most are cocky assholes, like this guy," I gesture my thumb to her mate. "Who would just stroll right up to you and start asking questions. I mean, it's not like you can tell that we're hunters unless you see the mark on the back of our necks. Or, you know, we try to kill you," I tell them both.

They look at each other for a brief second, seeming to have an entire conversation with their eyes. I wonder if they can communicate telepathically.

"Okay," Phoebe says at the same time as Alaric says "No," Phoebe gives him a death stare for a few minutes before his shoulders slump in defeat.

"Okay, you can come with us. But be warned: one step out of line, and I sick my brother on you," Alaric tells me.

Confused, I look at him with my eyebrows pinched. "Why would that scare me?"

"Because my brother was one of the shifters locked in the cages before the battle," he says. Oh, shit. Yup. Maybe I should be a little scared, even though I don't doubt my capabilities. I would imagine that a shifter feeling slighted would be extra motivated, and if said shifter had some friends or a mate... Well, let's just say, it would be extremely difficult to walk away unscathed.

"I swear to you that I mean you and those in your pack no harm," I tell him, making the sign of the cross over my heart.

Phoebe chuckles again before standing up and gesturing for us to follow. She leads me back to the motel. "Grab your stuff. You'll stay with us."

"The hell she will," Alaric growls out, grabbing her gently by the arm. "Did you forget who else lives with us?"

"No. Of course I haven't. But you need to trust me. I have a feeling in my gut that we need to help her," Phoebe tries to reason with him.

"You can help her while she sleeps somewhere that our children do not live," he bites back. I didn't even consider that they had children.

"You have kids?" I ask curiously.

"Yes," Alaric responds, not even bothering to look at me.

"Yes, we do. Two boys and one girl," she says to me before turning back to Alaric. "You need to trust me," she pleads again, rubbing a hand on his cheek. They have a mini stare down, but I see the moment he relents. His eyes close and he nods curtly before striding back to their truck.

"Alright. Let's get you packed," she says, clapping her hands together, before whispering to me. "I always get my way. He's a big pushover."

"I heard that!" He shouts.

"You were meant to," she calls back with a giggle.

It doesn't take long to pack up my modest belongings and return the key before we are driving to pack land. Goddess, how my life has changed in the past week. I'm no longer a hunter; instead, I'm sitting in a car on my way to stay with a pack of supernaturals. Hopefully, I'm making the right choice. I know I don't want to be a hunter anymore, but I hope coming here was the best thing to do. Maybe I should've just run on my own. But this is the absolute last place my dad or his cronies would ever look for me, and I can't not warn them. I owe Phoebe a debt. She saved my life that night; it's only fitting that I do what I can to save hers.

"If it's not rude to ask, what type of supernatural are you?" I ask Phoebe as we place my bag into the trunk.

"Don't answer that," Alaric growls from the front seat as we pack up and load the SUV.

"Actually, I'm a phoenix."

"No way!" I exclaim. My mouth drops open in shock. "But Phoenixes are extinct." Really, I should've guessed that is what she was when I saw her on fire, but our lessons on supernaturals only glossed over phoenixes because they are thought not to be around any more.

"That's what they tell me, yet here I am," she gestures to herself.

"I think you just broke my brain," I tell her, holding my head. "A Phoenix? Seriously?"

She nods again, a giggle slipping out. "Yupp."

My mind is reeling as we slide into the SUV. Holy shit! Maybe I was right in coming here. I'm sitting in a car with the most powerful supernatural known to the world. This is insane.

I half expect Alaric to put a blindfold on me so that I don't know where we're going, but I'm glad he doesn't. I like to be able to know all my escape routes.

Chapter Six

Rayne

Driving into the pack is surreal. I look around at all the homes, watching the children running from door to door, playing at the park. Just being kids. Tears come to my eyes as my mind whirls. How many kids just like this are now orphans because of someone in my family? How many parents have had to bury their child because of this misguided quest my father is on? How many kids, just like Dru, have been held captive? The tears flow faster the longer we drive as I think about how many lives I've ruined, even if indirectly. Sure, I have never actually killed a supernatural, but I've helped capture them. I've pointed other hunters in the right direction. I may not be the one who actually pulled the trigger, but I'm just as responsible for anything that happened to them as the one who did.

"What's wrong?" Phoebe asks, turning in the seat to look at me.

"Just thinking about how many lives I've ruined as a hunter. I don't think any of the hunters think of you as people with families, children, parents, brothers, sisters. They just think of you as animals. I wish I would've left years ago," I tell her honestly. I figure telling them the truth is the best way to get them to actually trust me. And from what I was taught, shifters can sense lies—or smell them—and as much as I don't want to admit, I need Alaric to at least tolerate me for the time being.

"We can't change the things that happened in the past. We can only focus on the present and work towards a future that we can live with," she tells me. I nod because that makes sense. And I hope to the gods that I am able to atone for the things I've done in my life.

We pull up to a large log house situated in front of a lake. It has a large wrap-around porch lined with seating, but that's not what catches my attention. It's the children sitting on the stairs waiting for us with a woman and a man behind them, both holding babies. Oh my gods. There are babies. I don't know why, when I realized there were children, that I didn't realize there would be babies. I'm a monster.

The two boys run up to Alaric and Phoebe as they get out of the truck. I stay sitting in the back seat with tears streaming down my face. I understand now why Alaric didn't want me to come here. Maybe he was right. What if I bring more hunters here sooner?

Phoebe opens the door to where I'm sitting. "Are you coming?"

"I think I should leave. This was a bad idea. I don't think I should've come here," I tell her, looking right into her eyes.

Her look softens. "It's okay. You're supposed to be here. I feel it in my gut. There is something bigger than us at play here. Come on, meet everyone. If you still want to leave in the morning, I won't stop you."

I search her eyes, wondering why she would be so compassionate toward me, but that's exactly what I find: compassion. Like she can sense all my inner thoughts and turmoil. I incline my head in agreement, hop out, and follow her to the stairs. She introduces me to Charleigh and Ashton, after Alaric ushers the boys, who

Phoebe tells me are Ryker and Riley, inside. Apparently, the babies are Cybil and Aurora, the cutest little girl. Although both Charleigh and Ashton let off a growl and snuggle the girls into their chest more at the mention that I'm a hunter, they both relax a bit when Phoebe explains about her gut feeling. Not sure why they're putting so much stock in her gut feelings, but I'm grateful. I know they will watch me like a hawk for the entire time I'm here, and that's okay. I have nothing to hide. I'll get them prepared for the fight with my father and disappear like I told them. All I need is their help to connect me with another shifter group somewhere in the world. That's the only way I'll be able to hide without my father finding me. If I were to attempt to stay hidden in the human part of the world, he would find me in less than a year. I have no doubt about that.

Phoebe gestures for me to follow her into the house but I pause, looking at Alaric as he walks out. "Is there a cabin or something where I can stay instead?"

Phoebe's eyes soften, and Alaric growls. "You can stay with us in the house."

I look at the door where the kids just walked through. Now that I understand why Alaric was reluctant to have me here, I shake my head, "I think you were right. I should stay somewhere where your kids don't sleep." Alaric nods and Phoebe goes to protest but I hold up my hand. "Just until I earn your trust."

Once again, Alaric nods in agreement while Phoebe looks like she wants to argue but dips her head in agreement as well.

After showing me to a small cottage just off to the side, built in such a way that it looks like it grew from the forest itself, Phoebe pulls me off to the side.

"Are you sure about this?" She asks, and I bob my head.

"Yeah, I am. But if I'm being honest, it's not really because of the trust thing. I don't know if I can be in the same house as your children without ending up a blubbering mess every time they walk in the room. The things my family has done..." I choke on my words, unable to finish thinking of how many children no longer have their parents because of my family?

She places her hand on my shoulder. "I understand." When I look in her eyes, I see that compassion again that I would never have expected from a supernatural to a hunter, which just proves even more that I'm doing the right thing.

* * *

The next few days go by pretty amazingly, if you ask me. It turns out Phoebe and I both have an extreme love of being snarky and have the ability to really put our feet in our mouths. Every time that I brought up talking strategy, Phoebe would blow me off, making some kind of excuse. I'm pretty sure she just wanted to get to know me first, or she wanted me to get to know them. Either way, I'm sure she accomplished whatever it was she intended, because I care more than I want to admit for every member of her family. Including Alaric, loathe as I am to admit it. Phoebe was right. He isn't so bad once I got to know him.

But today, we set up a meeting with the local supernatural leaders so I can give them all the information I have, and that's how it happens: I'm sitting at the dining room table with Phoebe and Alaric, waiting on the rest of the leaders when he walks in. Drake. The leading man in every single one of my fantasies lately. He looks shocked upon seeing me but recovers quickly. Gods, he looks just as sexy as the last night I saw him.

"Drake, I'm glad you made it," Alaric says, standing and clasping arms with him.

"Of course," he responds with a smile. Goddess, there's that smile again. Cue the gush, right on schedule, as my panties become soaked.

"This is Rayne, the one I told you about," Alaric explains, gesturing to him to take a seat.

"Rayne," he says my name like he's tasting wine.

"Hi. Nice to meet you," I say, meeting his eyes. Goddess, I wish I never did that. He looks pissed. No, not just pissed, furious. And all the gods help me if I don't find it the sexiest thing in the universe. I would love nothing more than for him to bend me over his knee and give me a spanking. Cue the gush again. Ugh, I really need to stop looking at him. At this rate, it's going to look like I peed myself.

"Rayne, would you like to accompany me for a walk? I'd like to get to know this hunter who wants to change sides before I put my trust in her," he questions. I know he just wants to talk to me without prying ears. I nod, not trusting my voice to come out in anything less than a seductive tone.

"Don't hurt her, Drake. I mean it. She's under my protection," Alaric growls out as we get up and move towards the door. Guess I'm not the only one who started caring.

"I promise she'll be in the same condition that she is right now when I return her," he responds without glancing back. He hovers his hand over the small of my back, leading me out the door. I so badly want him to make the contact and put me out of my sexually frustrated misery. My luck with being able to cum hasn't improved at all since coming here. The only difference being that I have been able to distract myself by talking to people.

We walk in silence through the woods for a few minutes. "So..." I start, but he cuts me off.

"Not yet." His tone is clipped, and I can see his jaw clenching from here. Why is this turning me on so much?

All of a sudden, he spins, grabbing me by the throat and pushing me up against a tree. Goddess, he really is strong. I'm about to complain when he pushes his mouth on mine, kissing me with a ferocious passion.

Not wanting to give in, I break from his hold and slap him across the face before spinning us both around. I push him up against the tree and move my mouth back to his in a hard and fast kiss.

We go back and forth like that a few times before I finally give in. I jump up, wrapping my legs and arms around him, rubbing my pussy over his very impressive bulge. I start moving faster, chasing my release that I know is coming up fast, when he pushes me away from him.

"No. Not like this," he says, stepping back and running his hand through his hair. He continues glancing at me in my spot by the tree, where I'm still reeling from the fact that I was so close, and he prevented it. Ugh.

"Hey! You started it!" I whine. I can see the very obvious desire to come back and finish what we just started, so I give him a little nudge. "Fine. If you're not going to help me, I'm going to help myself," I say as I sneak my hand down my body, into my pants, and begin rubbing circles on my clit. It's not as good as when he does it with his fingers, or even better, with his mouth, but it seems with him this close, it's actually going to work.

I watch as he visibly wars with himself, looking at my hand, then away, over and over, and I decide that I'm going to taunt him just a bit more. I shimmy my pants down so he can see exactly what I'm doing with the moon shining enough light through the trees to see. Or maybe he doesn't need that light at all. I don't know how well vampires can see in the dark.

"Mmm, Drake. This feels so good. But it would be even better if you came over here," I moan out. Closing my eyes, I continue, "You know what I'm thinking of right now? That beautiful cock of yours sliding in and out of my wet pussy." I insert a finger as I say the words, coating it with my juices before returning to my clit.

When I open my eyes, I see the moment I've won our little

battle as he's stroking himself under his pants. He takes no time at all, and he's kneeling before me.

"This doesn't mean anything," he says with a growl, before forcing my hand away and devouring my pussy.

"Oh god, Drake. Yes! Just like that," I scream as he takes my clit between his lips, stroking it fast from side to side with his tongue.

Seconds later, I'm screaming my release, coating his face in my juices. I don't even get a chance to come down from the high before I'm spun around, and he's entering me from the back.

"Oh yes!" I cry out, feeling the fullness that only he can provide, and the satisfaction that after days of being sexually frustrated, I'm finally able to cum.

I feel a smack on my ass. "This" *Smack* "Changes" *Smack* "Nothing," he says, each word through clenched teeth between smacks. I can't do anything but nod. He thinks he's punishing me, but I'm sure he can feel the way my pussy clenches with each one.

He thrusts in and out of me at a record pace, and soon I'm crying out my release once more.

"What the fuck is going on here?" a feminine voice calls out.

"It's not what it looks like," Drake says, stumbling back away from me and righting his clothes. I'm momentarily dazed, wondering if he has a girlfriend or worse, a wife, but shake that thought away. The bartender, Trevan didn't seem surprised that Drake and I were together, and I'm sure if he had someone, he would've made it clear I was in the wrong. Especially since I'm a hunter.

"Oh, good. Because I thought I just walked up on my brother fucking a hunter. You know, one of the people that stole me from my family and held me captive." Ah, 'Brother' not 'husband.' Wait. I know that voice...

I spin around, pulling up my pants. "Dru?" I question, and they both turn to look at me with shock.

"Rayne?" she questions, and at my nod, she rushes over, engulfing me in a hug. "Oh goddess, Rayne. How are you here?" She exclaims into my hair before leaning back, searching my body for any injuries. "Are you okay? What happened? I've thought about you every day! Wait," she says, stepping back. "Why are you here? Did the others come with you?" She looks around, concerned.

I place my hands on her shoulders. "You were right. They are monsters. I left. I'm never going back. That's why I'm here. But I never in a million years would've thought I'd find you," I say, wiping a tear from my eye. I always hoped I'd see her again, but it seemed like such a huge impossibility that I forced myself not to think about her. I wrap my arms around her once again, squeezing her tighter this time.

"Wait. What the fuck just happened?" Drake says, still concerned, looking between me and Dru from where he's standing, adjusting his pants.

"You remember I told you about that girl who helped me escape?" Dru says, gesturing to me, and I do my best 'that's me,' pose.

"Wait. What?" he says, still confused, although I'm unsure how. She literally just spelled it out for him.

"What's so hard to understand, Drake? Is it the fact that you just spanked the woman who helped your sister escape?" I tease with a wink. But instead of them finding it funny, Dru looks like she's going to puke, and he looks completely mortified. The laugh that leaves me isn't pretty; it's a full out hysterical laugh which causes them to both look at me with concern. But I can't help it. The thought of how he literally just 'punished' me for being a hunter, and then within minutes, I became the savior...It's just too ironic not to laugh. Plus, the looks on their faces are hilarious.

Dru recovers from her shock first. "Are you okay?"

I hold up my hand, gesturing that I just need a minute and force my giggles to die out. "Yup. Your brother here," I say, shooting my thumb at Drake, "thought I should be punished for not telling him I was a hunter when we met before." I use air quotes to put emphasis on 'punished' and 'met'. Obviously, she doesn't want to hear the details about how we got down and dirty without knowing each other's names, so I decide to tone it down for her.

"You what?" She wheels around towards her brother.

"I... I..." he stumbles with his mouth opening and closing like a fish and his eyes ping ponging between me and Drusilla.

I step back and watch as Dru's five-foot-two self walks up to her six-foot brother and stares him down. "Why would you do that?"

"I didn't know, Dru. Besides, it's not like she didn't like it," he tries to argue. She looks like she's going to puke again briefly before she recovers.

"Well, you won't be doing it again," she tells him before walking back over to me, linking her arm with mine, and together we walk back to the house.

"I missed you so much!" she tells me as we're walking.

"And I missed you," I respond and squeeze her arm a little.

"Drusilla?" Alaric says in surprise as we walk into the house.

"Hey, Alaric. Long time," she says in response, a small smile on her face. I look between her and Alaric in concern. They're both supernaturals, and obviously Drake and Alaric are allies, so why would it have been a long time since they saw one another?

"Hi. I'm Phoebe, Alaric's mate," Phoebe says, stepping up and reaching out a hand to Drusilla.

She takes it with a smile. "I've heard a lot about you."

"All good, I hope," Phoebe responds with a chuckle.

"Of course," She responds.

I pull Dru along with me, taking my spot back at the table,

letting her claim the spot next to me as Alaric and Phoebe tell her about their family.

We're still sitting at the table when some random woman I've never seen walks right in the house like she owns the place.

"Hey, guys," she says, walking up to Dru and wrapping her in a hug. "I haven't seen you in so long."

Dru hugs her back, though I do notice the flinch at the initial contact. "I know. Too long. But I heard you've been driving my brother crazy," she winks.

"Speaking of... Drake?" she says, her eyes glinting with mischief. Oh, I have a feeling I'm really going to like this one.

"Not today, Skar," he growls out from where he's sulking in the corner.

"Who put the stick up your ass today?" she asks.

"That would be me," I say from the table with an enormous smile.

"Did you need something, Skar?" Alaric says.

"Yeah. We need to be ready. A storm is brewing, and I think we're going to have a few battles to fight," she responds, being extra vague, and I'm sure that's due to me being here. But after I was finally able to release some of my pent-up sexual frustration, I can't seem to make myself care.

"You're right. We are. Especially with her here," Drake says with a snarl, pointing toward me. Instead of responding, I simply stick my tongue out at him.

To my surprise, though, Dru walks over and slaps him on the shoulder. "What did I tell you?"

Despite being berated by his sister, Drake doesn't stop the snarling. "Okay, what did I miss?" the newcomer asks, looking around.

"I'm Rayne. I was born and raised a hunter." As she steps back, I raise my hands. "Don't worry. I don't want to be one. I've never wanted to be one."

"She's the one who saved me," Dru says, stepping behind me and placing her hands on my shoulders in a show of support.

Now it's her turn to berate Drake. "You're picking on the woman who saved your sister? Shame on you."

He turns to look at her. "Just wait. She's worse than you at driving people nuts. On second thought, you two will probably end up being besties," he turns and walks out the door.

"He's just sour because his sister interrupted our hate fucking," I say, and Dru and Alaric look horrified while Phoebe and the new girl snicker.

"I'm Skarlyt," the newcomer tells me, wrapping me up in a hug. I was going to go for a handshake, maybe a high five. But I hug her back after my shock wears off.

"She's a hugger and doesn't know the meaning of personal space," Dru whispers, earning her own death glare from Skarlyt.

"Okay. I think this just turned into a girls' night. Dru's missed enough that I think one is in order. I'll text Trixie and Axel to reschedule," Alaric raises his phone, sending out a text message before looking back at all of us. I'm shocked, so is Dru, but Skarlyt and Phoebe grin like the cat who stole the canary. "I'll grab the wine and watch the kids. You girls have fun," Alaric says, placing a kiss on Phoebe's cheek and heading out of the room. All the women in the room walk towards the porch as Phoebe passes each of us a blanket to cover up with.

"What's a girls' night?" I whisper to Drusilla.

She shrugs, "I guess we'll find out." We both chuckle, each of us choosing a spot on the outdoor couches settled on the porch and getting comfy.

As Alaric walks out onto the porch, wine bottle and glasses in hand, he looks right at Skarlyt and says, "No funny business."

She places her hand over her heart. "I would never." But I can tell by the glint in her eyes that she most definitely would, so I snicker.

He gives her a look that says he doesn't believe her. "You forget that we've been friends our entire lives. I know you, Skarlyt Moon. Don't even think about corrupting my mate."

"As if I could be corrupted," Phoebe scoffs, making Skarlyt literally laugh out loud.

"I think you should be more worried about your precious mate corrupting me," she says.

Now it's Phoebe's turn to feign innocence by placing a hand over her heart. I have a feeling this could go on all night, and Alaric's a smart man as he just walks up, placing a kiss on Phoebe's head, before returning inside.

"Now that Captain Buzzkill is gone, let the fun begin!" Skarlyt says, swirling the wine bottle a few times with a mischievous look on her face. Oh boy. What did I just sign up for?

Chapter Seven

Drake

As I storm out of the house, I'm aware of two things: first, Skarlyt and Rayne are going to end up being the death of me, and second, my fucking balls hurt from being denied my release.

How could I have been so stupid to make the same mistake twice? And worse, Dru caught me. It doesn't matter who she ended up being, the fact of the matter is that Rayne is still a hunter, whether or not she wants to be one. Fuck.

I don't know what came over me. I had every intention of ripping her heart out if I ever saw her again. But then she was just sitting there with her pouty lips and perfectly sized tits popping out of her low-cut shirt, just begging to be fucked. My cock has been hard as a rock every morning for days after dreaming of this vixen. Seeing her in person did the exact opposite of what I hoped, which was to show me that she wasn't everything I remembered. Problem is she's all that and more. Goddess, just thinking about her now has my cock twitching in anticipation of touching her again.

Finally, the logical part of my brain fires up. It's too much of a coincidence that she shows up now, just after the battle. Then she runs into me at the bar, fucks my brains out, leaving me begging for more, like a little lost puppy, only to find out that she's a hunter who no longer wishes to be one. And then, just so happens to be the hunter who saved my sister. There are too many factors there for this to be anything but planned.

Shit. I just left Dru with her. Sure, she had Alaric, Phoebe and Skarlyt, but still. Rayne could have backup waiting just outside pack lands for a signal. Or she could convince Dru to go for a walk with her and lead her into a trap.

At that last thought, I pick up my pace and rush back to the house. I definitely don't expect to find the women on the porch laughing and drinking wine.

"Dru. Can I talk to you for a minute?" I ask, walking up the stairs. All laughter stops and eyes turn to me. I purposely don't look at Rayne. Even now, my body is trying to betray me and get closer to her. No. The need to protect my sister outweighs any desire to bend that little minx over and fuck her into next week. Maybe giving her a few extra spankings just because, and making her pulse on my cock.

Dru nods at me and together we turn to walk into the forest. I'm not sure how to start, so I stay quiet as I'm attempting to collect my thoughts. But Dru, being impatient as she is, blurts out, "What is it, Drake?" I can tell that she's still annoyed or angry with me, I'm not sure which. At first, I was worried about her finding out about me fucking a hunter, but now I don't know if she's upset because I was or because of the spankings. Either way I spin it, this is all way too fucked up.

I turn to look at her, taking in her innocent features. Sure, she's a grown woman now, but every time I look at her, I still see that little girl begging to go to meet a boy without her big brother. So innocent, full of life, in need of protection.

"I don't trust her," I say sternly.

"Who? Rayne?" she asks, and I dip my head in agreement. She waves her hand in the air, dismissing me. "We've been through this already. She saved me. What more do you need?"

"I understand that, Drusilla. But isn't it too coincidental that she shows up here after this long and happens to be in the place where you live? Come on. You have to see that there are some ulterior motives here," I try to reason with her.

"You know that's not true. Besides, even if it were, I wasn't the one caught fucking her, was I?" she bites back at me.

She's got me there, but it doesn't change anything. "That's exactly my point. She's put a spell on me or something. I can't seem to control myself around her. How many women have you ever seen that have that effect on me?" I pause as she thinks. "None. No woman has ever had me betray my entire species just to get laid. Come on, you know me better than that."

"Don't you think it could just be possible that she's your mate, and that's why you're reacting that way to her?" she questions, raising a brow at me.

"I admit that crossed my mind, but the goddess would never be that cruel to pair me with a hunter after what happened to you. And more than that, it was her family who did that to you. I have more faith in the gods than that," I tell her honestly.

"But she's not just any hunter either, Drake. She's the woman who saved me. She brought me extra blood to gain my strength, talked with me, treated me like a person rather than a monster. If it wasn't for her friendship, I would have been a shell when I left there, even more so than I already was."

I begin to pace, thinking over her argument. "Listen," she begins again, "even if what you think is true, and she does have some ulterior motive, I would be betraying my debt to her by not at least giving her the benefit of the doubt. You need to as well.

"If it weren't for that woman," she points back towards the

house, "you wouldn't have a sister to argue with right now. Think about that." She claps onto my shoulders to stop me from pacing. "I love you, Drake, and I know you blame yourself for what happened to me even though it's not your fault, but you can't push everyone else away because of something that might happen. Rayne could be your true mate, and you're ruining it by being suspicious. Why don't you try and get to know her before you make that judgment?"

Both our heads snap to the side at the sound of someone sucking in a breath. "Are you saying that Rayne is your mate?" Skarlyt says, walking out of the Shadows.

I shoot Dru a look that begs her to keep her mouth shut. "No. That's not what we're saying at all," I growl out.

"But," Skarlyt starts, but I cut her off.

"I don't know what you think you just heard, but that hunter is *not* my mate!" I say through clenched teeth.

She looks between Dru and me in confusion. "I don't understand."

"I think she's his mate. He seems to think differently. Either way, let's keep this to ourselves," Dru says, walking toward her. "Let's head back."

"This conversation isn't over, Dru," I call out to her.

"It is until you pull your head out of your ass. Not only did that 'hunter,' as you put it, save my life ten years ago, but she's saved it again by getting me out of the house and giving me the strength I needed to realize I need to live again. When you're ready to be grateful for the gift she's given you, you know where to find us," she spits back at me, continuing to walk away with Skar.

"Fuck," I whisper to myself. Could she be right? Could Rayne be my mate? No. That's stupid. There's no way. All I need is to find a woman to warm my bed and all my thoughts of her will be gone. That, and I need to watch her closely; she's going to fuck up sooner or later, and I'll be right there to catch her when she does. And not in the sexy way my body seems to want.

I head back to the new build and get to work. Since we're not meeting with the other faction leaders today, I have the time. All the apartments on the top five levels are ready to be painted, with the bottom five only needing the drywall finished. It's moving along a lot quicker than I expected, but with Axel's bear shifters working by day and the vampires working by night, we're getting double the work done each day. Within the next week, we will be able to move everyone in and figure out what to do with our current building.

I was surprised to see Dru out of her apartment, even more so that she was on pack land. And the way she stood up to me...I saw a bit of the fire in her that I haven't seen since before she was taken. I caught a glimpse of the woman she would've been. I guess I should be thankful to Rayne for that, if nothing else. She has my sister's loyalty, something not easily given. Even if she is a hunter and betrays us—which I'm sure she will do—I'll forever be grateful to her for setting Dru free both in the past and now.

Like every night for the past few, I get lost in the familiarity of taping and mudding the drywall, forcing myself not to think of Rayne and my traitorous body's needs.

Maybe I need to find Colleen and get her to take care of this for me. I contemplate doing just this, but as soon as Colleen's image flashes through my mind, my cock softens. Fuck! I would take care of it myself but for some reason, I haven't been able to complete the deed. Each time, I stand there, moving my hand up and down, trying lotion, lube, even water in the shower, nothing. It's like there's a block on it and the only thing that will let me cum is *her*.

What if I just use her for sex? She seems to enjoy it. I know I sure as fuck do.

No. No way. I'm not spending more time with her than I already have to. Although, if I use her for sex, it will allow me to get closer to her. Thoughts for another time. The way my body is betraying me already, I can't trust that I won't do something stupid like bond with her.

Chapter Eight

Rayne

We're sitting on the porch drinking wine from a bottle that seems to never be empty, even though I'm pretty sure it should have been three glasses ago. But that doesn't matter. What matters is the fact that, for the first time in my life, I'm sitting down, drinking, and laughing with a group of women, and I'm having fun while doing it. Sure, I went out for drinks with my coworkers before, but most of them were men, and it never felt as right as this does. This feels completely natural, as if I'm not a hunter and they aren't supernatural beings. We're just a group of friends telling jokes and laughing at each other's antics.

I watch Dru's face light up as she and Skarlyt reminisce, laughing at some of the pranks they pulled in their younger years. I have a hard time connecting Dru to the outgoing, mischievous older girl corrupting a younger Skarlyt. But the stories just don't seem to stop, leading me to believe them.

"Where was Drake in all this?" I question, unable to keep his name out of the conversation and kicking myself for it. Even saying his name seems to spark a fire in my core. There's some kind of connection between the two of us; I know it. I just wish I knew what it was or why.

"Oh, Drake didn't associate with anyone outside of our coven. When he was younger, he felt himself above all other supernaturals. Hell, he didn't even meet Alaric until recently," Dru admits.

"So, nothing has changed," I respond. From the few times I've been around him, that's exactly how I would explain his actions. Like he's better than everyone and everything. Skarlyt bursts out laughing at my comment, but Phoebe just shakes her head.

"Come on guys, he's not that bad," she tries to reason with us, but Skar and I just laugh even harder.

Even Dru laughs along with us. "It does seem like the stick in his ass has gotten longer or more pointy in the last week or so," she says, giving me a pointed look.

I shrug my shoulders. "I have no idea what you're talking about," I tell her, taking another drink from my glass. Maybe it was my comment or the way I said it, as if she didn't walk up on us fucking in the woods earlier, but she has tears flowing out of her eyes with her hysterical laugh.

I didn't realize just how much I missed Dru until I saw her again. Reconnecting with her in this setting is so much more than I could ever have dreamed. I reach over and clasp her hand, giving it a slight squeeze. She looks at me in confusion but returns the gesture. Maybe it's the wine or maybe it's just that the events of today are catching up with me, but I'm starting to get a bit emotional.

"Dru. Can I talk to you for a minute?" Drake's voice rings out, making my emotions jump from sappy to turned on in a matter of seconds. Gods be damned. Why does the simple sound of his voice send sparks straight to my clit? I can tell he is purposely not looking at me, and a pang of hurt slices through me. But then again, he had told me in the forest earlier that nothing would happen between us anymore. It still doesn't stop the pain at the thought of never touching him or having him touch me again. Dru gives my hand a small squeeze, and she gets up to follow her brother.

As I stare off in the direction they walked, Skarlyt snaps my attention to her by clapping her hands together. "Now that Dru is gone, what's the deal with you and Drake?" she asks with a raised eyebrow.

I shrug my shoulders in response. How do I explain something I don't quite understand myself?

"Come on. I may not have a wolf's sense of smell, but I could still smell the two of you all over each other when you came back earlier," Phoebe adds.

I sigh. "I'm not really sure."

"What do you mean, you're not sure? You guys had sex, right? You said Dru interrupted your hate fucking," she asks before taking another drink.

"Well, yeah. But it's more than that," I try to think of the words that would describe what is going on between us.

"Okay, try to explain it to us," Skarlyt says.

"Well, I went to Supernatural the other night to try and find a way to contact you," I gesture to Phoebe, and they both nod. "When I was there, before I talked to the blue-haired bartender..."

"Trevan," Skarlyt supplies.

I dip my head in thanks to her for supplying his name. "Trevan. Anyway, it felt like there was this magnet pulling me further into the club. I tried to resist it until I couldn't anymore, and it led me straight to a booth at the back. I was swaying to the music, trying to get the courage to walk over to said booth, when he came up to me. We didn't exchange names. We hardly even spoke to one another before the pull became electric, and he brought me to this room in the back, where we could be alone," a small smile graces my face at my memories from our brief time together in that room.

"And..." Skarlyt says leaning forward.

"We had the most mind-blowingly amazing sex I've ever experienced in my life. But then when it was done, he saw my hunter's mark and got all growly and weird. I guess it makes sense now that I know Dru is his sister, and was there for what happened to her, but in that moment, there was a brief feeling of pain at the disgust plastered on his face for being with me. I honestly thought that I'd never see him again.

"But then he showed up here, and we had a brief hate fucking session in the forest before Dru found us. Talk about awkward. Other than that, I don't know what it is. I feel this pull to him, but I can also feel his desire to stay as far away from me as he possibly can. So, I guess I just don't know." I take a large gulp of wine as I finish, and the two of them look at each other and back at me before barking out laughs once again.

"Wait," Skarlyt holds up her hand, attempting to speak between chuckles. "So, Dru walked up on you and her brother getting down and dirty in the forest?"

"Yup. More specifically, he had just got done spanking me and telling me that it would never happen again, while he was giving me the biggest orgasm of my life."

"Do you think it's never going to happen again?" Phoebe asks with sadness, lacing her words.

I shake my head *no*. I can't admit it out loud quite yet. "I just need to focus on something else. I have never reacted this way to a man. Never been the 'relationship' type."

"It could just be that you've uprooted your entire life, so you're subconsciously grasping onto the first thing that seems solid," Phoebe tries to reason.

"Yeah, that could be it," I admit, but even as the words come out of my mouth, it doesn't ring true.

"Well, this party just went from fun to somber. I'm going to find Dru and drag her ass back here so we can get back to having fun," Skarlyt says, grabbing the wine bottle and heading out into the forest.

"I wanted to thank you again for saving me and my family that day. You didn't have to, and they didn't respond the way any person—supernatural or human—should. But you did it anyway, and I'm grateful," I tell Phoebe.

She waves her hand at me as if it was no big deal. "I couldn't stand by and let humans, hunter or not, be at the mercy of those assholes. What you don't know about me is that I wasn't always aware that I was a Phoenix. In fact, I once thought I was completely human and married an evil man who sought to control me. He was mentally and physically abusive, broke me down until I had no one and nothing except him, or at least that's what he made me believe. We were married for just over ten years and had two children together. They are the lights of my life, and I wouldn't trade them for the world. But it wasn't until Alaric and I happened upon each other, in a grocery store of all places, that I realized what I had with Tanner wasn't what was meant for me.

"I'll spare you all the details, but long story short, Tanner ended up being a mage. He had me and my boys tethered, siphoning our power to fuel the coven, leaving us human. It wasn't until after he abused one of my boys that I found the courage to leave him. It's still strange to me, but it pushed me directly towards Alaric. When people used to say that you know the moment when you meet your soulmate, I thought they were crazy. But that's how it was. It was instant and electric. It was as if one day I was simply drifting by in a gray world, and then the next day, color took over. As if my life didn't truly start until I met him.

"Now it's been over a year. We have a beautiful daughter, Aurora, and a life that rivals even my wildest dreams."

As she finishes her story, my jaw is hanging open. I'm having trouble connecting the woman she described in an abusive relationship with the strong woman I've spent the past few days getting to know. Never in my life would I have thought she was anything but the confident, strong, absolutely fantastic woman sitting in front of me. But we all have our secrets, and I never once would've guessed that the boys don't belong to Alaric. They interact as a father and his sons should. He even purposely tries to keep them away from me, protecting them from the big bad hunter until he makes his mind up about me. Not that I mind.

I'm lost on what to say and luckily, Dru and Skarlyt choose that time to return. "What was all that about?" I ask, gesturing to her walk in the woods with her brother.

She and Skarlyt share a look. "He was just being his usual self. Don't trust the hunter. Blah blah blah," Dru says.

"It was about me?" I ask. I really shouldn't be surprised. He hasn't hidden his contempt for me. But then there's a traitorous part of my heart that flutters at the thought he was thinking about me as if it doesn't matter whether it's good or bad.

"Of course, it was. You're an unknown element in his life that he has no control over. And for a control freak like Drake, that's a huge deal. Don't worry. I set him straight," she says as she comes and sits next to me once more. For a moment, I'm lost in my thoughts of Drake and his distrust of me before I realize that what this one man thinks of me shouldn't matter. I'm fucking fabulous, and I'm going to enjoy it immensely when he realizes that. I'm going to make him get on his knees and beg for my forgiveness. What he does while on his knees...now, that is the question.

I stop my mental planning of what exactly Drake can do to earn my forgiveness and bring my awareness back to the present. The girls and I sit and drink into the wee hours of the morning when the sky is turning a slight pink, showing the impending dawn.

"I should go," Dru says, eyeing the sky.

"Stay downstairs. It's already all set up. And that way Rayne can stay with you," Phoebe offers.

Dru nods, and after saying a goodnight to Phoebe, Skarlyt leads us through the house and down the stairs to a keypad on the wall. After entering a code, the wall opens, and we enter a bunker of sorts. I want to explore every inch, but for now, I'm tipsy. Okay, maybe I'm a little more than tipsy, and tired, and probably won't even remember it in the morning.

"Through that door over there are the beds. The bathroom is to the left and there is food in the kitchen right here," Skarlyt says, walking us inside and pointing to the fridge.

"Can you show me how to open and lock the doors?" Dru says with anxiety coating her words and reminding me of the girl I found in that cage. I grab her hand and give it a squeeze. I want to reassure her that I will always protect her, but the fact that I can hardly stand up straight and need to lean on the back of the couch for support says otherwise.

"Sure," Skarlyt says, bringing her back to the door. I don't follow, mainly because I can't without falling down and wait until Dru returns, slipping her arm around my waist.

"Let's get you to bed."

Everything is a blur as Dru pulls me further inside. I feel something soft under my head just before everything goes black from me passing out. Hopefully they have Tylenol because my head is going to hate me in the morning.

Chapter Nine

Rayne

Waking up in a strange place with a pounding headache is not my idea of a good time, but it's what I got. I roll over once, right onto the floor. "Fuck!" That hurt. I hear a small snicker coming from my left, which quickly turns into a full-blown laugh.

"Aren't you even going to ask if I'm okay?" I scowl at Dru.

Between giggles she gets out, "Are" ha, ha "you" ha, ha "okay?"

I grab the pillow off the bunk and whip it in her direction. As usual, I hit my mark and her giggles stop. "Not so funny now, huh?" I snicker back at her. She throws the pillow back at me, so I sit up quickly, failing to catch it. Bad idea. The room spins and my head throbs. "Ah. Oh man, I haven't felt this shitty since I was a teenager," I groan.

"Sucks to be you," Dru chuckles at me, laying back down and getting comfy.

"How do you feel fine? You drank just as much as me," I question. "Wait, is it one of those vampire perks?"

"Yep. Never get hung over. Downside is that we can only get

drunk if we drink elderberry wine laced with blood. Literally everything else just comes right back up," she responds.

"Huh, interesting," is all I can say. I mean, I knew that there were some perks to being supernatural, but come on, never getting hung over? That's just unfair.

Don't get me wrong; there have been times where I've daydreamed about being supernatural. Maybe a wolf shifter or a witch, but never a vampire. Nothing against them, it's just that I don't think I would be able to have a blood only diet. I love my food way too much.

"Wait. Did I drink blood last night too then?" I ask, if she can only drink wine with blood in it and we all drank out of the same bottle...

"No. I put a few drops in my glass each time I refilled it."

"You had blood with you? Where? I didn't see any."

"I always keep a small vial of blood on me just in case. Though I've only ever used it once before last night." The way she says it makes me want to ask why she didn't need to use it before, but she yawns loudly and rolls back over. I'll save my question for another time.

My stomach rumbles at the thought of food, and I get all the way off the floor and stretch. As my bones creak and groan, my muscles remind me that I haven't trained in over a week and really need to find somewhere I can work out.

"Do you think Alaric has a gym in this place? I mean he must, to keep all those muscles, right?" I ask Dru.

She lets off another enormous yawn. "I don't know, go ask. I'm going back to sleep. Wake me up when the sun goes down," she tells me. I shrug my shoulders and head in the direction of the light, wondering how the hell she knows whether the sun is up or not. I look around as I walk and don't see a single window. Maybe it's another one of those vampire traits. I don't really remember much of last night after Skarlyt and Dru came back. But following the light pays off because the next thing I know, I'm walking into a large common room with a living room, kitchen, and bathroom.

I walk into the massive bathroom, immediately sit down to do my business, and take a look around. I spot the showers and, hanging just outside of each, is a big fluffy robe. Thank the gods, or Phoebe, you know, since it was probably her.

As soon as I step under the spray, my head throbs turn into a dull ache. I quickly wash myself, staying under the hot water for longer than I need, but the positive effect it has on my hangover outweighs my stomach's rumblings. Well, almost. When my hunger rumbles turn into hunger pains, I know it's time to get out. I wrap myself in the fluffy robe, squeezing as much water out of my hair as I can.

I glance around for something to wear when I head up the stairs, but other than my dirty clothes, I find nothing. I wrap the robe tighter around me and decide that this is the best I'm going to get until I can get to my bag from my cottage.

I walk up to the door in the wall and look around, unsure of how to open it; there's no handle. I spot a sticky note on the right side. 'Punch code into panel.' I see the panel and punch in the numbered code written on the bottom of the note. The door slides open.

After securing the door closed once more, I head out of the room. I'm momentarily confused as to where to go until I hear voices coming from the stairs. Guess I'll head that way. I slowly make my way up, clinging to the robe. The last thing I want is to have any of my bits shown in front of Phoebe or her family, especially after she's been so nice to me. As I crest the top of the stairs, I see two little heads turn in my direction with wide eyes.

"Good morning," I say to them with a soft smile.

"You mean, 'Good afternoon'," the older blonde boy corrects.

"Be nice. Rayne probably isn't feeling very well this afternoon," Phoebe berates them with a chuckle while handing me a coffee. "I wasn't sure how you took it, so I just made it like mine with milk and sugar."

I take a tentative sip because if I'm honest. I tend to use a little more sugar than the average person would deem necessary. "It's perfect," I tell her, taking a larger swig. She has perfected the sugar to coffee and milk ratio; I'm impressed. "I'm sorry about the robe. I left my bag in the cottage next door."

"Oh, shit," Phoebe starts.

"Mom, language," Phoebe's son, Ryker, who looks just like her, says.

She rolls her eyes at him. "I think you've been spending too much time with Constance." Turning back to me, she says, "Your bag is over there. Alaric brought it over from the guest cottage earlier. I would have brought it down to you, but I don't think I was feeling much better than you this morning."

"You weren't," Alaric says, walking in through the patio doors and giving her a kiss.

She scowls at him but leans into his embrace all the same. "It's all Skarlyt's fault. I wouldn't have drunk so much if she didn't spell the bottle to keep refilling," she says with an innocent look on her face.

"That's what you say every time. You know you don't have to keep drinking it," Alaric chuckles at her.

"So you say. You don't see the look she gives me if I tell her I don't want any more," she pouts.

"It's true. I think I vaguely remember Phoebe saying she didn't want anymore, and Skarlyt said something to the effect that she wasn't a true Phoenix," I speak up, coming to Phoebe's defense.

Alaric gives me a skeptical look while Phoebe looks back at him triumphantly. I simply shrug my shoulders in response. At the first sign that Alaric is going to call me on my bullshit, I quickly grab my bag and rush back down the stairs.

I take my time getting dressed so that Phoebe can steer Alaric to a different conversation. I allow myself to think back on the events of yesterday. Never did I think I'd see Drake again, nor did I think I would feel his touch once more, but I did and now I can't stop thinking about it happening again. But then I think about how he looked at me and talked to me, even during our throes of passion. Like I disgusted him. It sends a pang of hurt through my chest that I don't understand. Never in my life have I hated someone so much yet wanted them so badly it almost kills me. How could I, Rayne Chasen, allow a man this much power over me, supernatural or not?

If my father could see me now, I think he'd kill me himself for consorting with the enemy. But are they our enemies? I find myself questioning now more than ever before if a vampire truly did kill my mother, or if that was simply how it was made to seem. After meeting the few supernaturals I have over the last couple of days, I find it hard to believe that they could be as evil and corrupt as I've been taught. I'm sure like every species, there are good and evil beings, but I can not believe that they are all lumped into one category because of the actions of a few. Just like the old saying: don't let a few bad apples ruin the bunch. The actions of the few can not, and should not, represent the whole species.

I'm hoping that in time I can win Drake over. I know he doesn't trust me, given what happened to Dru, and I don't blame him. I don't entirely understand my need for his approval either, but at this point, I'm done fighting it. My body and heart seem to know what they want, and that is him. It doesn't mean that I'm going to be following after him like a lost puppy, though. I'm a strong, independent woman. I do not need a man, nor will I ever lower myself by begging for one's attention. No matter what my heart wants, if he does not change his tune, I won't be waiting around for him forever.

I give my head a shake to clear the thoughts. No sense getting all worked up over possible futures. I need to live in the now. For the first time in my life, I don't have some 'duty' hanging over me or someone's opinion of what is right or wrong to follow. I don't have to hunt. I just have to do what's best for me.

I head back up the stairs to find Phoebe, Alaric, and their kids sitting at the table eating. For a moment, I feel like I'm intruding, before I notice the empty place setting at the end of the table.

"Took you long enough," Phoebe says, turning around and gesturing to the empty seat.

I let out a little chuckle and take my seat. "Thank you."

One of the boys, Ryker if I'm not mistaken, is staring at me, cocking his head to the side, obviously wondering who the fuck I am. I've been here for a few days now, and despite Phoebe's insistence, I've tried to steer clear of the kids as much as possible until I could gain Alaric's trust. A normal person probably would've introduced themselves at this point or said something. But I'm not a normal person, so I mimic his movements instead: cocking my head from left to right, raising an eyebrow then the other, even opening and closing my mouth. It's really hard not to laugh, but it's now become a competition on who can hold out the longest. And I absolutely refuse to lose to a kid.

Finally, the other one speaks up. "Who are you?"

I stop mimicking his brother and turn to look at him. "I'm Rayne. Who are you?" I ask.

He looks at his parents and back to me, but instead of getting backed up by his parents, they both just give him a look that says, 'you made your bed.' "I'm Riley," he finally spits out.

"Well, hello, Riley. It's very nice to meet you. And who might you be?" I state, turning back to his brother for the last part of the statement.

"Uh...I'm Ryker."

"It's nice to officially meet you as well, Ryker," I state, turning to look at Phoebe. "And this little spitfire must be Aurora," I gesture to the bundle of cuteness sitting in her highchair.

"It sure is," Phoebe says, turning to look at her daughter with a sparkle in her eye that can only be described as unconditional love. What I wouldn't give to have known that look from my mother. Something so simple, yet foreign to me; my father definitely never gave me that look.

We eat our meal in a casual silence. Rather than being awkward as I expected, it seems natural, as if a hunter and some supernaturals share a meal all the time. Although now that I think about it, am I still a hunter if I'm no longer hunting? The mark on my neck would say so, but how at home I feel here begs to differ.

"Hey, Alaric, can I ask you something?" I try to catch him before he leaves again to do his alpha duties.

"Sure, what's up?" he asks. It's crazy how amazed I still am that he walks, talks, and looks like a normal person, but he can shift into a wolf. If I were to have believed everything I was taught, he would be a snarling beast, no matter which form he took, with only one desire: human blood. He wouldn't have a mate or children. He definitely wouldn't have a witch for a best friend or a hunter as a house guest. It makes me wonder if there's a way I can change the way other hunters view supernaturals as well. There's no way they can all be brainwashed nit wits.

"I was wondering if there was somewhere I could work out or train?" I ask him, "I have never gone this long without doing something, and my muscles feel like they're shrinking."

He chuckles at me. "I don't think they're shrinking after a week or two, Rayne, but yeah, there is. We have a gym over there at the building with the sign 'gym' on the front. Some people do spar every afternoon, but I'm not sure how many takers you're going to have."

I turn and look in the direction he's pointing. Sure enough, just down the street there is a large log cabin style building with the sign 'Gym' on the front. Well, don't I feel like an idiot now. "Thanks. But what about you? Would you be willing to spar with me? If I know my dad, and I do, he's going to attack here sooner rather than later, and I want to be sure that all of your pack members are aware of how we fight, the way we move and can anticipate your movements. Like all other hunters, I've been trained since I could walk on how to beat a supernatural in either form. If we can figure out a way for you to deviate from the norm, it might give us more of a fighting chance."

He sighs, rubbing his chin. "About that. Are you really going to be able to help us take down people you've known your entire life? Your own father?"

I pause, not expecting his question. "I've thought a lot about it, and even before I left to come here, I had to make sure it was something I am willing to do. Do I want to kill my dad? Absolutely not. Do I want him to die? Again, no way. But the others in his group? I couldn't care less about them. They're nothing but entitled pricks who deserve to be taken down a peg, or ten. Do I wish that there was a way to save my dad and get him to see reason? One hundred percent, but I also know that the chances of him changing his tune at all is zero.

"At the end of the day, I have to think about what is right. And what the hunters do is not right in any sense. If they were, say, directed to those supernaturals who were actually preying on innocent humans, sure, but they see any supernatural and think they're evil. That's not right, and it needs to be stopped. When they decide to attack, we'll be ready," I tell him with conviction in my voice.

"I appreciate you saying that, but I would never ask you to go against your family in battle. You can help us train, sure, but when it comes to the actual fight, you should sit out," he says, his eyes softening with something like pity in them.

"No. I want every single one of them to see me fighting on this side. I want all of them to second guess themselves. Besides, I can handle it. I know you don't know me well, and one day I hope to fix that, but for now, let's just say that I was the best hunter they had. If any of your men or women can beat me, they will literally wipe the floor with them. The real concern will be the weapons. If we can get the witches on some sort of spell to render them inoperable, it will end up being a very short battle," I tell him honestly. I want—no—need to be a part of this. Maybe it is possible to get some of the hunters to see reason. I know not all, and I know for sure my dad will not be one of them, but even if we can change a small few, it will go far in the future.

"I thought you were only stopping here until you could find somewhere to disappear?" He asks, and I freeze. That was the plan.

I look back at the house, envisioning myself looking through the walls and seeing the petite blonde-haired vampire sleeping in the basement. "I don't know anymore," I say turning to him. Rather than pushing me on it, he simply smiles knowingly.

"Okay. I will talk to Skarlyt to see if she can get some of the coven members to search for a spell to stop their weapons from working. But as for you fighting, let's just wait and see. It's one thing to talk about going up against your friends and family, and it's another thing entirely to actually do it," he says. I see his reasoning. I know I'm not going to change my mind, but I incline my head in agreement anyway. I'm sure he'll learn soon enough that when I set my mind to something, it generally happens.

I wave to Phoebe and head over to the gym after thanking Alaric for his advice. As soon as I walk into the building, gasps go around. A normal person would have felt shy or wary, but again, I'm not normal.

"Listen up. I'll make this brief. Yes, the rumors are true: I am a hunter." At the growls, I know I've got their attention now. "But it's also true that I have left my home and my family in order to help you prepare in the event that hunters ever attack again." I word it that way because I'm unsure what Alaric has told them and don't want to cause mass panic. "I will be working out here daily, sparring as often as I can with whoever is willing," I finish my little speech and throw my hair up into a bun before bending down and starting my stretches.

A surfer-looking man with shaggy blonde hair, sun-kissed skin and bright blue eyes comes up to me and puts his hand out. "I'll take the first spar. I'm Lennox, Skarlyt's mate."

I reach up and shake his hand. "I'm Rayne. I'm sure your mate has told you all about me," I tell him with a chuckle. "After all, I'm sure I spilled more than my fair share of secrets last night."

"No secrets that I know of. All she said is that you were here, had saved some chick named Dru, and were, in her exact words, cool as shit," Lennox says.

"Thank the gods for that," I respond. We quickly get to work sparring. For a shifter, he's extremely good at anticipating my moves and even took me down a time or two. By the time we're done, we have a large crowd, with others signing up to take me on tomorrow.

"Thanks for this, Lennox. It seems you broke the ice with the pack," I tell him as I towel off the sweat.

"No need to thank me. I was a newbie here not that long ago," he responds.

Huh. I wonder how that works. I always assumed that there was some sort of transfer happening between packs and what not, but I'll have to ask Alaric how that works.

"I call dibs tomorrow," a beautiful dark-skinned woman says while walking up to me. The graceful way she moves means she's definitely not a wolf shifter and too small to be a bear. She must be some sort of feline.

"Sounds good to me," I say, holding my hand out to her. "Rayne."

She clasps my hand back. "Samara." Her handshake is firm, and I can tell by the little bit of gold coming through her eyes that I'm going to have my work cut out for me. I can't wait.

Chapter Ten

Rayne

They say time flies when you're having fun or, in this case, time flies when you're kicking ass or getting your ass kicked. I would love to say that I won every round I went with the group of shifters that actually had the balls to sign up, but the truth is Alaric has some very talented fighters in his ranks. By the time I actually leave the gym, the sun has set, and my stomach is letting me know that I haven't eaten in hours. The burn I feel in my muscles, though, is phenomenal. After not training for almost two weeks, I expected some stiffness in my movements, but I was just as fluid as ever.

I head back to Phoebe and Alaric's home and pause at the door. Do I knock? Do I just walk in? I'm standing there contemplating my choices when a gorgeous blonde woman walks up. "Are you lost?" she asks.

"Huh?" I say, turning towards her. She gestures to the fact that I'm standing there staring at the door. "Oh. No, I'm not lost. I'm just debating whether I should knock or just walk in."

She looks at me in confusion. "I'm sorry, but who are you and why would you just walk in?" she asks, giving me a look that comes across as fierce.

"I'm Rayne," I tell her, sticking my hand out to her. "I've been staying here. I think we met the first day I got here."

"Oh the hunter... right... I'm Charleigh. Phoebe's best friend," she says skeptically, taking my hand. She was on the porch the first day when I came here, with her mate Ashton and the two babies.

Without another word, she opens the door and yells into the house, "Babe, are you expecting someone named Rayne?"

Phoebe comes rushing to the door with Dru hot on her heels. "Yes. We were just going to send out a search party for you. We expected you back a while ago. I mean, how long can one person work out at the gym?" she asks, wrinkling her nose.

I let out a small laugh, relaxing. "You'd be surprised," I tell her.

"I'm so glad you're back!" Phoebe exclaims, pulling Charleigh into a hug.

"Dude. I was only gone for two days."

"Two days too long," Phoebe pouts making everyone chuckle.

"Awe. You missed me," Charleigh smirks. "But you do realize I have some more training sessions coming up too right?"

"Yes. And I don't like it," Phoebe crosses her arms over her chest.

"Well, I happen to think it's important. Especially with all the traumatic events happening. The extra skills I learn about counselling people through trauma."

"I know it's important, but I still don't like it."

"You need to go shower. You stink," Dru says as she walks up to me, making everyone chuckle.

"Gee, thanks. I love you, too," I tell her, but after sniffing myself, I realize that she's right and head downstairs to shower.

After having a quick shower and getting dressed, the smell of something amazing cooking upstairs begins to assault my senses. I pick up my pace, with my stomach egging me on, wanting to fill itself with the yummy concoctions being prepared in the kitchen. But as I begin walking up the stairs, a voice has me pausing mid-step. Drake.

"You need to come home, Dru," he tells her.

"No, Drake. I haven't been out of our home in years. This is the first time that my anxiety hasn't had me paralyzed in fear. I finally feel safe enough to leave," she responds.

"But you aren't safe," he yells at her.

"Hey. You need to calm down," Phoebe berates him. Good for her. I hear a snarl, and then a growl, and I can tell that the growl is Alaric.

"Be careful how you act towards my mate, Drake," he spits at him.

"I apologize, Phoebe," he says, taking a deep breath and addressing Dru again. "I shouldn't have to tell you again, Dru: you aren't safe here. Not with that hunter staying here. What if she came to finish the job her father started?" I can hear him pleading with her. I can't hold my tongue any longer, and I stomp up the stairs.

"You!" I scream at him, moving to put myself between Dru and him. I'm desperately trying to ignore the way that my body is begging me to get closer to him and not to kick his ass like my mind is demanding. "First, I would *never* hurt her. Second, you don't know anything about me. How dare you judge me based on the actions of an entire group? You're no better than the hunters that you hate," I spit at him, pushing my finger into his chest. He's smart, and he begins backing up.

When he is backed into a corner, though, he snarls at me, his fangs dropping down. Acting purely on reflex, my arm snaps out and punches him right in the jaw. Either I surprised him, or he didn't care enough to stop me, but my fist connects, snapping his head to the left. A small amount of blood slips from his lip and he reaches up his hand to wipe it off, looking between me and his hand.

"See?" he says, looking at everyone in the room except me. "Once a hunter, always a hunter."

"No," I say, refusing to allow myself to feel bad for my actions. "It's just that you're an asshole who deserves to be taken down a peg."

"Your first instinct was to attack me. You can't tell me that wasn't drilled into you since birth. You're a hunter. Admit it," he spits at me.

Despite his accusations digging in a little and causing a small pang through my heart, I stand tall. "I am a hunter. I've never denied that. But I don't want to continue hunting in the same way that I have. And of course, I attacked you. You bared your fangs at me. I was taught to strike first," I spit back at him.

Dru walks over and puts herself between the two of us. "Now, now. You're both big and strong," she says, then she gets a kind of evil smirk on her face. "But if Rayne was a guy, her dick would be bigger than yours. Sorry, Drake," she says with a chuckle. He looks hurt by her statement, dropping his mask of hatred and indifference momentarily, allowing me a glimpse into the man that he could be if he wasn't hell bent on being such an asshole all the time.

"Fine. Do what you want. But don't come crying to me when she proves me right," he says, pointing towards me. I stick my tongue out at him triumphantly as Dru steps up and puts her arm around my shoulders.

"You know, you really shouldn't antagonize him. It's not going to make him change his mind about you," she whispers to me.

"If he wasn't such an asshole, I wouldn't have to," I say back to her. I shake out my body, trying to get all the stirrings Drake caused to leave. It doesn't work, and even though he's already gone, my body is still buzzing, wanting him inside me. What the fuck is wrong with me?

"I know that. But at some point, one of you is going to have to be the bigger person," she tells me with a sigh. She knows just as I do that hell will freeze over before either of us give up.

We sit down and eat with Alaric and Phoebe's family once again: Dru with her glass of blood that looks like wine, and us with a mouth-watering steak dinner. I've never tasted a steak so delicious. I don't think I say one word the entire time; I am too busy inhaling my food.

After our meal and some small talk with Alaric and Phoebe, it is time for them to put their kids to bed. Dru and I take that as our cue to head downstairs. As much as I don't want to admit it, I'm pretty fucking exhausted. Once downstairs, I change into my comfy sweatpants and hoodie and get cozy on the couch.

"What do you do all night while everyone is sleeping?" I ask Dru as she is flipping through the new releases on Netflix.

"Usually, I watch TV; sometimes I read," she states.

I've been waiting all night to bring this up, ever since her comment to Drake about not leaving the house. "What about hanging out with other vampires?"

"Um. I don't really care for any of the other vampires," she responds.

"Why not?"

"They all look at me with this pitiful look on their faces. You know, 'Poor Dru, she was taken by hunters'," she says, mimicking the look on her face.

"I understand that, Dru, but have you really not left the house since you escaped?" I ask.

She sighs, looking down at her hands and nods. "Yeah."

Tears spring to my eyes. "I'm sorry," I tell her.

She turns to me, surprised. "Why are you sorry? You're the only reason I'm alive right now!"

"Because I should have gotten you free sooner. I should've done more," I tell her, with tears flowing down my cheeks.

She moves fast and wraps me in a hug. "I have been grateful every single day that you helped me escape. You saved me. Don't ever think that you didn't do every single thing you could have. You were a kid yourself. You betrayed your family by freeing me," she whispers in my hair.

"Yeah but..." I start.

She pushes me back, keeping a solid hold on my shoulders. "Now, you listen here. You are the hero in my story, not the villain my brother continues to paint you as. You could have left me there to rot. Or you could have joined in on their 'fun', but you didn't. You fed me, you talked to me, you befriended me. And don't think I didn't know that you even donated your own blood to give me strength enough to escape when you couldn't steal an extra bag from the delivery guy."

I suck in a breath. "You knew about that?"

"Of course, I did. There was no way your father would have allowed you to give me two bags of blood, let alone three on some days. Plus, I could smell that it was your blood," she tells me.

"I just couldn't stand to see how starved you were," I whisper back to her.

"I know. And that is because you're a good person. I'm so glad we found each other again. Yesterday, when I heard a couple of coven members whispering that Drake was coming here to meet a hunter, the first thing I felt was panic, but then there was this overwhelming need to come and see for myself. And now I know why. It's because it was you. You and I are bonded in a way not many people will ever understand," she tells me, and I almost believe her.

"I love you, Dru. You were my first friend. Sure, I had the other hunters or kids from school, but they were never my friends. How can you truly be friends with someone while hiding your entire life from them? I have always felt like I could tell you anything," I say as I pull her into another hug.

"I love you, too, Rayne. And I feel the exact same," she whispers back to me. As we separate, she looks at me dead in the eyes with a serious expression on her face. "And that is why I have to ask about you and my brother," I go to answer, but she holds up a hand. "I don't want any of the graphic details."

I chuckle and wipe the tears from my eyes. "I really don't know what to tell you. He drives me crazy. One minute I want to punch him in the face and the next..." I stop myself before telling her that I want to jump her brother's bones.

"I get the gist," she shudders. "But what I really want to know about is when you two met," she asks.

I take a deep breath and get comfy on the couch, trying to think of how to explain it without giving her the graphic details she doesn't want. "Well, the other night, I was going stir crazy at the motel, so I decided to head out dancing and to try getting in contact with Phoebe. When I got there, it was like there was something pulling me deeper into the club. The feeling didn't go away until Drake came up to me. Without giving you the details, one thing led to another, and we ended up..." I try to think of a word other than fucking, "...um, 'talking'." I use air quotes on the word, and she nods in understanding. "When we were done 'talking', he noticed my hunter's mark and kind of freaked out."

"And then you guys 'talked' again in the woods?" she asks, and I chuckle.

"Yeah. He came to Alaric and Phoebe's when I first got here and asked to talk to me alone. I thought I would never see him again, but my body responded to him the exact same way it did the first time. Then you interrupted our 'talking,' and you know the rest."

"I have never seen him react this way to anyone. Ever," she responds.

I dip my head, not knowing what to say. It's not only him who has never reacted this way to another person. I still can't understand *my* reactions to him.

We spend the rest of the night watching cheesy chick flicks. Well, at least until I fall asleep half-way through the first movie.

When I wake up, I'm no longer on the couch but on a cot in the bunkhouse. I sit up and search for Dru, finding her fast asleep on the cot across from me, and I smile. She must've carried me in here and tucked me in. How this tiny slip of a woman has the strength to do that, I'll never understand. It's like her muscles, though smaller in size, are denser than mine. I can't wait to see how much of a bad-ass she is when I start training her. She doesn't know it yet, but I have big plans to show this beautiful soul just how strong she is.

After showering and dressing quickly, I head upstairs and visit with the Westwood family. Watching Alaric and Phoebe together with their kids is honestly the cutest fucking thing I've ever seen in my life. They have this ability to anticipate each other's movements and finish each other's sentences. while the whole family are constantly laughing and smiling with one another. The more I watch them, the more it cements the fact that I made the right decision.

As we spend the day together, I learn more about their family and their past. The amount of shit they have had to deal with in their short lives, especially the boys, is heartbreaking. It makes me want to go back in time and make their asshole of a father suffer. Not only that, but after spending time with Aurora, too, and finding out about the attempted kidnapping and Drake's involvement in it, makes me want to find him and make sure he understands how fucking wrong that was. It might not be in the same manner as the boys' father, but Drake will surely learn his lesson when his tongue is unable to move due to overuse.

I shiver at the thought of Drake and his tongue. His expert

tongue that he knows how to use extremely well. My clit begins to throb, and I have to squeeze my thighs together to try and stop the sensation. After all, I'm sitting here with Phoebe and her family.

When I finally gain some semblance of control, I decide that it's a good time to head over to the gym. I'm so excited about sparring with Samara. I think she is really going to give me a run for my money.

At the gym, I find Samara already stretching in the ring. "Ready to get your ass kicked?" she asks me over her shoulder.

"We will see," I respond, not wanting to come off as cocky since, by the looks of her toned muscles, me getting my ass kicked could be a very real possibility.

"Good to see you again, Rayne," the blue-haired bartender, Trevan, says, walking up and grabbing Samara's bag, giving her a kiss.

"You, too, Trevan." Huh. Guess that's his mate. I didn't realize that there was cross-species mating. He's obviously a Fae, and she's a feline shifter of some sort with my money being on Mountain Lion. I wonder how that works. Questions for another time. Though Lennox is a wolf and Skarlyt is a witch, and Phoebe is a phoenix and Alaric is a wolf. So, I guess I really shouldn't be surprised; it's obviously more common than I was taught.

As promised, Samara gives as good as she gets. Holy shit is she strong. I haven't ever had to try that hard to beat someone, if 'beat' is what you would even call it. At the end of the fight, I have more bumps and bruises on my body than I've ever had. Samara, the lucky bitch, has her shifter healing to take care of her injuries.

Just as I'm about to say just that, Skarlyt pops into the gym, grabs Samara, and pops away. "What the fuck?" I question, spinning around in a circle.

"You get used to it," Trevan says while he's gathering up Samara's things.

"You mean that happens a lot?" I question.

"Skarlyt believes in asking forgiveness rather than permission. You'll see the longer you're here. But good job with the fight. Samara has been looking for a sparring partner who can keep up with her. Alaric is the only one who can match her so far, and even that is very close. Be prepared. She's going to want to spar all the time," he tells me.

"I'll be fine with that. She was the best opponent I've ever had," I respond, grabbing my own stuff and heading back over to Alaric's and Phoebe's. Rather than knock, I walk straight in and say my greetings to everyone before heading downstairs to shower.

I find Dru downstairs waiting for me, and after my shower, we briefly go upstairs to eat dinner and head back down to watch movies. It seems like we're falling into a nice routine, one that I hope my father and his cronies don't jeopardize.

Chapter Eleven

Rayne

Two more days pass with the same routine: wake up, spend the day with Phoebe and the kids, spar at the gym, eat dinner, watch movies with Dru, then fall asleep before we even get to the good parts. Tonight, though, she wants us to socialize. She has convinced Phoebe to invite all the girls over after dark so we can have some drinks. My first thought at her suggestion is, 'What the fuck. Didn't she learn her lesson the other day?' But then I remember her vampire healing. And it turns into 'Oh shit. She's trying to kill me.' That's the only explanation for why she would want me to drink with the girls again, and has absolutely nothing to do with the fact that she is enjoying spending time with them. At least that's what I'm currently telling myself.

I head to the gym to get my ass kicked by Samara once again. I have to say that she is one tough chick. If I would have known that she was as good as she is, I probably would have thought twice about getting in the ring with her. Actually, probably not. Hate to say it, but I'm a glutton for punishment.

"Ready to get beat again?" Samara asks me as I step into the gym.

I chuckle. "Are you?" I ask.

She laughs out loud. "You're delusional."

"That may be true most days, but not today. Today, I'm going to kick the shit out of you," I respond and begin getting myself pumped up for our fight.

We trade blows back and forth for what seems like an eternity with neither of us relenting. This is one of those times where, in the movies, the hero would deliver a particularly deadly blow and take the win. That doesn't happen here. We both throw right hooks at the same time, falling to the ground, and end up laughing hysterically. We must look like a couple of idiots. Both covered in blood, each other's and our own, rolling on the floor of the ring.

"You both look like fucking psychopaths," a voice calls out.

Our laughter dies out just enough to gain some composure, and we turn to look in the direction of the voice.

"You realize you are laughing like a couple of hyenas covered in blood, right?" Lennox asks from the side of the ring.

I nod while trying and failing to gain some control over my laughter. When I turn and look at Samara, my laughter starts all over again. She has blood all over her face and is rolling around on the ground, clutching her stomach and laughing. It's not until Trevan walks in that she finally stops.

"Samara," he says in a scornful tone of voice.

She sobers up quickly. "It's not what it looks like."

Now I'm confused and my gaze ping pongs between the two of them.

"It doesn't look like you and Rayne got in the ring to beat the shit out of each other again, after you told me you were going to take a couple days off?" Trevan asks.

"No?" she responds, trying and failing to feign innocence.

"Wait. You told him you weren't going to get in the ring with me for a couple of days?" I ask Samara. Then I turn to Trevan, "Why wouldn't it be okay for her to get back in the ring with me?"

Samara stands and begins dusting herself off while Trevan sighs dramatically. "It's not that it wouldn't be okay. It's the fact that even though she has shifter healing, every day after she spars with you, she's so sore she can hardly walk. She promised that she was going to take at least *one* day off," he tells me, ending with a look in Samara's direction.

I start laughing and look at Samara myself. "You said you were fine after our fights."

"It's not as bad as he's saying," she tells me.

"Yes, it is. Don't let her fool you," Trevan speaks up. "Come on. You need to get in the bath before you go get drunk with the girls *again,*" he tells her as he walks over and helps her out of the ring. I stretch out my muscles and feel how tight they are. Maybe I could use a bath as well to loosen them up.

After the longest, most relaxing bath I've ever taken, I begin to feel like myself. My muscles are still tight, and I feel like I look like a velociraptor when I'm walking, but I just hope that Samara looks worse when she comes walking up to the house. A smile forms on my face at that thought. Samara always talked so much shit about how she was never even sore after our sessions, giving me all kinds of grief about my groans when I'd move certain ways. I can't wait to return the favor. I'm going to have to watch her closely. I'm sure that there will be signs of soreness that I can exploit.

Dru walks into the room as I finish getting dressed. She grabs my face and turns it to the side to look at the bruises rising there. "Samara?" she questions.

"Yup. But apparently, I'm not the only one with sore muscles after our fights. Trevan let it slip that Samara was supposed to take a couple of days off because she's been so sore," I tell her with a grin.

She grins back. "Still. Her bruises fade a lot faster than yours," she tells me, turning my face from side to side to get a good look at the marks.

I reach up and touch the tender part of my cheek. I know she's right, but it's still worth it.

"Come on, let's head upstairs."

There's a flurry of activity as we head up the stairs, with Alaric yelling and screaming to people on the porch and on the phone, asking where Phoebe is.

"What happened?" Dru whispers to Charleigh's mate, Ashton.

"I don't know. We just got here, and Darren, Alaric's brother, called and then Phoebe went on the phone with her sister. And now both Skarlyt and Phoebe are missing. Alaric's losing his shit," he whispers back.

"Maybe they just went to get some of Skarlyt's special wine?" I offer as a reason.

"No, I don't think that's it," he replies.

"Where is she?" Alaric screams into the phone. There's a brief pause before he speaks again. "Phoebe? Thank the Mother, you're okay. Wait, why the fuck are you on Darren's phone?" His tone is clipped and then another brief pause. "Put Skarlyt on the phone." There was a pause then he says sternly, "Come get me now."

He hangs up the phone. Seconds later, Skarlyt is standing in front of him. He turns to Charleigh. "Watch the kids?" he asks.

"Of course," she replies, and he and Skarlyt disappear.

After a time, I can't handle the silence anymore. "What the fuck just happened?" I ask.

"I honestly couldn't tell you," Charleigh says grimly.

"All I know is that Phoebe came out, put a phone in Skarlyt's face and demanded she take her somewhere," Lennox speaks up from the doorway.

"Well, shit," I say. What the fuck do I do now? I feel like the shit is about to hit the fan. Not sure if it's going to be my shit or their shit. Either way, a whole lotta shit is about to go down. I only hope that both of our shits don't blow up at the same time.

"At least I won't be hung over tomorrow without Skarlyt's devil wine," I chuckle. That breaks any tension there is in the room and we all let out a little laugh.

"I've never heard it called that before," Lennox adds with a chuckle, handing me a vial and whispering. "Skarlyt said to give you this." I eye it warily but at his nod, I down the drink. Skarlyt would never do anything to harm me on purpose. At least, I don't think she would. Shit. Maybe I shouldn't have drunk that.

I'm not worrying for long before my sore muscles begin loosening. I can even feel the split in my lip stitching itself back together. I raise my hand to my face, feeling the perfectly smooth skin. "What the ...?"

"I told her what happened at the gym this morning, and she made you a potion. That way you can rub it in Samara's face tonight that you're all healed and she's not. Except that Sebastyn came and got Samara and Trev straight from the gym, so they'll be gone for a week."

"Please thank her for me."

"I will. But I'm going to get this little munchkin over to his grandmas so his mommy can come get me." He says, lifting Kayne higher in his arms.

"Why don't you come stay at the coven with me for a few days. Just until it calms down here a bit?" Dru asks quietly.

"I'm not so sure your brother will be okay with that," I reply to her.

"You leave my brother to me," she responds with a wink.

Together, we head downstairs to gather our things before heading to her coven. I'm still not sure this is entirely a good idea but with Alaric and Phoebe already having some stuff to deal with, having me here is much more of a burden than I want it to be.

* * *

Walking into a den of vipers is exactly what it feels like as I walk into the coven with Dru. Between the looks of fear on the faces of the children, and the looks of distrust and contempt on the faces of the adults, it's almost too much. As I look at each of the little faces peeking out from behind their mothers or fathers with wide eyes, a tear slips from my eye. How did this happen? Why would the hunters who came before me not realize that there are families with children, mothers, brothers, sisters, fathers? How could they allow this to happen: to have an entire race both fear and hate us just from a single glance? It was the same when I arrived at the pack. How could I have not realized that they would have died out if they were unable to have children?

The crowd seems to get thicker the further inside we get. When we get into a large common room, we get boxed in with people on all four sides.

"Move," Dru commands.

"Why should we?" a snooty blonde bitch asks.

"Colleen, Rayne is my guest. She will be treated as such," Dru spits, stepping up to her.

"I don't think so, Drusilla. Your brother is the coven leader, not you," she hisses back, poking Dru in the chest.

Seeing this Colleen bitch step right into Dru's face spurs my protectiveness, and I insert myself between them.

"You will not touch her again," I snarl at her.

"Or what?" Colleen asks, raising a brow at me, seeming to dismiss me as a threat.

"Rayne, it's not worth it," Dru pleads with me, grabbing my shoulder and trying to pull me back.

"No, Dru. You will not be disrespected in front of me," I tell her, giving her hand that is now on my shoulder a small pat.

"And just what are you going to do about it?" Colleen hisses right in my face with her fangs out.

Instead of reacting instinctively like I did with Drake, I get a smirk on my face. "Well, if you insist on being a bitch and disrespecting my friend, I'll have to teach you a lesson you're not going to forget anytime soon."

I anticipate her fist moving before it actually does. Something I attribute to my years of training. I grab her fist in my palm. To my surprise, I can hold her off. Maybe there was something extra in that potion Skarlyt made for me. She looks between my face and my hand in shock before pulling her fist back.

Before her shock wears off, I slam my fist in her face, hitting her square in the nose. I feel her bone break under my knuckles and watch as blood spurts out.

"You bitch!" she screams while using her hands to snap her nose back into place.

I don't let her theatrics distract me, and I reel back and slam my fist into her face once more, catching her eye once, twice, and then a final third time.

"Do you think you've learned your lesson yet, or shall I continue?" I ask, wiping my fist on her shirt to get the blood off.

Rather than respond, she hisses in my face again, and I get ready to give her a few more shots to her face, but before I can, Drake's voice rings out.

"I'd say she has. Colleen. Leave." At the sound of his voice, shivers run down my spine in anticipation of seeing his face. My body needs to be close to him.

As he walks towards us, I keep my eyes trained on Colleen. I learned many years ago never to turn my back on an opponent. Colleen walks up to meet Drake, running her hands over his shoulder and chest. "Drake, baby. It's all her fault. Look what she did to my face," she coos, and my blood boils. Who the fuck does this bitch think she is touching him?

"Seeing that my sister is standing right beside Rayne, seeming to support her actions, I'd wager that you are more than likely at fault, not her," he responds, grabbing her hands and pushing her away.

"You don't mean that," she tries again. This time she gets so close that their bodies are touching. The heat that spreads through my body at the sound of his voice quickly dissipates, being replaced by a range of emotions: rage, disgust, jealousy. What the actual fuck? Since when do I get jealous over a man who is nothing to me? At least until he pulls his head out of his ass. I lock eyes with Drake, and I'm sure that he can see the emotions flit over my face. Dru can, too, it seems because she reaches out a hand and places it on my shoulder once more. I can feel the rage flowing through me with every stroke of Bimbo Barbie's hand on his chest and the shimmy of her body against his, so much that I'm shaking.

"Calm down," Dru whispers into my ear. I try and fail to calm, but I admit as he once again takes her hands off his body, a smugness at his rejection settles into me.

"Colleen. I will deal with you later. Go," he says forcefully to her.

Instead of being upset as I suspected she would be, she gets an evil grin on her face. "I can't wait," she responds with a wink and sashays away. Apparently, she enjoys Drake's punishments just as much as I do. And just like that she has graduated from a thorn in my side to Enemy Numero Uno.

"As for you two, I'll deal with you now," he says, turning to me and Dru.

"Uh oh," I say to Dru in a snarky voice. Drake looks exasperated at my comment but leads the way to his office anyway.

Once tucked away in the privacy of his office, he turns to both of us. "Right. What the fuck is she doing here?" he asks Dru, pointing at me.

"I know we discussed staying at Alaric and Phoebe's, but it seems that they have some issues they are dealing with at the moment," Dru responds to him, sitting in the chair across from him.

Drake sighs loudly and rubs his hand over his face. "Be that as it may, you know my feelings about this. You could have brought her anywhere, literally anywhere else besides here."

"And just where do you propose we go that would allow me safety from the sun?" Dru snaps back.

"I didn't say you had to go with her. Just that *she* couldn't come here," he responds.

"How about you don't talk about her as if she isn't standing right here in front of you," I berate him. His head snaps up at me, and my knees go weak with the heat in his eyes. Whether it be from sexual tension or anger, either way, it's making my pussy weep.

"Well, it can't be helped now. You're here. Just keep to yourself, don't make waves. Or else," he threatens me.

"Or else what?" I challenge.

He looks caught off guard for a moment, but the desire lining his eyes is more than obvious. He seems to like my snarkiness, despite his protests to the contrary. "You'll see."

"Can't wait," I mimic Colleen's earlier comment and walk out the door with Dru. It's not a lie. I actually can't wait for a repeat of my forest punishment, even though he seems to think it'll never happen again.

Chapter Twelve

Drake

"Everything's just about finished at the new compound. We'll be ready to move the coven in within the week," Colin says, walking into my office for the hundredth time tonight.

I nod at him. "And what's the general consensus?" I could probably ask the coven themselves to see how they're feeling about the move, but I doubt they would answer me truthfully. But Colin? They have no issues voicing anything with him.

"On the whole, it's positive. There are some that don't want to move, of course, but when I pointed out we will be much closer to the academy, they changed their tune. The older students are so excited about moving in that they haven't even unpacked," he says, taking a seat in the chair opposite me.

"And you still believe that is the right move?" I ask. When Darren and Alaric brought it up at the last board meeting, I didn't want to agree because I thought it wouldn't be safe. When Colin's eyes lit up at the mere mention, I changed my mind and agreed to it on a trial basis because I know I have some major making up to do with the members of my coven.

"I do. The younger kids will still go to and from with the teachers each night, but the older ones are craving independence. With us being locked inside more often than not, lately, I think it's the right move."

"I'm only trying to keep everyone safe," I supply as an excuse.

"I know that, so do they. But after you sided with the mages against the pack, then pulled us into not just one, but two, separate fights against the mages, let's just say: you need to do something positive."

I scrub my hand across my face. "I already agreed. Is there something else you want?"

"Actually, I want to lower the age of the kids that stay at the school during the week from sixteen to thirteen. I've had petitions, both from students and parents, requesting it."

"What?" I hiss and shake my head. "That's too young. No."

"Listen, Drake. I know that you believe they're too young, and you may be right, but if the parents agree to sign a waiver showing them the risks, I think we need to do this."

"And on the waiver, you will spell out every single possible thing that could go wrong living outside the coven: attack, getting lost, injury, hunger. What if we can't get blood there for them to drink? The older kids can control themselves by sixteen, but imagine starving at thirteen: what wouldn't you do at that age to get a single drop of blood?"

He pales but dips his head in acknowledgement. "I will make sure it is all spelled out for them."

"As long as every single thing is listed, then fine. I want to see it before you give it to the parents, though. And I think that we should hold an information session with the parents of kids aged thirteen to sixteen to make sure they are very clear on the risks."

"That's a good idea. I'll set it up for a week from Saturday," he says, pulling out his phone and putting it in his calendar.

"Just so you know, I'm only doing this to try and make up for my past decisions. In no way do I support this," I tell him, looking directly into his eyes.

He inclines his head. "I know. But it doesn't change the fact that I think this is the right thing for the coven."

"Anything else?" I ask, ready to distract myself from the magnetic pull that starts in my chest.

"Nope. That's it," he says as he leaves.

I wait a minute for him to have walked far enough away before I make my way out the door, keeping to the shadows.

I know exactly what the pull in my chest means: Rayne is here. Whenever she's near, there's this pull that I can't describe trying to get me closer to her. I stand in the shadows, watching her as she walks through the coven. I see the stray tear that slips from her eye when she thinks no one will notice; there was a fleeting look of sadness and regret cross her face and then when Colleen starts her shit, I see the protectiveness for Dru overtake her as she steps between the two. I should have stopped it right there, I really should have, but Colleen has always been a thorn in everyone's sides. She deserves to be taken down a peg or two. That's not to say that she doesn't have her uses. She is the most beautiful woman in the coven: with her luscious blonde hair that runs down to her plump, perfect ass, a face like an angel, and tits that any woman would be jealous of. There was a time not so long ago when just the thought of Colleen and the things she can do with that mouth of hers would get me hard as a rock, but now? Nothing.

But the mere thought of Rayne has my dick standing at attention, ready to go ten rounds with Mike Tyson. What the actual fuck? Even though I don't want to admit it, it was hot as fuck watching Rayne wipe her blood-filled hands off on Colleen's shirt rather than on her own.

I decide I can't stand by and watch any longer, so I step up to the three women. Colleen rubs her body up against mine in an attempt to persuade me that their interaction was Rayne's fault. It doesn't work, of course, but being this close to Rayne and being able to smell her delicious arousal has my little soldier painfully erect. If the wink that Colleen throws me as she is leaving is anything to go by, she believes that it's because of her, rather than the petite brunette with blood on her hands standing beside my sister. Ugh, what am I doing?

I lead them both into my closed office, where I can basically hear her pussy weeping, and my mouth begins to salivate. I may have been more curt with Dru than necessary, but having Rayne this close to me without being able to touch her or taste her is absolute murder. When she gets all fired up and challenges me, as if it weren't impossible, my dick gets even harder and is begging to be sunk deep into her pussy. Goddess, help me. There is no way I will survive her staying here.

"Thank the goddess," I whisper as they walk out of the door, and I sink down into my chair.

I reach my hand down to try to relieve some of the pressure in my groin when there is a knock at the door.

"What is it?" I call out.

"I think we should talk," Rayne says as she walks through the door. She pauses and locks the door before continuing inside.

"I thought we just had," I respond tersely.

Rather than stopping on the appropriate side of my desk, she continues over to me. "What are you doing?" I ask, a slight tremble in my voice. I'm normally in perfect control but if she comes any closer...

She continues her saunter over to me. "Trying to relieve some of this tension between us. We can't function this way," she says as she turns my chair toward her and straddles me. My brain tells me to push her off, but my body doesn't seem to get the memo, and I find my hands sliding up her thighs to grip her hips. "We both love Dru, and us being at odds is hurting her. She feels like she needs to choose between us." She starts to slowly grind on me.

My eyes roll into the back of my head at the extreme pleasure I feel from her touch. But as amazing as this feels, I can't forget my personal feelings about her. "I don't trust you," I say through clenched teeth, trying and failing to keep the moan from my voice.

"I know. This doesn't mean there is anything between us. It's simply a way to relieve this tension before we kill each other," she responds with a moan of her own.

She stands from my lap and slowly sinks to her knees in front of me. "We don't need to fuck. We can just help each other out. I don't know about you, but ever since I met you, I can't seem to cum without you," she says as she unzips my pants, freeing my painful erection. At the first swipe of her tongue, the moan that escapes me is loud and surprising even to myself. As she engulfs me in her mouth, increasing her suction as she moves up and down rhythmically, a moan escapes her as well as if she's getting just as much pleasure from this as I am.

"Oh, goddess!" I cry out, and she quickens her pace. Moments later, I'm exploding into her mouth while she swallows me down. When she makes eye contact with me, licking her lips as if that was the most delicious thing she's ever tasted, I lose control. There's desire apparent in her eyes, the scent of her arousal in the air, and a flush to her cheeks. This woman is going to be the death of me. I finally lose my composure and run my hands through her hair.

Chapter Thirteen

Rayne

I admit, when I ventured back into Drake's office, I expected more of a fight. But it pleasantly surprised me when he not only allowed me to straddle him but taste him as well. And what an amazing taste it is.

As I stand, he grips my waist and pushes me onto his desk. When his mouth fuses with mine, I'm momentarily stunned but recover quickly, thrusting my tongue into his mouth. Our kiss is full of passion.

He slips my pants down my legs and runs his fingers over my core. Oh, goddess! What I wouldn't give for these panties to just disappear and feel him touching me uninhibitedly. My wish is granted as he slips my panties down my legs, over my knees, and to my feet, giving him complete access. He thrusts his tongue in time with the movements of his fingers as he circles my clit.

"Drake," I pant as he removes his mouth from mine and sinks to his knees in front of me. He doesn't wait or toy with me but dives right in, sucking and flicking my clit with his supernatural speed. As he inserts two fingers, curving them upward, I cry out. "Gods!"

A few more swipes of his tongue and thrusts of his fingers, and I climax, my pussy gripping his fingers, sucking them in deeper. I thought that this would satisfy the tension between us, but it only intensifies it. I grip his head and pull him up to me. I merge my mouth to his, and our tongues mix with our combined tastes, creating a delectable concoction.

"We shouldn't," he says as he pulls back.

"Please," I beg. Gods, when did I resign myself to begging a man to fuck me? I grab his cock and guide it into me. His previous reluctance seems to disappear as he thrusts in and out of me with vigor.

Just as I am about to reach my peak, a knock sounds at the door. "Drake, baby. I'm here for my punishment." That blonde bimbo again!

"Later," Drake groans out, never losing pace.

When we hear a key being placed in the lock, Drake slips out of me, and I slide under the desk. He takes his seat just as the door opens. I smile when I notice his pants are still laying in a pile on the floor.

"Colleen, I told you later," he says. I hear the lock click back into place and her footsteps come closer to the desk. "Stop!" he yells at her.

"But Drake, it's been over two weeks. You have needs, as do I," she says before the sound of clothing dropping onto the floor. Rather than being aroused as I assumed he would be, his dick starts to deflate. Good boy.

To reward him, I move forward and slip him back into my mouth and stifle a moan at the combined tastes of us. His hands grip the armrests of his chair. "It doesn't matter how long it's been. I said to leave," he grinds out. If I didn't know better, I would not be able to tell that he was distracted at all. But his flaccid dick begins to get bigger between my lips making me smirk.

"It's because of that hunter, isn't it?" she pouts.

His fists slam on the desk. "That hunter has nothing to do with anything. I am simply tired of you."

I hear her sniffle. "Why are you being like this?" she asks.

I increase my suction on his cock, rubbing my tongue along the vein below the head and hear his sharp intake of breath. "Leave!" he demands, and I smile around his cock.

I hear her pause and pick up her clothing before rushing out and slamming the door behind her.

"That was very naughty, Rayne," Drake coos to me.

I remove his cock from my mouth and smile at him deviously. Within seconds, I'm lifted up and spun around so that I'm bent over his desk. A quick smack on my ass followed by a quick thrust of his cock inside me has me crying out in both pain and pleasure.

He slams into me harder and faster than before, and without warning, we both tumble over the edge with our releases.

"This will not happen again, Rayne," Drake says as he removes himself from me and gets dressed.

"I agree," I respond while replacing my own clothing.

"I mean it, Rayne. You can not come to me like this again," he says, spinning me around to face him.

I sneer in his face. "I promise you, Drake. This will not happen again. Not until it's you begging for it."

"That will never happen," he snaps back at me.

"We'll see, won't we?" With that said, I pull up my pants and head off to find Dru. As much as my body is demanding that I return to Drake and continue our sexcapades, I meant what I said. I will not proposition him again until it is him who comes to me. I just may need to find another way to satisfy this unrelenting hunger that my pussy seems to have developed.

"What took you so long?" Dru asks when I return to her apartment.

"Your brother and I came to an agreement to be civil while I'm here," I respond, heading straight to the bathroom.

"You mean you two kissed and made up, literally," she responds with a gag.

"Actually, there wasn't very much kissing at all," I reply with a wink over my shoulder. Watching as she clutches her stomach and mouth, suppressing a gag, I laugh and enter the bathroom.

Reluctantly, I hop in the shower and reminisce on my time with Drake. Each time, I have said it will not happen again, and each time, I know it's a lie. This time, though, I am confident that I will stand my ground. I will not go to him again, no matter how much my body craves his touch.

After throwing on some pajamas, I head back to the living room and find Dru perched on the chair, reading a book. She sets it down, looking up at me. "So, you and my brother? I feel like I need to know even though I don't want to."

I sigh, knowing she wants to have a serious conversation. "I honestly don't know what to tell you, Dru. It's like I can't control myself when he's around." She nods like she understands but there's no way she actually can. "I mean, I can't decide if I want to punch him in the face or fuck him." Her sharp intake of breath has me wincing. "Sorry. But you know what I mean. It's like my body and my mind have two different opinions of him. My mind can't stand his cocky attitude and hates how he obviously dislikes me, but my body... well, it lights up like the Fourth of July."

"You know, I think you and him could be something good," she says, shocking me.

"You'd be the only one," I snort.

"No, I'm being serious. Think about it: you're both strong, independent people with a protective streak a mile long. You both love fiercely with everything you have."

"Don't compare me to him. I'm nothing like him," I challenge.

"You only think that because he's only shown you the one side of him. He is so much more than that."

"Yeah, well, I doubt he's going to show me any other side of him anytime soon." She raises a challenging eyebrow, but I'm done with this conversation and change the subject. "So that Colleen chick unlocked his office while I was in there."

She shifts in her seat, pulling her legs up and leaning forward excitedly. "Really? And how did that go?"

I chuckle. "She had a key, so she walked right in. We were quick enough that she didn't see anything, though." I say, and she starts laughing.

"She could probably smell you though."

"What? You guys can smell that?" Horrified, I think of how I must've smelled to her when I walked in here. Now the gagging really makes sense.

"Yup. She probably knew exactly what you two were doing. What did she look like when she saw you?"

"She didn't see me; I hid under the desk. She came in and stripped down naked, but Drake told her to leave." She laughs even harder. I purposely leave out how Drake deflated at seeing her naked body, but I'm sure she would get a kick out of that, as well, if he wasn't her brother, of course.

"Oh, my gods! What I wouldn't give to have seen her face. I bet it was priceless. I'll have to ask Drake next time I see him."

"I'd like to be there when you do. Seeing his face when you ask should be even better," I say with a smirk.

"On second thought, maybe I'll just imagine it."

I dip my head, agreeing with her on that one. "So... what are you reading?" I probe, gesturing to the book.

"It's Suzanne Wright's Mercury Pack Series. It's sooo good." My brows crease as I try to think of what it could be. She sees my confusion and takes pity on me.

"It's a paranormal romance about a pack of shifters finding their mates. Each book focuses on a different couple. It's amazing. You should read it," She supplies, and I shrug.

"Maybe, I will. But I've been meaning to ask about that. The only thing I know about mates was what my father told me: the mate is a supernatural's greatest weakness."

She pushes the book away and gets comfy on the couch once again. "Well, every supernatural being has a true mate out in the world somewhere. Shifters know the instant their eyes meet who they are to each other. Witches learn once they're intimate for the first time because their magic instantly flares together. With vampires, it's the first taste of our mate's blood that confirms for us. At eighteen, there is a ceremony that is preformed where everyone who is unmated attends. The women take a drop of blood from each male to see if they're true mates."

"Wait. Hold on a second. You mean to tell me that the women just go down a line, sucking on a drop of each man's blood?"

She nods. "Yeah. It may seem weird to you since you're not a vampire, but it's the quickest and easiest way to find a true mate pairing within the coven."

"Did you do that?"

She shakes her head. "No. I was still a captive on my eighteenth birthday and then when I was finally home, I was too broken to have anyone want me for a mate."

I see her head drop at the word 'broken,' and I move over to her couch and wrap my arms around her. "You are not broken. You are stronger than you give yourself credit for. Any man, vampire or not, should be lucky to have you as a mate."

She sniffs and inclines her head, but I know she doesn't believe it. Not yet. But she will if I have anything to say about it. That's my new mission, to make her see herself how I do: as the strongest woman I've ever met.

Chapter Fourteen

Rayne

Two days go by once more, and as promised, when I see Drake, I simply pretend he is not there. But at night–or more accurately during the day–when I'm alone, I imagine all the things we could be doing to one another. Though, like before, no matter how hard I try, I can not find my release. I've tried everything with no success, and I can feel my resolve begin to wane.

"We're going out dancing," I tell Dru when I get done working over the punching bag she had brought into her room for me. I've taught her a few things, too, so she could be able to protect herself if I'm not around. I'm hoping that, if she has the ability to take care of herself, she will be more willing to leave the coven on her own.

"What?" she asks from her armchair where she's reading.

"I need to relieve some tension, and since no man in this place is willing to help me, I need to look elsewhere," I respond while grabbing my towel and heading to the bathroom.

"What about Drake?" she asks.

I spin on my heels. "What about him?"

She looks almost pained as she speaks. “Well, wouldn’t he be willing to ‘relieve your tension’?” She gags out the last few words.

“I refuse to ask for his help. Besides, he has made it painfully clear he has no desire to help me in that regard,” I respond, and quickly close the door to the bathroom before my face or my voice gives away the hurt I feel at that comment.

By the time I’ve finished showering and my hair and make-up are done, Dru is completely ready with a dress for me all laid out on the bed. It’s a skimpy blue dress that covers pretty much nothing once it’s on. Absolutely fucking perfect!!! If Drake won’t give me what I need, there won’t be a man in Supernatural that will be able to deny me while I’m wearing this.

“I’m ready,” I tell Dru as I step out of my room.

She gives off a whistle. “Damn, girl, you look fucking hot.”

I give a little spin, which causes the bottom of the dress to fly up, showing off my bare ass. “I know, right?”

We both walk out of the apartment toward the front of the building. “And where do you two think you’re going looking like that?” Drake asks from a doorway.

“We’re going out dancing,” I respond with a raised eyebrow in challenge.

“Looking like that?” he asks, looking us up and down.

“Is that a problem? Last time I checked, we are both free women and can come and go as we please,” I adjust my stance defiantly.

“You’re just asking for trouble going out looking like that,” he responds.

“No. I’m asking to be fucked, and that’s precisely what I plan on doing,” I respond and spin to show off my ass before grabbing Dru’s arm and continuing on our way.

“He’s just jealous, you know,” Dru whispers to me.

“Well, he has a shitty way of showing it,” I whisper back.

Her phone dings. She pulls it out, getting a huge smile on her face. "Oh perfect! Phoebe just texted: they're all meeting us there for a surprise congratulations mating party for Skarlyt's brother, Sebastyn."

"Is that normal?" I ask, as we hop in the back of some car. I'm assuming it's safe because it was waiting outside the coven which is in a very secluded area.

"Depends. Sometimes, people just wait for the mating ceremony and celebrate there. Others have taken a page from the humans' book and thrown Stag and Doe's, and even more have bachelor and bachelorette parties."

"So, is this like a Stag and Doe? Should I be bringing extra money? I only grabbed enough for drinks." At a normal Stag and Doe, there are games and raffles, all the money going towards the bride and groom to help pay for their upcoming nuptials. I've been to quite a few, though those were for humans; I don't know if supernaturals do it differently.

"No. It's just a last-minute celebratory party. Just enjoy yourself." I nod, hoping that she's right. I want to tell the driver to turn around so I can run back in and grab a few hundred dollars just in case, but I don't, trusting that she's right.

Not long after, we arrive at Supernatural. I can tell that Dru is nervous by the way she is continually wringing her hands. "Are you okay?" I ask her.

"Yeah. This is just the first time I've been out dancing since..." she starts. Shit, I didn't even think about that.

"Shit, Dru. I'm so sorry. I didn't think. We can leave if you want to," I tell her.

"No, I need to do this," she responds, steeling herself to enter.

I'm just as awestruck as the first time I entered here. It's so beautiful with all the greenery making it feel as though we've been transported into another world. We head toward the bar and order our drinks, and I turn to look over the crowd. There, standing off to the side and nursing his drink is a tall drink of water. Broad shoulders, strong jaw, short-cropped hair, not bad on the eyes. Looks like I just found my conquest for the night.

Dru and I slam back a couple shots in quick succession, getting some liquid courage, not only for me but for Dru as well, before we head out on the dancefloor.

I move my body in time with the music before being pulled back to the bar. I turn quickly, my fist already cocked and find Phoebe looking at me with concern. I drop it quickly and we step across to where the sound is lower.

"Sorry," I tell her.

"No. I'm sorry. I should know better than to have startled you. But I did try to get your attention," she says, and I pull her into a hug.

"All good. I'm just glad I pulled the punch."

"Me, too!" She laughs. "Come on; let's do some shots."

We walk up to the bar and find it already lined with shots and a bunch of women standing around. I recognize Skarlyt and the woman with strawberry blonde hair looks vaguely familiar. When I glance back at Phoebe, I realize who she is: this must be her sister.

"To Sarah!" Phoebe cheers, and we all clink our glasses together and down the liquid.

"Thanks, ladies!" The beautiful brunette in the group says, followed by a hiccup.

"Sarah, I'd like you to meet Drusilla and Rayne," Skarlyt says, pulling both me and Dru forward.

Dru sticks out her hand first. "You can call me, Dru. Everyone does."

"Sarah. It's nice to meet you." She responds, releasing Dru's hand.

I step up next. "I'm Rayne. Thank you for letting us crash your party. I needed to get out tonight," I say with a wink, sticking my hand out to hers.

"Sarah. But you already know that," she chuckles, and I join in while stepping back into the group.

"And this is my twin sister, Sophia," Phoebe says, slinging her arm around the strawberry blonde's shoulder.

Both Dru and I introduce ourselves to Sophia and, once again, the women in this group make me feel like I'm supposed to be here, that I was always meant to be part of their group.

We do another shot and all of us head back to the dance floor. Dru and I move further into the crowd, and the magnetic pull I have begun associating with Drake starts to tug, and I turn toward the booths. Sure enough, I find him sitting there, glaring at me like I'm personally offending him. I send him a wink and move my body seductively. He's not going to stop me from doing what I came here to do.

The song "Sexy Bitch" by David Guetta and Akon comes on and everyone cheers, me included, and I throw myself into the song, swaying my hips and rubbing my hands up and down my body.

Within seconds, the tall drink of water I had been eyeing earlier and his friend approach us, and we begin dancing. The smile on Dru's face shines brightly, and I can see that she's actually enjoying herself, so I let loose. I take Mr. Tall Dark and Handsome's hands and bring them to my thighs, guiding them upward. It doesn't take long for him to catch onto my intentions and take over. As I grind my ass onto his raging erection, his hands roam my body, and he moves his mouth to my neck. Rather than being wet as I assumed I would be, my pussy turns as dry as the Sahara Desert.

I turn toward him, hoping that switching my position and using my pussy to grind on his impressive cock might reignite my arousal. With this new position, my dress rides up so that the only thing protecting my overly dry pussy from him is the black thong I chose to wear. Unfortunately, it does nothing to help the dryness situation. But it doesn't stop me from lifting my leg and using the leverage to grind my pussy all over it, closing my eyes and moving in time with the music.

Just when I think it might actually be working, I'm ripped away from him and briefly pushed up against a hard wall of muscle, before I'm pushed behind the same wall of muscle. There, standing in front of me, is Drake, hissing at the man I was just dancing with.

"What are you doing?" I say to Drake, pulling on his arm to try to get him to face me. He fights me momentarily before turning toward me.

"This is what you want, isn't it?" he questions as he pulls me toward him and puts his hand up my dress and strokes my clit.

"Drake," I warn as I push him away.

"No. This is what you want, right? You came here tonight to get fucked, didn't you? Then, let's fuck," he says.

"Why are you being like this? You didn't want me. Why shouldn't I be able to go find someone to scratch my itch?" I demand, extremely confused. My mind is telling him to fuck off but my body is humming in anticipation.

"You two are making a scene," Dru whispers to us. We both look around and it seems we have gathered a crowd. Luckily, our friends have surrounded us in a protective circle, keeping everyone else from seeing.

"Fine," Drake says, grabbing me by the arm and leading me outside.

"What the fuck is your problem? You don't want me, but you don't want anyone else to have me either?" I question.

He runs his hands through his hair as he paces. "I don't fucking know."

"Seriously, Drake. You're giving me whiplash. One minute you're fucking my brains out, and the next you're pushing me away. Just make a decision. What do you want?" I scream at him.

"You. But not you as a hunter. Just you," he whispers as he turns to face me.

"Well, that won't work. I am a hunter, no matter if I choose to embrace it or not. If you want me, you have to accept me. All of me," I tell him.

"I'm not sure if I can," he admits.

"Well, then, you need to leave me alone," I tell him and turn to walk back into the bar.

"I can't," he admits. He pushes me back up against the wall and secures his mouth to mine. Despite my mind objecting, my body has other ideas, and my legs wrap around his waist.

"Rayne?" I hear a voice calling my name. I turn my head toward the voice and remove my legs from Drake's waist.

"Price?" I question, momentarily dazed, before getting my wits and realizing my mistake. Fuck.

"So, this is where you've been. You left home to be some vampire's whore?" he spits at me. Drake, feeling threatened, pushes me behind him and hisses at him.

"She's no one's whore," Drake growls out, once again confusing me. I never expected him to stick up for me.

Price completely ignores Drake and continues talking to me. "Your father has sent hunters out in every direction searching for you. He is convinced that some type of supernatural faction has taken you hostage."

"Well, that's his problem, isn't it?" Drake answers for me.

"We can't let him get word back to my father," I whisper to Drake.

With supernatural speed, Drake moves and grabs Price around the neck, lifting him from the ground.

"Don't kill him," I plead.

Drake turns to me in confusion. "What exactly do you want me to do with him, then?"

That's an excellent question. I don't want to be responsible for

Price's death, especially when his only crime is happening upon me and Drake at an inopportune time. I don't particularly like the guy, but still. "Let's keep him captive," I say, and Drake raises an eyebrow. "Just until we can figure out what we can do with him."

Drake doesn't seem convinced, but he dips his head in agreement all the same. He lowers Price to the ground and the two shifter security guards from the club rush over and secure him in bindings. "Take him to the coven and tell them to secure him for interrogation." The shifters nod and get to work.

Once the shifters leave, Drake turns to me. "Now, where were we?"

"Really?" I ask. He can't be serious.

"What is so surprising to you? I thought we were in the middle of something," he responds.

"We were, but Price showing up here changes things. If my father is sending people out looking for me, it means that his attack is going to happen sooner than expected," I tell him honestly. This is going to be all my fault. "I need to leave Parry Sound. I need to be seen somewhere far away from here, otherwise you, Dru, the covens, the pack, you'll all be in more danger than ever. I'm sorry. I should never have come here."

As I turn to walk away, he grabs my arm. "Wait. Don't go. Let's just have tonight," I search his face for the truth of his feelings. This is so unlike him. I'm expecting to see the mask he always wears, but instead, I see vulnerability and desire.

Reluctantly, I nod my head in agreement, and I allow him to lead me toward a building off to the left. He lifts me, and once again, I wrap my legs around his waist and my arms around his neck. Somehow, even though his attention seems to be solely on me kissing and licking my way up his neck and sucking on his earlobe, we make our way into a simple apartment. He closes the door and leans my back up against it, returning the favor by licking and sucking on my neck. I feel his fangs poke me, not enough to draw blood, but enough that I can tell they have descended, and a shiver flows through me.

I whisper two words that I never thought would come out of my mouth, "Bite me." He pulls back in shock.

"Are you sure? You were pretty adamant when you said no biting that first night," he asks.

"I am. If this is our last night together, I want to experience everything," I pant.

He carries me to the bed and lays me down gently while removing my dress. I reach out and unbuckle his belt and unzip his pants, freeing his erection. He moans slightly as I dart my tongue out to taste him, but he pushes me back onto the bed. His eyes roam my body, licking his lips in anticipation before removing his shirt and lowering his mouth to my center. He pushes my thong to the side and swipes his tongue, lapping up the juices that have already leaked out, and now it's my turn to moan.

As he sucks my clit into his mouth, his fangs descend and sink into the flesh just above. The slight pain from his fangs piercing my skin gives way to the most amazing pleasure, like nothing I've ever felt before. Drake has brought me to climax over and over again, but I have never in my life felt like this. It feels like a continuous orgasm, and as he slides two fingers inside me, my pussy clenches them.

"*Goddess*!" I cry out as the orgasm peaks, but he doesn't stop, he doesn't slow, he continues his assault on my clit, sucking and flicking it with his tongue.

It could have been an hour, or it could have only been a minute. Either way, I've never felt ecstasy like this before. His demeanor changes when he removes his fangs, and rather than spinning me around and having intense hate sex like I'm used to with him, he makes love to me. Sliding his cock in and out while kissing me from my mouth to my neck and back again. I've fallen over the edge so many times I've lost count as his cock hits the delicious spot inside of me.

Finally, I can't take his tenderness any longer, and I roll him over and thrust myself up and down at an impossible rate. Each time I lower myself, I rock slightly so that not only is he hitting my G spot from inside, but my clit rubs up against him as well. This time when I cum and my pussy clenches down on him hard, I feel his balls tighten, and he tumbles over that edge with me.

I rise back up and feel the loss immediately as he slips out of me. "Don't go," he whispers to me.

"I have to. You know that." I clean myself up with a towel I find on the dresser and get dressed.

"No. You don't. I can protect you," he tells me.

I turn to face him, so confused I can't even explain it. "Sure, until you decide you want nothing to do with me again."

He scurries off the bed to stand in front of me. "That won't happen. I promise," he pleads.

"I wish that were true, Drake. You don't know how much I wish that. But the fact of the matter is that since I've met you, all you've done is want me to leave. Now that I'm giving you exactly what you want, you change your mind?" I ask him, removing my arms from his grip.

"Rayne. Please," he says, and for the first time since I met him, I see a hint of sadness in his expression and in his voice. It almost breaks my resolve. Almost.

I kiss him passionately, trying to put as many of my feelings into this one last kiss as I can. "I have to go, Drake. Please be ready. My father will launch an attack sooner rather than later. Protect Dru." I leave as quickly as possible before I change my mind, only stopping momentarily at the coven to grab my bag. I scribble a small note for Dru, apologizing and telling her how much I love her and to stay safe. I hope she's not too mad at me.

Chapter Fifteen

Drake

I stand there staring at the door in my birthday suit, seemingly unable to move. I fucked up. I fucked up so large this time that I don't think there is a way to fix it. My mate just walked out of my life, and it's all because of me. Dru was right. She saw what I didn't want to. As soon as I tasted Rayne's blood, I knew. But when I think about it, I guess I've really always known. Why else would I have been so drawn to her? Why else would the thought of being with another woman have been such a turnoff? Or the thought of her being with another man throw me into such a murderous rage?

Rayne is my mate, and she just walked out of my life for good. Not because she wanted to, but to protect me. To protect my family. How could I have been so wrong about her? Instead of spending the last week with her, enjoying each other, I spent it pushing her away, making her feel unwanted.

"*Fuck*!!" I scream out.

The door slams open, and for a single moment, I allow myself to think it's Rayne returning. Instead, it's Dru. "What happened?" she asks, looking around for danger.

"She's gone," I reply, hanging my head.

"What do you mean 'She's gone'?" Dru asks.

"I mean just that. She's gone. She's not coming back," I slowly sink to the bed and cover myself as I realize I'm still naked.

Dru rounds on me. "What did you do?"

I place my head in my hands. "You were right."

"Of course, I was." She waves her hands in the air. "But what was I right about?" she asks in confusion.

"She's my mate," I tell her.

I hear Dru suck in a breath, and then I feel her sink to her knees and wrap me in a hug. "What happened?"

"Well..." I start and raise my face to look into her eyes.

"Spare me the dirty details. Just explain to me why she's gone. Did you tell her that you're her mate?"

I shake my head. "No. When we left the club, we were outside talking, and one of the hunters from her father's group happened upon us. He recognized her immediately. Turns out her father has been scouring the province looking for her, believing that she's been taken captive. She left to keep us safe. I tried to convince her to stay. That's what we were doing here when I figured out that she's my mate. I tried Dru. I really did," a wetness forms in my eyes as I speak.

She nods, tears forming in her own. "That would be a reason for her to run. She's got a protective streak in her a mile long, just like you. It's going to get her killed."

"She's protective of you, Dru. She left to keep them away from you. I see it now, what you see in her. She's fierce and loyal to those she cares about, and she loves you," I tell her, taking her face in my hands and wiping the tears from her eyes.

"I know. I love her, too. She's snarky and bullheaded, but she also gives everything she is to those she loves. That's what I tried to tell you. I tried to make you see reason before it was too late. Now that she's in the wind, you won't find her unless she wants to be found," Dru says.

"I know. I just hope that the hunter we took captive can give us some answers."

"What hunter you took captive?" Dru asks, confused.

"The hunter that saw us; Rayne didn't want me to kill him, but we also couldn't exactly let him go. So, I had him sent back to the coven," I tell her as I get up to get dressed.

I try to focus on the task at hand as we return to the coven. I need to find a way to keep Rayne safe and make sure that I prepare us for the battle that is bound to come this way. Problem is: I don't know how to do either of those things while Rayne is on the run.

"Drake, baby. I was looking for you," Colleen coos, rubbing her body up against mine as we enter. I look over at Dru, and she gives me a look that tells me to handle this now.

"Not now, Colleen," I tell her and brush her off me.

"Why not now? When then, Drake? You've been saying 'not now' for days, but now never seems to come," Colleen pouts.

I breathe out heavily. "You're right. I don't mean 'not now.' I mean *never*. I'm not interested in you. Aside from being your coven leader, I don't want anything to do with you," I tell her straight, watching the hurt cross her face. I know that she had convinced herself that she and I would eventually be together, and she would help me run the coven. That has never been the case, but I also never told her that either.

"You can't mean that," she pleads.

Dru steps in at that moment. "Take the hint, you blonde bitch. He just told you he doesn't want you. Don't be so pathetic."

Well, that was the wrong thing to say. Colleen grabs Dru by the hair and forces her head back, hissing in her face. Before I can step in, Dru twists her wrists and takes her down to the ground, placing her knee on Colleen's neck. "Don't ever fucking touch me," Dru spits in her face.

Colleen is shocked at the strength of Dru, if her mouth opening and closing and wide eyes are any indication. Though, I'm sure there's a similar look on my own.

"You'll pay for that," Colleen says as Dru lets her up.

"Not likely," Dru responds, wiping off her clothes as if she got dirty just from touching Colleen.

"Where did you learn to do that?" I ask once Colleen is gone.

"Rayne. She thought I should know how to protect myself, just in case," Dru responds sullenly.

"Well, it was extremely impressive," I tell her, throwing my arm around her shoulder, and together we continue to make our way towards the cells.

The coven isn't large by any means, but it's home. It's a design of my own. Above ground, there are twelve floors of office buildings where we rent out the spaces to different companies, but below ground is a ten-story apartment building. I still need to figure out what to do with them once our new home is done. The bottom ten levels at the new compound are the same as here with minor adjustments, mainly for security. Each floor holds thirty apartments with a full-size swimming pool, gym, and rec center, with a playground on the bottom floor. It should be impossible to have built this in Parry Sound due to the rock sediment scattered; however, thanks to our supernatural strength, we were able to remove or crush any of the rocks we came across.

As we descend the staircase, I watch as many of the coven members go about their evening. Parents are walking toward the playground with their kids; teenagers are shooting pool or playing video games; others are reading or taking their lessons. Everybody is just going about their lives as if nothing is going to happen. For the first time in a lot of years, I look at the coven in a new light. Sure, I've always been responsible for them and cared for their wellbeing, but until Rayne, that's all it was: duty, responsibility. Now, after meeting Rayne and finding out that she's my mate, I look at the couples and see love; I look at the families and feel envious. I never wanted to meet my mate. I couldn't fathom how one person could change another in such a profound way like the other couples I've met have. Men I grew up with became completely different people once they met their mates. But that's what happened to me, and now she's gone.

Goddess. She hasn't even been gone an hour and here I am feeling like it's been years since I saw her face, looked into her eyes, felt the touch of her hands, tasted her mouth or other places, touched her luscious body, ran my fingers through her long locks.

I didn't realize I was standing still, lost in thought, until Dru grasps my shoulders. "Drake."

I shake my head to clear the thoughts of Rayne. "Yes?"

"Are you sure you're up for this?" she asks, concern lining her features.

"Why wouldn't I be?" I challenge.

"Because you just found out that Rayne is your mate, and she left," Dru points out.

"Thanks for reminding me," I respond curtly.

"Drake. I'm being serious," Dru stops me from continuing to walk toward the cells. "Do this another time."

"I need to do this, Dru," I say to her, and she raises an eyebrow at my attempt to brush her off. Letting out a sigh, I continue. "Rayne is gone. There is nothing I can do about it. I need a distraction. This is just the thing to do that."

She still looks at me skeptically, but nods. "Okay." Together, Drusilla and I walk up to the cell, peering in the small window before I reach for the door handle. I turn back to look at Dru and find her frozen, her entire body trembling.

"Are you okay?" I ask, gripping the top of her arms.

Her eyes flit from the cell window to mine, and she shakes her head. "I can't go in there."

"Okay," I tell her rubbing her biceps. "Why don't you go back to your apartment, and I'll meet you there."

She lets out a relieved breath before spinning and using her vampiric speed to rush away. For the last couple of days, I seemed to have forgotten about all her trauma. It seems that Rayne really was the one giving her the strength to come out of her shell. With her gone, I can't help but worry that Dru will revert back.

I enter the cell and find the man, Price, sitting on the bed. "Do you find your new accommodations up to your standards?" I ask.

"I have nothing to say to you, leech," he responds.

"That may be. But I have some things I need you to answer by any means necessary," I advise him while running my tongue along my fangs.

"I'll only speak with Rayne," he tells me. A pang of hurt hits my chest at her name coming out of his mouth.

"Well, Rayne is gone, so you'll have to make do with me," I respond.

"Gone? Gone where?" he asks.

"None of your business. Though it seems that seeing you made her decide to leave," I tell him deliberately, keeping as close to the truth as possible. If he wasn't a hunter, I would have already compelled him to forget seeing us earlier, but there is something in the hunter's bloodline that prevents them from being susceptible to it. It's a well-kept secret by the hunters. One day, if Rayne ever returns, I'll have to ask her about it.

"Good for her. Probably just couldn't stand to be around you leeches," he spits at me.

I don't even know what to say in response to that. The only thing I want to do right now is throttle the man sitting in front of me.

"Besides, you'll all be dead soon anyway. The hunters are coming for you. We know where you live, where the pack is. What did you think? That we would just allow you to continue to breed like rabbits and infect the earth?" he says.

As long as he is talking, I'll just keep standing here and listening. That is, until he starts to laugh maniacally.

"And when is this attack going to happen?" I ask.

"When you least expect it," he responds. "We're going to exterminate every last one of you from this earth," and that's it. That's when I snatch him up quickly by the throat.

"Threaten my family again, and I'll be the monster you've been claiming me to be," I hiss in his face. To his credit, he doesn't seem scared, just more determined than ever.

I throw him down on the bed and swiftly leave the room, heading straight to Drusilla's apartment. "Well, did you get anything from him?" Dru asks.

"Just that the hunters are coming like Rayne warned. We need to be ready," I respond.

"We will be," she replies, much more determined than I've ever seen her. I give her a smile and a kiss on her head before walking out the door.

When I head back to my office, I find Colleen completely naked and on my desk. This is exasperating. "Colleen. We already talked about this."

"No, you talked. I just know there is no way you could have meant what you said. We are meant to be together," she states.

"I meant what I said. There is no *we*. There never will be," I tell her forcefully.

"Ever since that hunter came here, you've changed. What happened?" she asks.

"This has *nothing* to do with her," I growl out.

"*It has everything to do with her*!" she screams at me.

"Get the fuck *out*!" I scream back at her, my fangs dropping down. She scrambles to grab her clothes and rushes out of the room with her eyes welling up with tears.

She's right, though. If she had shown up on my desk two weeks ago, it would have been more than welcome. But since I met Rayne, I have no desire to have any woman warming my bed. Well, any woman except Rayne. If only there was a way to get her to come back. The hunters are coming here whether or not she is with us. It seems that we may stand a better chance with her, rather than without her.

I scrape everything off my desk with a groan. Throwing myself in my chair, I pull out my phone and bring up Alaric's contact. Although I'd rather be finding a hole for myself to hide in, I press call and bring the phone up to my ear.

"Drake?" Alaric says gruffly, answering the phone.

"Yeah. We need to talk." I tell him and hear Phoebe giggle in the background. Obviously, I've interrupted their private times once again.

"Can it wait?" He asks.

"That depends. Rayne and I ran into a hunter outside Supernatural. She left to try and lead them away. I have a hunter in my cells who's telling me the attack is coming sooner rather than later. What do you think? Can it wait?" I question.

"Shit. I'll be right there." I hear sounds of Phoebe protesting in the moments before he hangs up. I send a quick text off to Colin informing him that Alaric is coming over and I set my phone down on my desk to pick everything up off the floor and set it right.

I'm just placing the paper weight on the desk when Alaric walks in with Darren beside him.

"Alaric. Darren." I nod to both of them. They dip their heads in greeting, both with annoyed looks on their faces. Maybe Alaric wasn't the only one who was interrupted.

"Drake. So, what exactly happened?" Alaric asks, and I sigh. I give them a play-by-play of what happened after Rayne and I left Supernatural, leaving out the details of our bedroom antics.

"Let me get this straight: this hunter recognized Rayne and she convinced you to capture him rather than kill him? To do what with?" Darren asks.

I shrug my shoulders. "I honestly don't know. She just said she didn't want me to kill him, but we couldn't let him go either. I had him brought here instead."

"And then you and Rayne bumped uglies, and she left saying she's going to lead them away? And you trust that?" Alaric challenges, and I growl. He raises an eyebrow. "I thought you hated her. What changed that?"

"She's my mate," I tell them, placing my head in my hands.

"What?" Darren asks, leaning forward as if he didn't hear me.

"She's my mate," I say again, looking up at them both. They share a look before turning back to me with pity on their faces. Both of them have met their mates, and, although neither of their mates left like Rayne did, they each had their own struggles in keeping them, so if anyone knows how this feels, it will be these two.

"It will work out, Drake. Don't worry," Alaric says, and Darren nods but I'm not sure I believe them. I don't see how it will.

"Let's go talk to the prisoner," Darren says, standing up.

"I'll take you two down there, but I don't think you'll get very much information. Maybe you should ask Skarlyt to make a truth potion like she did with that Joe guy."

"That's not a bad idea. Okay, new plan. We'll head home and come back tomorrow night with the potion," Alaric says. I lead the two of them up the stairs and out of the house.

"I don't even know if he really knows anything. Trust me: I tried to get as much out of him as possible," I tell them.

"I'll have to ask Skarlyt if it will even work. If vampires can't compel the hunters, it stands to reason that magic may not work either." With that, the two of them leave, and I head back inside to try drowning my sorrows in a bottle or two of Faerie wine.

* * *

After drinking for hours, I must've passed out because when I wake up, Colin is pounding on my office door.

"Come in," I call out, and he opens the door to allow both Alaric and Darren to walk in.

"Shit," I say, running my hands through my hair in an effort to smooth it out.

"Did we wake you?" Darren says walking up to the desk with a chuckle.

I wave him off. "Shut up."

"We brought the potion," Alaric interrupts our stare-down.

"Let's try it then," I say, standing up and leading them back down to the cell area.

After pouring it down the sleeping hunter's throat and startling him awake, the three of us step back and wait.

"Now, let's try this again. When is the attack going to happen?" I ask.

"As soon as Ulysses finds Rayne." His hand slips over his mouth like that's not what he meant to say, and I smile.

"Who's Ulysses? And what is he to Rayne?"

I ask, and he smiles. "Her father and your worst nightmare."

"And if he doesn't find her. Then what?"

His mouth clamps shut, but he can't seem to help opening it back up. "The other bloodlines are going to force the attack in two weeks with or without him." Once again, he pulls his hand to his mouth.

"And how many will there be?" I ask, leaning forward.

"Not even I know that. It depends on how many answer the call," he says with a smug look on his face.

"What's your best guess?"

He struggles momentarily as if he doesn't want to answer. "Over a thousand. And they're going to drain each and every one of you, starting with your women and children." Alaric's fist snaps out, punching Price in the face, knocking him out cold.

"Well, that was unexpected." I say, looking between Alaric and knocked out Price.

"Sorry. Couldn't help it," he admits, and I shrug my shoulders. Hell, I probably would've done the same.

"I'd say we have just been given two weeks to get ready. We'll meet up again tomorrow night. We could all probably do with some training," I say, and they both agree, knowing that we'd be in a much better position if Rayne was here to help us train.

I walk them both back upstairs, not one of us speaking. I'm not sure there is much to say. If I thought my outlook on life was bleak without Rayne, it's even worse with the number of hunters heading this way.

When we reach the door at the top. "You should probably call the bears, mountain lions, and witches, too," I tell them.

"I definitely think it's an 'all hands on deck' situation." Alaric agrees with Darren also dipping his head in agreement.

They both turn, shifting into their black wolves and running through the forest back to the pack. I pick up their piles of folded clothes, depositing them in the bin just outside the doors so that they don't get wet and head back inside to get my coven ready.

Chapter Sixteen

Rayne

I've been on the run for just over two days and have purposely been seen by countless hunters; although, I haven't let any get close enough to talk to me. Word should have reached my father by now. At least that's my hope. I miss Drake and Dru more than anything. I miss the sound of his voice, the feel of his skin on mine. I especially miss having Dru to confide in, watch movies with, or just be together without doing anything at all. They're my home. Wherever the two of them are, that's where I belong. I didn't truly realize that until after I left.

But alas, it's what needs to be done, so here I sit, in a dark corner in this dive bar, trying to overhear the conversation between these two hunters, whom I have conveniently nicknamed Tweedle Dee and Tweedle Dum, sitting at the table next to me.

"I can't wait," Tweedle Dee says.

"Me, neither. We're going to kill every last one of those leech scum and shifters," Tweedle Dum responds.

"We sure are. And we don't have to wait much longer. Two days and we will attack. There will be so many of us they won't stand a chance. It's just too bad we have to travel all the way to

Ontario to do it." Tweedle Dee says. I suck in a breath. Two days. There is no way that my new friends will be ready in two days' time. The entire coven, including the women and children, will be slaughtered.

"Yes. And thanks to Price, we now have their numbers and locations." Thanks to Price? What does he mean by thanks to Price? I want to spin around and interrupt the two of them to get all the information. I know, without a doubt, that I could take them, but it could cost me precious time that I need.

"Exactly. I still don't trust his explanation of a blonde blood sucker releasing him, but I suppose it doesn't matter now."

I quickly down my drink and make my way out of the bar without being seen. I need to get back to Drake. They need to be ready. And if what Tweedle Dee or Tweedle Dum said is true, the only blonde bloodsucker stupid enough to release Price would be Colleen. If she is working with the hunters from the inside, they won't stand a chance.

I hop in my rental car and drive through the night. By the time I reach Parry Sound, it's early evening. I decide to go to the pack first as most of the coven will be sleeping since the sun set is still around thirty minutes away, but rather than the bustling community that I've grown accustomed to, I find no one. Not a single soul. Where could everyone be? I park my car next to Alaric's pick-up truck and begin to walk around.

After a while of searching, I finally find a woman rushing around. "Excuse me. Where is everyone?" I call out to her.

"They're at the clearing over at the Coven of the Moon for the mating ceremony," she responds as if I should already know.

"How do I get there?" I ask.

She looks at me for a moment before saying, "I suppose you can come with me." She says, gesturing for me to follow her.

A not-so-short thirty-five-minute walk later, we arrive in the clearing, and the sun has set. "Thank you," I tell the woman as we both rush toward the crowd. As I'm walking up, a dragon lands and shifts into a man. I'm awestruck. "A dragon shifter," I whisper to myself and watch as he walks over to a group of people. Upon closer inspection, I recognize Alaric, Phoebe, Skarlyt, Darren, Sophia, Sarah, Dru, and Drake. I step a little closer, intending to make myself known, but I pause and listen as the dragon shifter begins to speak.

"When the daughter of the storm and the son of the moon become one;
A hunter and her prey put aside their differences;
The lost daughter of air mates the first son born of magic and fire;
A son and daughter of fire join together;
The dual natured son and the dawn cement their bond;
A new age arrives where supernatural beings will need to come out of the shadows as a new enemy awakens."

What the fuck? Is that some sort of prophecy?

"Well, we can assume that Sarah and Sebastyn are the daughter of storm and son of the moon, given that Andres has already confirmed as such," Skarlyt adds.

"And Drake and Rayne are the hunter and her prey," Dru states.

"I'm not so sure that one will come to pass," Drake adds. What does that mean? The hunter and her prey? And it won't come to pass?

"What do you mean?" Alaric asks. "You are true mates, aren't you?" I suck in a breath. True mates? I thought only supernaturals had mates.

My gaze lands on Drake as he answers. "Yes. But she's gone, and I don't think she's coming back. Why would she after the way I treated her?" he responds.

"M.m.m.ates?" I stammer as I walk closer. His use of that word is impossible. There is no way that I could be a mate to a supernatural, especially not an immortal like Drake.

"Rayne," Drake whispers, and takes a step toward me.

I hold up my hand to halt him. "Explain," I demand.

"All supernaturals have a true mate. Like a soul mate," he begins.

"I know what a true mate is," I snap back. "I just don't understand how I can be yours."

"True mates can be any species. Take me and Lennox. I'm a witch, and he's a shifter. Or Samara and Trevan: she's a shifter, and he's a Fae. Just because you're a hunter doesn't mean that your mate can't be a supernatural being," Skarlyt adds.

I roll that statement over in my head. I guess I never thought about it before. "But hunters don't have mates."

"Are you saying that soul mates don't exist in the human species?" Dru asks. Again, I mull that over for a moment. I guess if I really think about it, people all over the world have claimed to have found their soulmate. It would stand to reason that it could be possible.

"Okay. Let's say I believe you," I tell them and turn to face Drake. "Just how long have you known?"

"Since the moment I tasted your blood," he responds, while looking ashamed.

"So instead of telling me that you were my mate, you let me leave?" I accuse. Of course, I know that it wouldn't have made a difference, except possibly urging me to leave even more, and that is if I actually believed him.

"If you remember correctly, I tried to stop you from leaving," he snaps back. There's the Drake I know.

"Well, you could have tried harder," I snap back. Then I round on everyone else. "And you all knew?"

Every single one of them, apart from the dragon shifter, nods. I thought these people were my friends. To me, friendship means you don't keep things like this from one another. Not a single one of them thought it might be important for me to know that they thought I had a supernatural mate. They didn't need to specifically say Drake. "When?" I ask these people I considered my friends.

"I suspected when I caught you and Drake in the woods," Dru tells me, and my mouth drops open in shock.

"You suspected?" I challenge the person I believed to be my best friend.

She lowers her head, looking a little ashamed of her actions. "Yes. I suspected. But I didn't want to tell you without knowing for sure," she reaches for me, but I step back, just out of reach. How could the person who claims to be my best friend—my family—keep something from me so important like me possibly being bonded to her brother? Not from anyone else. Just me. "I was afraid it would scare you away." Tears begin to line her eyes at her admission and a pang of hurt flows through me. I don't want to hurt her, but I'm not sure how I can trust her right now either.

"I don't want to become a vampire. I have no desire to be turned," I tell them, with my gaze ending up on Drake.

"That doesn't matter. We can make it work," he pleads.

"How?" I ask.

His mouth gapes open and closed like a fish unable to answer. "It won't work. I will grow old and die. You will stay young and alive forever. What kind of life would that be for either of us?" I ask, my own sadness seeping through.

"Rayne, please," Phoebe begins, but I hold my hands up to stop her.

"No. I refuse to believe that I am a part of whatever trick this is. I came here to tell you that the hunters are coming in two days and that Price escaped. I've done what I came here to do," I say and watch as shock registers on their faces.

"That's impossible. I locked him away at the coven's compound," Drake counters.

"Really? Well, apparently Price escaped with the help of a blonde vampire. Can't you think of any blonde vampires who would want to help your enemies hurt you?" I ask.

"Colleen would never," Drake responds.

"Ha!" I laugh. Of course, he defends her. He should've kicked her out solely based on the way she dared to treat his sister.

"Listen, I've done what I need to do. I thought I had found the place where I finally belong. I thought I had found friends..." I look at each one before landing on Dru. "Family. But it turns out I was wrong. I'll be going now." As both Dru and Drake take a step forward to stop me, I turn to them raising my hand. "Don't follow me."

With that said, I turn and walk away. I allow the tears to flow at their betrayal. I know that I'm being hasty in my judgment and that I will probably gain clarity after a while. Right now, the fact that they didn't tell me there was a possibility that Drake and I are mates cuts me deep. Especially when I had confided in Dru, Skarlyt, and Phoebe about how I didn't understand why I was so drawn to him. Add in the fact that Drake knew and just let me leave without saying a word, and I feel like there is no way that I could ever trust any of them again.

Oh, yeah, there's also the nonsense with that prophecy thing that I am apparently part of, some big threat looming over the world. Maybe my father was right: not in the reasoning why all supernaturals needed to be eradicated, but in the fact that the world would be safer without them in it. After all, if there are no supernaturals, then those mates in the prophecy can never bond, and the big baddie won't be able to come to fruition.

"Rayne?" Dru calls out to me, but I keep walking. "Please," she uses her speed to get in front of me.

"I told you not to follow me," I spit at her.

"I know. But please, just listen," she begs. Reluctantly, I nod, not being able to stand the sadness on her face.

"I have lived in fear since the day you helped me escape. When I was being held captive, the only light in my life was you. Maybe it's like a Stockholm Syndrome type of thing, but I didn't leave my home at all until the day I found you and Drake in the woods. Seeing you again fixed something inside of me that has been broken since I was taken. It gave me the strength to start living again. It's no excuse, but I was afraid that if I told you I suspected that you were Drake's mate, you would leave, and I couldn't lose you." She steps forward and I step back. "I *can't* lose you. I guess I understand now why I have such a pull toward you. Because we were meant to be family. We *are* family. If you don't want to be turned, we can figure it out. Maybe the witches have a spell to extend your life. We can find something. Please, just don't go."

I wipe the tears from my own eyes. "Dru. It's not just that you didn't tell me your suspicions. I will eventually get over that. It's this whole prophecy thing, too. If Drake and I were to mate, as you call it, we would be taking another step closer to fulfilling it, and I can't allow that to happen," I tell her and clasp her hands in mine. "I love you, Drusilla. You are my best friend in the entire world, and I will always be there when you call me. But I also care for your brother, and I know that I'm not strong enough to deny him for long. I need to go."

"Please don't," I hear Drake whisper from behind us.

I spin around to face him. "Drake." His name comes out as a whisper, tears already welling up in my eyes. I don't want to leave him. As mad as I am about him not telling me we are mates, it doesn't change the fact that somehow he wormed his way into my soul and I've developed extremely strong feelings for him. I won't say I'm in love with him, but I'm not *not* in love with him.

He takes a few small steps toward me. Rather than backing up this time, I hold my ground.

"Please. Don't go," he says as he reaches out and takes my hands in his.

"I'll give you two a minute," Dru says, giving my shoulder a squeeze before walking away.

"Drake. As confusing and exciting as our time together has been, it can't go any further. You will have to find another to be your mate, someone who is more like you," I tell him while removing my hands from his.

"Rayne, I don't think you understand. There will be no other for me. I can't simply decide to take another mate. My soul will not even allow me to think about being with someone else, let alone actually committing the act. In hindsight, it should have been the first sign for me.

"Ever since I met you, I have been unable to get even slightly aroused by anyone other than you. Unless you formally reject me and reject our bond, I will never be able to be with another woman" Drake tells me. That shouldn't change anything. I should still leave, but the thought of causing him pain or to be the reason he lives the rest of his life alone hurts more than I thought it would.

Curiosity gets the better of me. "What does a rejection do?"

"One of the mates verbally rejects the other. It is excruciatingly painful. It's our souls severing from each other permanently." He says, and I frown. I don't want to cause him any pain.

"But Drake, I don't want to become a vampire. Surely that changes things for you," I try to reason with him.

"Would it be preferable that you turn? Of course. But it's not a deal breaker for me. I'll take you anyway I can get you—human, hunter, vampire—for as long as I can have you. Who knows, maybe after a decade or so, you will change your mind," he grasps me around the waist. "What is it about being a vampire that turns you off of it so much?"

I let out a sigh and melt into his body for a moment. It feels so nice to have him touching me after being away from him for the last few days. "It's the little things like never seeing the sun again or eating a pepperoni and cheese pizza when I'm craving it. You don't miss those things because you've never experienced them. I have and I can't imagine my life without either of those things. Besides, it's not just the issue with species. It's this whole prophecy thing."

"I just found out about that, too. I admit it's a scary thought, but like all prophecies, some come true, and others don't. Who's to say that this one won't be the latter?" Drake asks.

"I suppose that's true. But what if it does come true? We could be part of the reason the world is in danger.".

"Rayne," he says, grabbing me by the hands. "Even if it does come true, we are just one part of that prophecy. If it's even about us, it can still go on even if we don't mate."

I walk over to a tree and slide down to sit on the ground, holding my knees to my chest. I was so sure that I was doing the right thing, but Drake makes a good point. Just because one part of the prophecy doesn't come true doesn't mean that it won't be fulfilled. Besides, if I stay, I know I can't resist Drake, but I also don't want to become a vampire. What the fuck do I do now?

"How about this..." Drake begins, coming to squat in front of me. "Let's just focus on the immediate threat. Let's get through the hunters' attack, and after that, we can focus on us," he reasons with me.

After thinking about it for a few minutes, I dip my head in agreement. "Fine. But while we train, you need to make sure you do everything I say if we are going to stand any sort of chance."

"Deal," he tells me and moves in for a kiss.

I hold my hand up to his lips. No matter how much my body is demanding to reciprocate his kiss, my mind wins out. "We said we'd wait."

Reluctantly, he leans back with a sigh. "You're right. Let's go talk to the others about the plan of action."

Chapter Seventeen

Drake

Walking back to the clearing with Rayne next to me while unable to touch her is almost as painful as if she wasn't here at all. I know I agreed to wait to focus on us being together until after everything is settled with the hunters, but I didn't anticipate how hard it was going to be. And it's only been a few minutes. My hand hovers behind her lower back, not touching but still close enough that I can feel the heat emanating off her.

As we enter the clearing through the trees, I catch Alaric's gaze. The smile on his face is wide as he notices Rayne walking next to me. It is a foreign concept to me, but the fact is, I have a friend for the first time in my life that seems to genuinely care about what happens to me. Not that I haven't had friends. I just haven't had anyone that I've trusted enough to let in as I have with Alaric and Darren. But when he sees the look on my own face, his smile drops. I want to be able to tell him everything, but not with everyone else here.

"Rayne," Phoebe exclaims, rushing over and wrapping her arms around her.

"I'm sorry I overreacted," Rayne says, returning the hug and the rest of the women join in. "I know you guys just didn't want to scare me away."

I leave the girls to talk and walk over to Alaric. "Seems like you were able to convince her to stay."

"For now. I have a lot of making up to do, but she's agreed to help us with the attack, and we will figure out the rest after," I tell him.

He places his hand on my shoulder. "It will all work out. You need to trust in the Mother."

I nod at him, actually believing him this time and turn to the newcomer. "Andres, right?"

He puts his arm out for me to clasp, which I reciprocate. "Yes. And you are Drake, the leader of the vampire coven?"

"I am. What is this business about a prophecy?" I ask.

"Long ago, before I took my sleep, there was a witch who had the gift of foresight. In her last days, she had one last vision. In this vision, she saw certain things coming to be. She said there would be a time when the supernatural factions would need to reveal themselves to save the world from an enemy thought defeated long ago," Andres tells us.

"And if these pairings don't come to be?" I ask, trying to get clarity on Rayne's theory.

"She was very clear on that point. If the pairings noted in the prophecy don't come to be, the world will have no hope of survival," he responds solemnly.

Well, there goes Rayne's theory. "Are you sure?" I ask.

"Yes. On that she was very clear," Andres states.

"Who was clear on what?" Rayne asks from behind us.

"Andres was telling us more about the prophecy," Alaric responds.

"Oh, I want to hear about that, too," she says and looks at Andres expectantly.

"As I explained to your friends, the seer that predicted the prophecy was very clear about what happens if the steps within the prophecy failed to come to be," Andres starts, but Rayne cuts him off.

"And what would that be?"

"That the evil said to come out of the shadows will overtake the world and there will be nothing on this earth able to stop it," he tells her pointedly.

Rayne sucks in a breath and goes a little pale. Unable to stop myself, I wrap my arms around her waist. "So let me get this clear, if Drake and I were not to go through with our bonding, the prophecy will come to fruition, regardless?" she asks.

"Yes. But rather than the humans and supernatural factions standing a chance, there will be nothing in heaven or on earth able to stop it." At Andres' statement, if it was possible, Rayne goes even more pale, as do the rest of our group as we share concerned looks.

Skarlyt is the first to recover, "I guess we need to figure out who else is in that prophecy."

"No. First we need to get through the situation with the hunters," Rayne speaks up.

"She's right," Sophia says. "If the hunters are indeed coming, we need to be ready. Who knows how many they will be bringing with them."

"They are, and based on what I've learned, they're bringing numbers the likes of which we've never seen," Rayne tells her, and I instinctively pull her into me. This time she doesn't fight it as much.

Darren and Sophia share a look and I already know what they're thinking. When Darren was captured, he witnessed first-hand what cruelty the hunters are capable of.

"Well, that Price guy said that they're bringing numbers in the thousands," Darren speaks up, "so I say we move the coven into the compound on pack lands and make a plan."

"I agree. That is, if Alaric is okay with that," I tell them and look at Alaric, who nods.

"Sebastyn, Sarah, and I will head to the coven and get all the witches ready. I've been working on replicating the shields the mages were using on a larger scale," Skarlyt adds.

"Actually, I have a spell for that," Sebastyn says, and Skarlyt turns to him with a surprised look on her face.

"What?" she asks.

Sebastyn looks a little ashamed. "We can discuss it later." At least Skarlyt is pissed at someone else for a change.

"I can train the pack in the afternoon and the vampires at night. But Colleen will need to be dealt with. If you could find a spell to make all the hunters' weapons inoperable that would be great," Rayne more to Skarlyt than anyone else; Skarlyt bobs her head in agreement.

"I suppose I could continue my travels to search for some allies," Andres adds.

"What about Kenji and the pride?" Sebastyn's new mate, Sarah, speaks up.

Alaric looks at her and then at Phoebe. "I suppose it wouldn't hurt to ask," Phoebe responds.

"Some of the Amazon coven are here now. Let's go see if they would be interested in staying and helping," Sophia says, pulling Darren along with her.

Rayne wriggles out of my hold and turns to face me. "We still have to wait until this is all over before we can talk more about us."

I sigh. I had hoped finding out that it will happen either way would change her mind, but I guess not. As I lift my hand and place a stray hair behind her ear, she leans into my hand and closes her eyes. On second thought, maybe there is some hope after all.

A throat clears next to us. "What do we do with Colleen?" Dru asks.

Rayne's look turns murderous. "I know what I'd like to do with her."

"We need to find out exactly what she told the hunter. Although I still have my doubts that it was her to begin with," I say.

"Of course, you do," Rayne responds with a roll of her eyes.

"What does that mean?" I snap. But Dru holds her hand up, interrupting before Rayne can respond with what I am sure was going to be a snark-filled comment.

"Come on, let's go figure it out then," Dru placates us both.

After saying a quick goodbye to everyone in our group, the three of us head back to the compound. "We need to move the coven over to pack land tonight," I tell them.

"Not the traitor," Dru adds.

I am still having trouble believing that anyone in my coven could be a traitor, but if that Price guy has been released, it's the only explanation. I did royally piss off Colleen the other night, so she would want to get some sort of revenge. I just can't understand why she would want to punish the entire coven when she was only mad at me.

"No. We will lock the person responsible in Alaric's cells," I tell them.

I look over at Rayne, and I see the gears in her mind turning. "What are you thinking?" I ask.

"Just wondering if there is a way we can use Colleen's betrayal to our advantage. Is it possible that we could feed her incorrect information somehow?" Rayne asks the two of us.

I think about it for a moment. "In any other circumstance, I'd say yes. But we can't move the entire coven to pack lands without her knowing, and we can't let her stay free if we do that. So I think for now we just hope we stand enough of a chance with your training."

"I suppose you're right. It would just be great if we could buy a little more time," she admits.

The entire coven is bustling when we arrive, with people running around, gathering their belongings. "What the fuck is going on here?" I shout.

Every single person in the coven stops and stares at me with fear plastered on their faces, but they don't say anything. "I asked a question, what is happening here."

"We were told that the hunters are coming," Colin tells me. "We have tried to keep order, but everyone is in a panic. As you can see."

"And who said this?" I ask him.

"Colleen. She told us you tasked her with getting everyone ready. Didn't you?" Colin asks.

"No. I most definitely did not," I growl out. "*Everyone to the common area now*," I shout out loud enough that everyone can hear me.

Everyone seems to stop what they are doing and heads down to the common area. While this is happening, I'm searching the crowd for the blonde-haired traitor, without success. I didn't want to believe that anyone in my coven could have been capable of betraying us, but I especially did not want to believe that someone I spent a great deal of time with could be the one. She was my consort for almost ten years. Perhaps that was my mistake. I gave her hope that we would preside over the coven together. Sure, I never told her that outright, but I never dissuaded her musings when she would talk about it. Fuck. This is all my fault. And after this, there is no denying that Colleen is the traitor for sure. I'm going to have to do some grovelling.

I turn to look at where Rayne was walking beside me, only to find no one there. I turn and search the crowd once again, finding neither of the people I'm looking for, and as much as I want to go searching for Rayne, the coven has gathered, and I need to trust that she can handle herself.

"I'll go look for her," Dru says from behind me. I give a nod in her direction, and she uses her speed to rush away.

"Quiet down, everyone," I call out and, as always, the entire room goes silent. "It's true that there is a group of hunters coming soon." Everyone starts murmuring once again, but I raise my hands to silence them. "However, we already have a plan in place. We will be moving over to the pack land, once again using Alaric's bunker. Please only bring necessities; everything else can be brought another time when we aren't under a direct threat. We want the hunters to believe we haven't abandoned our home if they are to breach our compound. We will leave in groups. The families with the youngest children will travel in an hour, then we will continue every half-hour with groups of no more than twenty leaving, based on the age of the children. By dawn we will all be settled into the bunker. Please see Colin for your sleeping assignments. He will have a list printed off for each of you before you leave here. I also spoke with Alaric, and he has assured me that the border is still erect so that no hunter will pass."

"What about the hunter you brought in here?" someone calls out.

"The male hunter that I placed in the cells has been set free by one of our own while I was at the mating ceremony," I respond.

"No, the woman," another voice says.

Before I can respond, a very familiar voice rings out. "That woman is the one who saved Drusilla when she was taken. She is not our enemy but our savior, and whoever treats her differently will deal with me," my father yells out as my mother rushes and wraps me up in a hug.

"But Colleen said..." Someone yells, and I scrub a hand on my face not wanting to deal with those questions quite yet. Especially when the traitor in question could still be around listening.

"That is all. Colin, please ensure they follow my orders," I say quickly before hugging my mother back.

"My darling boy. How I've missed you," my mother coos.

"And I, you," I tell her and turn to my father. "When did you get back?" I ask, clasping his arm.

"Just now. Drusilla called us the other day and explained that Rayne had surfaced here. We had to wait until we could get a flight that departed and arrived at night; otherwise, we would have been here sooner," he explains.

"Well, where are Rayne and our daughter?" my mother asks.

Once again, I look around the coven, searching for them. "I'm not sure. But among the three of us, I'm sure we can find them. They probably went after Colleen."

"Colleen? Your consort? Why would they do that?" my mother asks with shock lining her face.

"Because it seems Colleen is a traitor," I tell them, trying to avoid my father's eyes. He never liked Colleen. He thought she was a wolf in sheep's clothing, a status climber. Turns out he was right. Another person I need to apologize to about not believing them about her.

"Then we better get to it," he says, not waiting for an explanation as to how she's a traitor.

Chapter Eighteen

Rayne

As I'm walking down the stairs with Drake and Dru, out of the corner of my eye, I see that blonde bimbo hurrying down one of the side corridors. I can't let her get away. She must realize since we're back that we have figured out—or will figure it out shortly—that she is a traitor.

Even though she is fast, it seems I have no problem catching up with her. She screams as I reach out and snag her hair, pulling her back toward me. "Where do you think you're going?" I snap at her.

"I thought you were gone," she responds.

"No, you *wished* I was gone," I tell her as I throw her to the ground.

"Why would I wish that? You're nothing but a disgusting hunter. You may have Drake and Drusilla fooled, but I see through you, and I'll make sure everyone sees who you truly are," she spits back at me.

I jam my fist into her face. "And just who do you think I truly am?" I ask.

"A killer," she states.

"Ha. Maybe your killer," I tell her with a chuckle. "I don't understand why you would betray your entire coven by setting Price free."

"Oh, it wasn't me. It was you. While you tricked everyone into believing you were gone, you slipped back in, allowing him to escape with all the blueprints to the coven." She gives a sinister smile and spits blood onto the floor.

"What?" I say with a chuckle once again. "No one is going to believe that."

"Everyone here seemed to believe it. And once I turn on the waterworks and convince Drake of it, he'll be back in my bed, and you'll be six feet under." With her delusional statement, I laugh out loud. "What? You don't think I'll be able to convince him of your guilt?" she asks.

I try to stop my laughter, truly I do, but the fantasy world that she is living in is just too funny. "No," I wheeze out, clutching my stomach.

She takes offense to my laughter and stands up. "He was mine for ten years before you ever came into the picture, and he will be mine again."

As she goes to take advantage of my distraction and strike me—not that she would've been able to—a blur flies past me, knocking Colleen into the wall.

"Thought I might find you with her," Dru says, stepping up beside me.

"Aww, Dru, you ruined my fun," I pout.

"Don't worry, we have plenty of time to have fun with her," she pats me on the shoulder as I walk past her to Colleen.

"I can't wait," I say with a wink at Colleen.

"Drusilla, surely you don't believe this hunter over me?" Colleen pleads.

"Of course, I do. Unlike you, she is loyal and is..." I know what Dru is about to tell her, so I cut her off.

"Can I tell her? Pretty Please?" I beg. Dru gives me a smirk and a nod. "And it just so happens that Drake is my mate."

I don't know how I said it with a straight face as I watch the horror show come across her own. "That's right. You royally fucked up. Not only are you trying to frame me for something I didn't do, but you're trying to steal my mate. Now, Dru, how would someone accused of trying to seduce another's mate be punished?"

"Well, Rayne, in this coven, women accused of trying to seduce an already mated male are exiled, but in this case, with your mate being the coven leader..." Dru begins.

"The coven leader is her what?" A woman who looks similar to Drake says from the hallway. It's the eyes. I can already tell that she must be Drake's mother or another very close relative because their eyes are exactly the same shape, size, and color. Their hair is similar, too, but it's the eyes that give it away.

"Mother," Dru whispers and rushes over to the woman.

"My sweet girl. So nice to see you." Her mother hugs her. "There's something different about you," she says as she pushes Dru back, gripping her shoulders and giving her an extra squeeze.

"And this must be Rayne," she says. I stick my hand out for her to shake, but she slaps it away. "You are family, my dear girl. Not only did you save my daughter, but if what I just heard is correct, you will be my daughter in your own right soon enough."

"Well, about that..." I contemplate how to explain everything with Drake and me, but she stops me.

"Hush now. We will have all the time in the world to discuss everything. Right now, we need to deal with this traitor," she says pointing at Colleen.

"Yes, we do," Drake growls out from the hallway. "Colleen, what the fuck were you thinking?"

"Drake, baby, surely you don't believe I could be capable of betraying you or our coven. It was her. She's tricked you," she pleads.

"Enough of your lies," Drake spits at her. "I will not have you talking about my mate that way."

"Your mate? So, it's true? Impossible. She must have tricked you somehow, maybe a spell or something," Colleen begs, grasping at ways I could have tricked him.

"And how exactly would she have tricked me into believing that she is my mate?" Drake questions.

"Well, I'm not sure. Maybe she got a witch to," she tries to reason.

"A witch to what? To change her blood into that of my mate? Do you not remember how we identify our mates?" Drake says, grabbing her by the neck and raising her up against the wall.

"Drake, please," she begs, tears streaming down her cheeks.

"Enough, you viper. You will get what has been coming to you for many years," a different man says. He seems to have materialized out of nowhere and is now standing in the doorway.

"Daddy!" Dru exclaims, running and jumping on the man.

"My little Drusilla. I've missed you so," he says, cooing into her hair while rubbing her back.

"And I've missed you," she whispers. I can hear Dru's voice break and her emotions bleed through.

Watching the two of them embrace warms my heart. I wish more than anything that my father would have embraced me like that. But that was not in the cards for me, I guess. My father is as cold as the winters in Northern Ontario.

"And this must be Rayne," he says, releasing Dru and stepping toward me.

"Yes," I respond and stick my hand out toward him.

"Nonsense. We don't shake hands with family," he says, wrapping me up in a hug. I should've known he would react the same way as Dru's mom.

I return his embrace and allow myself a moment to pretend that it is my own father hugging me with such tenderness.

"Rayne is more than our daughter's savior it seems, Roderick," Drake's mother says.

"What do you mean, Margaret?" he asks, letting go of me and taking a step back.

"Well, it seems that Drake has finally found his mate," she informs.

"You have?" Roderick says, looking at Drake, surprised.

Drake looks back at his father, never removing his hand from Colleen's neck, then his eyes meet mine in question. I dip my head slightly in agreement. There's no use keeping it from him. Even if I don't give Drake the go ahead to tell his father, his mother surely will.

"Yes, I have," Drake confirms.

His father seems to catch on quickly, looking between the two of us. "You?" he questions me.

"It seems so. But it's a little more complicated than that," I tell him.

He waves his hand and repeats the same phrase as Margaret. "We have all the time in the world to discuss everything."

I look at Drake, urging him with my eyes to explain to his parents that it's more complicated than they think before they get too excited. Drake simply shrugs rather than speaking up. I shoot daggers at him with my eyes. It doesn't do any good, though. I mentally go through what I'm going to have him doing to punish him for that. I wonder how long it would take for his tongue to get tired... only one way to find out. Clearly, we're able to have sex without bonding. So maybe it doesn't need to be as slow as I thought.

"Let's get Colleen to the pack and make sure the rest of the coven gets safely to the bunker," Drake says. Although I agree with him that we need to ensure the coven's safety, it's still a huge piss off that he's not explaining the situation. I can already tell that Margaret especially is going to get too excited about this whole mate thing, and with so many unresolved issues between Drake and me, if the mating were to not take place, I won't just be hurting Drake now.

As Drake and his parents drag a kicking and screaming Colleen away, I stand rooted in my spot. Fuck. How can I make a decision without worrying about the feelings of others?

"What's wrong?" Dru asks.

I let out a soft sigh. "I'm worried your parents are going to get over excited about the mating before Drake and I have had a chance to come to a final decision."

"I'm sorry. I know you and Drake decided to wait until after the attack to discuss the whole mate thing," she says, placing her arm around my shoulder.

"I just worry that rather than being able to make the decision based on my own feelings, I'll have to consider the feelings of everyone else as well," I tell her.

"Not necessarily. My parents would never fault you for wanting to make a decision that is best for you," Dru says.

"Be that as it may, it still won't change the pressure I feel to take everyone else's feelings into account," I respond sullenly. "But let's leave that for now. It's my fault I spilled the beans to Colleen. I should've kept my mouth shut." She looks like she wants to say something, but I turn quickly. "We better go catch up."

"If you're sure," Dru says.

I nod. Together, Dru and I quickly catch up with the others. I watch as Drake manhandles Colleen, and I hate to admit how much it turns me on. I squeeze my thighs together to try to stop the juices that are leaking out of me. Of course, it doesn't work. Drake's head whips in my direction with a seductive smile. I can tell that he can sense just how much it's turning me on.

"Father, perhaps the three of you can get Collen locked away while Rayne and I keep things moving around here," he says to Roderick.

He looks surprised but recovers quickly after looking between the two of us. "Absolutely son. We will see you soon." He claps Drake on the back before returning to secure Colleen in the back of the SUV, sliding in next to her while both Dru and Margaret enter the front seats and drive away.

Drake walks up to me and pulls me into him so I can feel just how my arousal is affecting him. "Rayne, if you want to wait until after the attack, you can't smell like this," he says, sniffing up and down my neck.

"It's not my fault; it's yours," I respond with a small moan as he pushes his cock up against me.

"And just how is it supposed to be my fault?" he continues as he backs me up against the wall, lifting me under my ass, urging me to wrap my legs around his waist.

"Because..." I start, but he moves his mouth to my neck and begins using his expert tongue to tease me.

"Because what?" he taunts, removing his mouth from my neck briefly enough to say the words.

"Because just looking at you makes my body go to mush," I moan and begin to rub myself on him, causing him to moan right along with me.

"Maybe just this one time," I tell him. Without pause, he moves his mouth to mine and kisses me with a passion I've never felt from him before. It's as if he's kissing me for the last time, savoring every moment, every stroke of our tongues.

Hearing voices to the left of us makes me realize that we are in front of a building, grinding on each other for all to see. "Maybe we could go somewhere more private?" I whisper to him, my voice husky with need.

He doesn't need any further encouragement, as he uses his vamp speed to run us back into the building and into a large apartment. I want to look around to see his home. You can tell a lot about a man from his home, but his hand snakes into my pants as he sets me down. His fingers are rubbing lazy circles on my clit, and I forget what I was doing.

"We have to be quick. We really do need to ensure the coven gets to the pack safely," he whispers.

"Better get on your knees and get to work then; you have a lot of grovelling to do." I tell him, stepping back up against the wall and lowering my pants.

He looks at me for a moment before doing exactly as I ask. Once again, he sucks my clit into his mouth while sinking his fangs into the flesh just above. "Drake," I cry out as my orgasm overtakes me. Just like before, it doesn't stop or slow down. The pleasure I feel from the combination of Drake feeding from me as well as his tongue stroking my clit is almost too much to handle.

When he finally releases me, I begin to drop to my knees, but he catches me before I can. "No. I need to be inside you," he demands and, with a quick thrust, enters me as he lifts me up.

"Oh, goddess!" We both cry out as he begins to hammer into me over and over, harder and faster with each one. He's so fast that I'm sure anyone watching wouldn't be able to tell where one of us begins and the other ends. He adjusts his angle so that the tip of his cock hits me right where I need him to while snaking his hand around the back and rubbing my other hole.

"Gods, Drake. I'm going to cum!" I cry out. I never thought I would enjoy anyone touching my 'out only' hole, but oh, goddess, was I wrong. As he circles his finger around, massaging but never penetrating, I cum. My greedy pussy squeezes his cock, milking him and dragging him further inside me until he is groaning out his own release.

"Well, I wasn't expecting that after the day we've had," he admits as he slips from me. He speeds off and returns seconds later with a washcloth to clean me up.

"It's never been that part that's the issue, Drake," I tell him. "We've never been able to keep our hands off one another, even when we didn't want to admit it."

"I guess that's true. But..." he pauses, seeming to think about what to say.

"But what?" I ask.

"I know that we have a lot of things we still need to work out, and I promise not to complete the bond until we both agree. But do you think it would be possible for us not to try and pretend we're nothing to each other?" I get a little confused about what he's talking about, but then the realization sets in. That's exactly what I was asking him to do. In the woods, I wouldn't let him kiss me, even though it was just our body's natural reaction to each other. I know it was hard for me to have him so close yet not be able to feel his touch. I can only assume it was the same for him.

"Okay," I agree. "But no bonding. Not until after we've worked out everything." At his nod, I begin to get dressed. "Wait. How do vampires bond anyway?" I ask, figuring I should probably know.

"We exchange blood." Drake responds, pulling up his own pants.

"That's it?" I ask.

Drake smiles. "If we weren't true mates, there is a ceremony that needs to be performed by the coven leader, but because we are, a simple exchange of blood and the bond settles in."

"But wouldn't that turn me into a vampire?" I ask.

"No," he chuckles. "You would need to be almost completely drained of your human blood and then take in some of mine to become like me."

I dip my head in understanding. "Would it hurt?"

"Becoming a vampire?" He asks. "Anyone that I've spoken to who has been turned, which isn't many in this coven, said that it actually feels quite pleasurable. Think about how my bite makes you feel and then imagine feeling that for thirty minutes or more," Drake explains.

"Thirty minutes?" I ask. There is no way I could handle the euphoric feeling for that long. I would internally combust.

"Give or take. It all depends on the amount of blood actually in the body, and the suction rate of the vampire. But thirty minutes is a general rule of thumb," he tells me.

After I'm dressed, I walk up and wrap my arms around his neck. "Thank you for explaining it to me."

"I'll always make the time to tell you anything you want to know," he promises.

I kiss his lips, slowly and seductively, and my body is already ready to go another round.

He pulls back with a growl. "If you keep kissing me like that, we will not make it to pack lands before dawn to ensure that the coven is safe."

I let go of his neck with a chuckle as a knock sounds at the door. "Duty calls."

"But perhaps Skarlyt can be persuaded to allow us to use her bedroom at Alaric's in the basement, so we don't have to share with the rest of the coven," he teases me, wiggling his eyebrows.

"I'm sure I can get her to do just that," I respond with another quick peck on his lips. Now, I'm ready to go find Skarlyt. Even if she won't readily agree, I'll use the guilt of her not telling me about the whole mate thing. She'll definitely give in, then.

Drake opens the door wide and greets a tall, lanky brunette. He's handsome like most supernaturals but doesn't hold a candle to my Drake.

"Colin, this is Rayne," he says as he gestures to me.

I walk up and stick out my hand to him. He looks between Drake and I momentarily before taking it. "It's nice to meet you."

"You, too," he replies, but I have a hard time believing that's true.

"Colin is my second in charge." Drake explains to me, turning back to Colin. "Rayne is my true mate."

I'm momentarily shocked at his statement. I know we told his parents, and I let it drop to Colleen, but I didn't think we were going to be going around announcing it to people. I give him a 'what the fuck?' look.

"Colin needs to know these things so that he can do his job properly," Drake says, coming and wrapping his arm around my shoulder. I look back at Colin and notice that his entire demeanor has changed. Where he seemed apprehensive toward me before, he now has a warm smile on his face.

"That explains a lot," he chuckles.

"We're not telling many people just yet. Not until we've sorted some things out," I tell him. I need to ensure that it remains quiet.

"I completely understand. This is going to be a big deal," Colin says, staring off as if he's running through different scenarios in his head.

"You wanted to talk to me about something?" Drake interrupts.

Colin shakes his head as if clearing it. "Yes. Most of the coven has left for the bunker. They're wondering if it's possible to move straight into the new compound rather than coming back here. A lot of them are uneasy living here with the location compromised."

I look at Drake who is pulling out his phone and sending a text, presumably to Alaric. It dings a moment later, and Drake raises his head. "Alaric agreed that we can stay until the new compound is ready."

"Will do. It really shouldn't take more than a couple days if we can get enough help," Colin says, turning to leave. "Oh, and congratulations," he adds, before heading out the door.

I spin to Drake and pin him with a stare. "What the fuck?"

"He was wary of you because of what Colleen said before we got back. Most of the coven is wary of you, actually, but once they learn you're my mate, they'll see what Colleen's comments really were: those of a jealous woman," he explains, wrapping his arms around me. Unable to stay mad at him, I melt into his body.

"Okay. But no one else can know," I say. We split apart and head out to make sure the rest of the coven gets to the pack before leaving ourselves.

Chapter Nineteen

Rayne

We make it to pack lands without a hitch, ensuring every single member of the coven had left before we did. And as luck would have it, I was able to convince Skarlyt to let us use her bedroom, which allowed us to spend some more time together 'talking.' If I were to explain it to myself, I would call it an entire night—or, more accurately, day—fucking each other's brains out. Turns out he can go an extremely long time without his tongue getting even the slightest bit tired.

After only a couple hours sleep, I wake and head upstairs to begin training the pack. "Good afternoon, everyone," I say as I enter the kitchen.

"Did you have a good sleep?" Phoebe asks with a wink while handing me my coffee.

Rather than be embarrassed, I shoot her a wink of my own and smirk. "To be honest, Drake and I were up most of the day 'talking.'"

"Is that what the kids are calling it these days?" Alaric asks.

"It sure is," I tell him while taking a sip of my perfectly made coffee.

Alaric starts coughing at my response, "Well then. We should probably get ready to train."

"Alaric, let her finish her coffee first," Phoebe states.

I gulp down the rest of my cup. "He's right. We only have one more day to get everyone ready."

As we go into the gym, I recognize quite a few of the shifters waiting. "Rayne!" Samara exclaims.

"Oh, Samara. I'm so glad you're here. We've sparred enough that you could train some of these shifters as well," I say, pulling her into a hug.

"I don't know about that," she tries to protest.

"Well, I do. The number of shifters and vampires combined that need to be trained is way too many for me to do all on my own. Perhaps if you take a group and I take another, we will be able to get a larger number of people ready," I explain.

"I guess," she relents. She's not enthusiastic about it, but she agreed, and that's all I care about.

"Perfect!" I exclaim. "Everyone, if we could have your attention. Samara has graciously agreed to assist me, so we're going to separate into two groups." She shoots me a small glare, but I ignore it.

We spend the next few hours going over basic fighting techniques, and I demonstrate how hunters use the body movements of their opponent to predict and anticipate their next movements. I also try to give them tips on how to move in unpredictable ways that may take the hunters by surprise. There are a few very promising fighters who surprised even Alaric. Perhaps if we had more time, we would be able to get everyone ready to defeat the hunters. But as we only have another day, we'll have to make do with what we've done so far.

"I need to talk to Skarlyt," I tell Alaric as we walk out of the gym.

"She was coming to the house. I'm sure she's there now. She and Phoebe wanted to talk to you," he responds.

Sure enough, as I walk up, both Skarlyt and Phoebe are sitting on the porch. "Rayne. Can we talk to you for a minute?"

"Sure," I tell them, a bit confused as to what they could have to talk to me about.

As I sit on the bench, they sit as well. "We need to apologize," Phoebe tells me.

"For what?" I question.

"Because we didn't tell you that we thought Drake was your mate," Skarlyt says.

"Dru already explained that. I don't blame either of you," I tell them, trying to wave off their apologies.

"Still. You were right to be upset. I would have been upset. We would both like to apologize to you and start over if you're okay with that," Phoebe adds.

"Of course, I am. And again, you don't need to apologize. I was upset and overreacted when I found out. I never expected to be the mate of a supernatural, let alone a vampire. Not that there's anything wrong with that. It's just that I have never..." I trail off, not sure how to finish the statement. I don't want to say that I have never wanted to be a vampire and have someone from the coven accidentally overhear. That would just give them one more reason to hate me.

"Wanted to be supernatural?" Skarlyt asks.

"No, of course, like any ordinary human, I've fantasized about being a witch or shifter or even a phoenix but never a vampire," I admit.

"What is it about being a vampire that has you so set against it? I think having the super speed and the power to compel people would be really cool," Phoebe asks.

"I'm not insane, both those things would be very cool, and if it were just that, I would jump at the chance. But, could you imagine never seeing the sun again or never having a steak and potato dinner? The negatives far outweigh the positives, and I just can't get past it," I tell them both.

"When you put it that way, I suppose there are quite a few negatives I didn't think about," Skarlyt says. "What if there was a way to help with one of those things?"

"What do you mean?" I ask.

"Well, maybe I could find a spell to allow you to walk in the sunlight for a time, or we could try to figure out a way for you to be able to enjoy food once in a while. I can't make any promises, but I will look into it for you if you want," Skarlyt tells me.

"Really?" I ask excitedly. That would fix my dilemma because if I'm being truthful to myself, I'm not sure how I would ever be able to live without Drake. And being young and beautiful for the rest of my life wouldn't be too bad either.

"Like I said, please don't get your hopes up. But I will look," Skarlyt explains, and I nod.

"I would really appreciate that. Even if you don't find anything, just the fact that you're willing to look into it for me is more than I ever expected," I tell them. "But I also wanted to ask you for something a bit more pressing: do you think there is a way to erect the barrier around the pack so that only supernaturals are able to cross?"

"I suppose. Currently, it is linked to members of the pack and covens. But there is already a clause linked in there for those that don't mean anyone within any harm. That's why you were able to get in. Why do you ask?" she responds.

"Well, I was thinking that there may be a chance of other supernatural beings being held captive and able to escape. I want them to be able to cross into safety," I say.

"That's a good point. I'll get working on it with my mom," Skarlyt says, rubbing her chin in thought.

"There you are," Dru says from the doorway.

"Yupp, just talking with the girls," I tell her.

"Mind if I join you?" she asks.

"Of course not! Get over here," I tell her and shift over to make room next to me.

The four of us sit and talk for a while. It is nice to get my mind off the impending attack and pretend we are just four friends having an evening chat.

"It's time, Rayne," Drake says as he comes out of the door. "Everyone is making their way over to the gym now."

"Sounds good. I'm going to run over and get Samara first," I tell him before starting down the stairs.

"I'll come with you," Drake says, reaching my side and holding my hand in his. At the brush of his fingers, tingles spread throughout my entire body.

We gather Samara and head to the gym. There are just as many vampires as there were shifters this afternoon. Once again, Samara and I split everyone into two separate groups. The vampires, with their speed, have a leg up on the hunters, being able to outrun them, but it doesn't necessarily help them fight.

I walk over to Drake. "We need two teams of ten. The fastest vampires we have."

He looks at me in confusion. "Why?"

"Because I had an epiphany when I was watching some of your vampires spar. What we really need to do is take the hunters out one by one. We can station each team of ten on either side, swooping in and grabbing the hunters and securing them one by one. We could have ropes or something to tie them up. Oh, even better, a cage," I say and chuckle a bit at the visualization of putting the hunters in a cage.

"I suppose that could work," he agrees with me.

"It will. If we had more time, we wouldn't need to resort to this, but we don't. I also would prefer to have the chance to convert some of the other hunters. Surely there are others who are questioning just like I was," I tell him.

"Okay," he says. "I'll get your teams together, and you get Alaric to get the cages built. I can't say for certain that they will all be happy about taking the hunters alive, but I will make sure they understand our wishes."

"I'm sure they will get their chance to exact their revenge," I tell him.

A few hours before dawn, when we are finally done training for the night, I'm completely dead on my feet. My eyes are burning because I'm so tired. I thought my daytime sexcapades with Drake were worth being tired, but now that I'm hardly able to stand upright, I feel perhaps I should have gotten a little more sleep.

"Come here. Let's get you into bed," Drake says, scooping me up, carrying me to bed, and tucking me in. I would love to say that I pull him down on top of me and have my wicked way with him, but alas, that would be a lie. The truth is that I fall asleep within seconds.

That afternoon, I wake to the sound of an alarm ringing out. "What the fuck is that?"

"It's the border alarm. Someone or something has breached the wards," Drake says. I rush out of the room and up the stairs briefly before rushing back down.

"It's still daylight. You have to stay down here," I tell him.

"I know. Please be careful," he says before grabbing and kissing me.

"I will," I tell him before rushing back up the stairs again. This time, I have to share the stairwell with the throngs of people heading to the basement.

I walk in to see Alaric whispering to Darren.

"What's going on?" I ask, and both Alaric and Darren turn toward my voice.

"We haven't officially met. I'm Darren and this is my mate, Sophia," he says to me, sticking out his hand for me to shake.

"And I'm Rayne. I wanted to say that I'm so sorry for how you were treated during the last battle with the hunters," I tell him while shaking his hand and then Sophia's. Though we briefly met at Supernatural a while back, I don't expect her to remember me.

"We know it wasn't you. I trust my sister's judgment and her *gut*. She says you are genuine and that we can trust you," Sophia says, the way she emphasizes that she trusts Phoebe's gut—which isn't the first time I've heard it—has me questioning some things, but I'll wait to ask until the apologies are done.

"Plus, I saw you there. You were the only one who looked conflicted about what was happening," Darren says and my mouth drops open in shock.

"You did?"

He nods. "I even pointed you out to one of the teenagers in the cage beside me to show her that not everyone was on board with what was happening."

"Still. I'm so very sorry," I say to him. I can't think of anything else to say but I feel like if I let it, we will continue to apologize to one another over and over, so I turn to Sophia instead. "Okay, what is all the nonsense about trusting Phoebe's gut, and why is everyone putting so much stock in it?"

Everyone laughs, but it's Alaric that answers. "Let's just say that her gut has yet to be wrong. We've learned to trust it."

"Well, that explains nothing and everything all at once," I say with a chuckle. "But what is with the alarm?"

"It seems that the hunters are testing our weaknesses while the vampires are unavailable," Darren says.

"That would make sense. My father is not a stupid man. He has to know that the shifters and vampires are allies," I tell them.

"Blaze!" Sophia exclaims suddenly and rushes to a beautiful

red-haired woman at the door standing next to a large, dark-skinned man. The two women embrace.

"We just saw each other last week." Blaze giggles.

"Let's go see what we are dealing with," Alaric says to our group.

"Wait. That's what they want. They want us to rush out there so they can ambush us and garner our reaction time. We need to send scouts. Do you have anyone who is able to stay hidden to gather intel?" I ask.

"I can," the large man with Blaze says.

"And Samara. They can use the treetops to stay hidden," Sophia says.

"I understand how Samara could use the treetops being a mountain lion, but a shifter of his size... no offense..." I say to the man.

"None taken," he responds.

"Would not be able to remain hidden," I finish.

Within seconds, the large man in the doorway shifts into a perfectly proportioned black jaguar.

"Well, that works," I tell them all.

"I'll go get Samara," Sophia says, rushing off.

"Now what?" Darren asks.

"We wait. We need to know if they've brought everyone and if they're in one or multiple locations. We need as much information as we possibly can get before we decide anything," I tell him.

Blaze gives the jaguar a kiss on the head before he runs off. She turns to me, "I'm Blaze."

"Rayne," I tell her and shake her hand.

We, along with a rather large group of witches and shifters, gather in front of the house and wait for the information we need in order to make a plan. If I know my father, and I do, this is a ploy, a distraction for his true motives.

"Do we have anyone else we can send?" I ask as my mind begins to whirl.

"Why?" Alaric questions, pulling me off to the side.

"I was just thinking. My dad is fond of using distractions to mask his true intentions. If they are all focusing on one location, which I suspect they are, we need to look in the opposite direction," I tell him.

Alaric dips his head in understanding. "What about a phoenix? If we had one of the girls fly above the trees, do you think the hunters would try to shoot them down?" he asks.

"Well, if the Phoenixes are on fire as Phoebe was the night of the battle, it would gain their attention and there is a very real possibility that they would shoot. Not that they would hit their marks, but they would shoot nonetheless," I tell him.

Before I can continue, a loud screech sounds overhead, and we turn toward the noise. "Who is that?" I ask.

"Sophia. She must have heard us talking," he responds.

Well, shit. She's going to be a rather large target.

Chapter Twenty

Rayne

We stay gathered on the front lawn, anxiously watching the sky for Sophia's return before Darren begins to pace. "She'll be alright," Alaric tries to reassure his brother.

Samara and the jaguar return, both shifting back on the run. "There are about fifty or so attacking the north. They seem to be shooting wildly at nothing, as if they aren't truly trying to hit anything," Samara says.

"It's as if they are trying to draw our attention there deliberately," the jaguar adds.

"Sounds about right," I say. "But also, what is your name? I can't keep calling you 'Jaguar' in my head."

"Oh, right. I'm Kenji," he tells me with a thick Portuguese accent.

"Kenji. I'm Rayne," I tell him. I keep my eyes firmly locked on his to avoid drifting downward because of his nakedness. I admit he's a beautiful man: dark chocolate skin and firm muscles. But he doesn't hold a candle to my Drake.

"Yes, the hunter. They told me about you," he states then turns to Alaric. "I see what your mate meant; meeting her does make a difference."

Confused by his statement, I look between the two of them. Alaric sighs. "Phoebe wanted you to accompany us to the Amazon last week, but..." He pauses looking to Kenji, "Let's just say, some of the jaguars were worried about having a hunter in close proximity. She argued that if they were to simply meet you, then they would know that you weren't a threat. Seems Kenji now understands what she meant."

"Oh, I see. So that's where you guys went. Sometime soon you'll have to tell me what happened down there," I tell him.

"I'm sure the girls will enjoy telling you their tale on your next girls' night." I get excited for a moment before I remember the extreme hangover I am bound to have the next morning. Maybe I'll be able to limit my intake. Who am I kidding? I won't, but I can try.

Sophia lands in front of us moments later. "You were right. There were a handful of hunters on the south side setting up some type of device. I'm not sure what it does. I couldn't get close enough without being seen."

"A device?" I ask.

"Yes, it was a small box with a number of batteries and wires linked to it. It was emitting a high frequency sound, like the kind you would hear from a dog whistle," she responds.

"A high frequency pitch, you say?" I ask. "This may be ignorant of me to ask, but would a dog whistle affect you when you're shifted?" I turn to Alaric.

"I honestly don't know," he responds.

"Well, we should find out," I tell him.

"How? No one here has a dog whistle because we don't have any dogs here," Alaric states.

"You're right," I say as I begin pacing to think of another option. "Got it! What if you send a couple of shifters in wolf form, as well as a couple in human form, to the south to see how close you can get without being seen or the sound affecting you?"

"Darren and I will go shifted. Phoebe and Sophia can follow. That way, if needed, their tears can heal us, or they can fly us back to safety if it comes to that," Alaric advises.

The four of them leave immediately, leaving no room for anyone to get a word in. While they're gone, I look at the time: five o'clock. There's still a couple more hours until the sun sets. There has to be a reason for this early attack, more than just figuring out the weaknesses of the pack. I just can't fathom what that reason could be. If only I would have got more intel from the hunters before I came back. I could've stayed hidden and gathered more information. Damn it! But I let my feelings cloud my judgment. Granted, we are more prepared than we would have been, but still.

When Phoebe and Sophia return carrying limp Darren and Alaric, I fear the worst, but they come to as they land, and my worries abate a bit. "What happened?" I ask as I rush over to them.

"Seems whatever that device is causes us to shift back to human and renders us unconscious but otherwise unharmed," Alaric says weakly.

"So, it's safe to say that they specifically designed it for shifters. I wonder if it affects only canine shifters or feline shifters as well," I think out loud.

"I'll go," Samara speaks up, already shifting and heading into the trees.

"I will go with her," Sophia adds.

Before I can tell them to wait, they both rush off in the device's direction. If the device is being set up there, it's safe to assume that is where the battle will take place, and perhaps we have a much better chance than I had originally thought. Well, as long as they have no other devices to be set up.

When they both return conscious, with Samara running alongside Sophia, a plan begins to form in my mind. "Do we have any other feline shifters?" I ask Alaric.

"As of right now, we only have Samara and Kenji. I can ask Trixie again, but I don't think she's going to change her mind." Alaric begins.

"She won't," Samara says, shifting back to human. I don't know if it's just me, but the growl in her voice seems to hold an awful lot of hatred.

"But if Skarlyt or Sebastyn are willing, we could get a few more jaguars to join us," Kenji pipes up.

"That would be fantastic. We need to set the battle at night, so that the vampires can help. Having the jaguars who can blend in with the forest in the dark would be extremely beneficial," I say.

Over the next hour, Skarlyt and Sebastyn go back and forth to the Amazon, bringing shifter after shifter. Our slim chances are becoming better by the minute.

"Kenji?" I say, walking over to him.

"Yes?"

"Is there any chance you could have some of your shifters run the perimeter to see if there are any other devices being set up?" I question.

"Sure. But what are you thinking?" he asks.

"I'm thinking that they are trying to steer the battle to one specific spot, but that doesn't make sense to me." I say, beginning to pace. "Why would they put all their eggs in one basket? It would make more sense for them to have more devices set up around the entire boundary," I tell him.

"That does make more sense. Besides, they wouldn't know about any shifters other than wolves being here," he quickly sends a few of his shifters off to run the perimeter.

"That's not exactly true. because the bears and mountain lions fought alongside the pack last time. But do the feline and bears have a weakness to the higher frequencies like wolves do?" I ask, looking around.

"It bothered my ears and made me want to turn around, but I was able to push through it," Samara says, now wearing a pair of sweatpants and a t-shirt. I nod. That works in our favor but without the pack able to fight, our numbers will be greatly depleted.

The unseen dome over the pack flickers, becoming visible for a few seconds, and I look to Skarlyt for answers.

"It seems that they have something or someone sucking the magic out of the boundary." As it flickers once again, she and a few of the witches with her raise their hands and begin flooding it with magic. "We won't be able to hold this for long," she says, sweat beginning to bead on her forehead.

We all begin to move. "Okay, since the vampires won't be able to come out for another hour or so, we need to use the shifters in their place."

"For what exactly?" Alaric asks.

"You have the cages ready?" I ask.

"Almost," he responds.

"I need Skarlyt to spell them so that the locks are unable to be picked," I tell him.

"Skarlyt needs to keep her power flowing into the boundary," Alaric advises.

"You're right," I say and continue thinking. "Okay. New plan. You all know what to do. I will go try to talk to them. See if I can get them to stop sucking the magic out of the boundary and distract them for long enough so that you can get everyone mobilized."

I turn and walk toward the northern part of pack lands where the hunters are attacking.

"Wait, Rayne," Phoebe says, rushing to me. "Are you sure about this?"

"It's the only choice," I tell her. "I'll be okay. They won't hurt me."

She dips her chin reluctantly and wraps me up in a hug. I hold her back a little longer than necessary because the truth is that I truly don't know if they will hurt me or not. They could open fire as soon as they see me. I have faith that my father won't want that, but it's always a possibility.

It takes me longer than I wanted to get to the group of hunters, but once I make my way through the trees, I see a sizable group. On the ground is a large something. I'm not quite sure how to explain it. It looks like one of those toys that makes a tornado in the water when you turn it on. This must be what's syphoning the magic.

"There's the traitor!" Price yells out upon seeing me.

"Sorry, what did you say?" I call out.

"I said, there's the traitor," he yells out louder this time.

"What?" I respond, bringing my hand up to my ear. "I can't hear you over that noise."

He rolls his eyes at me in exasperation but does exactly what I want him to do and turns off the generator powering that machine. Immediately the flickering barrier disappears, but I know it's not gone, just simply hidden once again.

"That's better. Now what did you say?" I ask.

"Never mind that now. What do you want, traitor?" he spits at me.

"Come now, Price. That's no way to speak to the person who saved your life."

"Saved my life?" he yells. "You had me imprisoned in a vampire coven and then took off like the coward you are."

"Would you rather me let them kill you?" I question. I can see the gears in his head turning. It wasn't my intention to make them think I'm working from the inside, but I suppose it will work better than my original plan, which was basically to bullshit my way until I figured out what to do.

"Where is my father?" I say, looking around the group and not seeing him.

"He's busy," Price replies with more snark.

"Now, now, Price. We just discussed this. I know you've always been jealous of me but come now. This is bigger than your ego," I respond.

"Bigger than my ego?" he exclaims.

"Yes. Bigger than your ego, which is saying something," I reply. "Now where is my father?"

"Like I said, he's busy. Far too busy to be bothered by a traitor," he says, giving me a look that tells me everything I need to know. In his escape, he has somehow weaseled his way into being my father's new apprentice, essentially taking my place and getting exactly what he's always wanted.

"I see. And you know what he's busy doing?" I ask.

"Of course, I do. Your father now sees who his loyal followers are and who is not," he tells me with an evil grin.

"Rayne!" my father shouts while hurrying closer.

"Stop!" I tell him, holding up my hand. "Don't come too close to the boundary. I don't know what it will do to you, but it probably won't be good."

At my words, he stops just short of the boundary. As I take in his appearance, I note he has large dark circles under his brown eyes and his auburn hair is unkempt, completely different than his normal perfectly put together self. "I thought I lost you," he tells me, with tears brimming in his eyes.

"Didn't Price tell you?" I question, and my father looks between Price and me. "I have infiltrated the supernaturals in the area. He knew of my plan. I asked him to tell you so you wouldn't worry." As he turns to Price, I shoot him an evil look of my own. Check and mate, mother fucker.

"You lying bitch!" Price shouts. "You never told me shit and had me imprisoned." As he rushes toward me, my father grabs him by his neck. I kinda wish he would've let Price run into the barrier and hopefully fry his ass.

"I knew you were ambitious and jealous of Rayne's position in our ranks, but to allow me to worry for weeks? That is unacceptable," he spits directly into Price's face. "Take him away. We will deal with him after," my father says, throwing Price to waiting hunters to take him who knows where.

"What is your plan?" I ask my father once he turns back to me.

"We..." he begins but is cut off.

"We can't tell her anything. She's with them now," one of my father's enforcers calls out.

My father waves his hand at him. "Nonsense. If she were, there is no way she would be here speaking to us. She would be hiding with those monsters."

I shoot the asshole who dared speak against me, a triumphant look before turning back to my father. "Exactly. But in order to help you, I need to know what you have planned. Price was supposed to get word to me before your attack so I could prepare on this end," I say, shaking my head to try and show that I'm pissed. Obviously, I'm a really good actress because my father frowns while looking behind him at where they took Price then turning back to me with pride shining in his eyes.

"We have two devices set up—one in the south and one in the west—to funnel them here to the north, where we have set up our ambush," he begins.

"Devices?" I play stupid. "What devices?"

"Oh, Rayne, you'll love them. They are designed to ensure those beasts are unable to shift and must remain in their human form. The last thing we want is for them to be able to tuck tail and run away from us. If any of them dare to attempt a retreat, they will find themselves in range of the other devices," he tells me with a chuckle.

I plaster a fake smile on my face. "That is genius. Where did you find those?"

"We have a lab that has been developing different weapons we can use against them," he informs me.

"Lab? You've never told me about any lab," I say with concern lining my face. Though I'm hoping that he takes it as confusion.

"Not many know about it. Only the head of the bloodlines are privy to that information. You were supposed to get your first tour on your next birthday," he responds.

"And what exactly do they do at this lab?" I ask, unable to keep the anger out of my voice. It works because he thinks the anger is at not being informed, but in fact I can only imagine what exactly goes on there, and I have a feeling I'm not going to like it.

"Experiments," he says.

"What kind of experiments?"

"You'll see. After we defeat these supernaturals, I will take you there, and you'll be able to see for yourself," he says. I know that I will rouse his suspicions if I continue this line of questioning, so I change tactics.

"What do you need me to do?" I ask.

"I didn't plan on having someone on the inside. But it will help us to know numbers. We have the numbers of the coven thanks to you and Price, but not the pack," he tells me.

I think for a moment and begin to pace. I need to give him a large enough number that he believes me, but smaller than what we actually have. "The pack is quite large. From what I can tell, they have just over two hundred shifters in their ranks."

"That little?" he questions with a skeptical look on his face. Fuck. Think, Rayne. Think.

"Yes. It seems that after our last battle, quite a few left out of fear of another attack and their allies have all refused to help," I plaster a smirk on my face going for evil, hoping that he believes me. My father's face stays stoic and for a moment I'm worried that he doesn't believe me, but then an evil smile crosses his face.

"That's just like them, to run like the cowards they are. No matter. We will find them all in time," he says, rubbing his chin. "Okay, Rayne, I want you to go back now and keep up the ruse. I'll give you a sign when the time comes, and you know what to do."

"But I don't know what you want me to do," I respond shaking my head.

"Point out the leaders to us. If we cut the head off the snake, so to speak, the rest will fall."

I nod in his direction and turn to head back towards the pack. I only hope that was long enough for Skarlyt and Alaric to complete what needed to be done. I look up to the sky as I walk and send up a small prayer for night to fall quickly and for us to survive this night. My father may have told me part of his plan, but I know him better than he thinks. There is no way he's told me every trick he has up his sleeve.

"Please keep us safe," I whisper, and watch as the sky darkens with the setting of the sun. We have to win tonight. Otherwise, the supernaturals that are bound to be kept in that lab have no hope. We have more reasons to win than I thought. Hopefully it's enough.

Chapter Twenty-One

Drake

Sitting in the bedroom in Alaric's basement, not knowing what is going on up there, not being able to help even if I did, is a new form of torture. One that I wouldn't wish on my worst enemies. I know Rayne is a strong, capable hunter. No. She's a strong capable *woman*, not hunter, not anymore, who is able to take care of herself and doesn't need me to save her. That's part of the reason I'm falling in love with her.

Wait, what? Is that true? Am I truly falling in love with her? As I contemplate that thought, I realize the truth in it. I don't know when it happened or how, but I, Drake Dunkan, am falling in love with a hunter, and not just any hunter, but one of the Chasen bloodline.

With that thought in mind, my worry becomes more urgent. My mate is up there right now with enemies attacking, and I am unable to do anything to help. What if she's hurt? What if she's captured? Or if Price tells her father what he saw us doing, what will he do to her? I need to get up there.

I leave the bedroom and begin pacing the living room, just away from the stairs, where I can see the sunlight streaming through the bottom of the door. Damn this sunlight! Now I can see why Rayne may find this a hindrance.

I pick up my phone and dial my sister. "Drake?" Her groggy voice comes through the line.

"I need you and Colin to come out into the living room." I growl quickly before hanging up, not allowing her a moment to argue.

Moments later, the door opens and a sleepy Dru and Colin walk out. "What is it? What's going on? Dru says, looking around. "Wait. Where's Rayne?"

"She's up there. The hunters started attacking this afternoon. Because of the sun, I couldn't go with her, and now I'm going crazy."

Colin steps up to me and places his hand on my shoulder. "She will be okay."

I shake his hand off my shoulder and begin pacing once more. "You don't know that. You *can't* know that. She could be up there hurt or dying."

"Wait. Let's check the cameras in the bunker," Dru offers, and the three of us walk back inside quietly so we don't disturb the rest of our coven.

Only two of the cameras are still in operation, showing nothing but forested area. "The hunters must've taken out the cameras somehow," Dru supplies, sitting at the keyboard. She begins typing away, trying to get them back up. I stand behind her watching, hoping and praying that they will start working again so I can catch a glimpse of my mate to know she's okay. But no such luck. And the two that are working, don't tell me anything.

I hiss and walk back out the door, resuming my pacing. I am paralyzed with fear of the unknown. I want to trust that our friends will keep her safe; after all there are two adult phoenixes upstairs, a coven of witches, and a pack of wolves, but it does nothing to alleviate my anxiety. Until I can see for myself that she's safe I know that the feeling isn't going to go away.

As the stairway darkens with the setting of the sun, I creep my way up stair by stair until I'm at the top. I watch from the doorway as the shadows make their way down the front door. "Come on," I say to myself impatiently.

"It's okay. She's okay," Dru says from beside me. I didn't realize she followed me up the stairs, but I'm glad she's here.

"I know that. She's more than capable of taking care of herself. But it doesn't stop me from worrying. She's been out there all afternoon, and I have no idea what is happening."

"If you would've come back to the bunker, you would've known. The two cameras are still working, and I was able to get the one working from in front of the pack house," she tells me.

"Why didn't you come get me?" I demand.

"Because I told Colin to go back to sleep so he's well rested. And I didn't want to look away."

"What did you see?" I ask.

"It seems the hunters are here, and Rayne and Alaric were planning something, or that's what it looked like. But..." she pauses.

"But what?" I ask.

"A little while ago, Rayne walked off out of view of the cameras. I waited to see if she came back, but nothing so far. When I saw that the sun was setting, I figured it was time to go get her," she tells me and flinches back.

"She what?" I yell. I'm not yelling at Dru. I know it has nothing to do with her leaving the safety of the front lawn. But when I get my hands on Alaric for allowing my mate to walk off, it's not going to be pretty. "I swear to all the gods if she's hurt in any way, I'll kill every single one of them with my bare hands!" I growl out.

I turn back toward the door and go back to watching the

shadows of the setting sun. It could have been seconds or minutes, but either way, as soon as the sun is low enough that I can safely make my way to the door, I run. I throw the door open and stomp onto the porch.

"*Where is she?*" I bellow. As everyone turns toward me, my eyes lock with Alaric, and I rush to him, wrapping my hand around his throat and lifting him from the ground. "Where the fuck is she?" I growl out through my clenched teeth.

"Drake. Stop," Phoebe pleads with me, but my eyes do not leave Alaric's. "I don't want to hurt you, but if you don't release my mate right now, I *will* set your ass on fire."

As her hands alight with her flames, I release Alaric, allowing him to drop to the ground. "You let my mate go out there alone. *Alone.* Alaric. Was it so long ago that you were upset with me for suggesting the same of your mate that you don't remember?" I hiss at him.

Phoebe's fire grows larger at my tone, but Alaric sighs and places his hands on hers. "He's right. We shouldn't have let her go alone. If it were you, I would be acting worse than Drake."

"But she's the one who suggested it," Phoebe tries to explain.

"It doesn't matter whose idea it was. Which way did she go?" I growl.

"To the north boundary," Alaric says.

I don't respond; I take off with my supernatural speed towards the north. Alaric better be praying to the goddess right now that she is unharmed.

As I'm running, I catch her scent and veer off in that direction. As it gets stronger, my speed increases and within moments, I see her. She's distracted, looking up at the sky.

"Rayne!" I call to her. Her eyes meet mine mere seconds before I grab her and pull her close to me. "Never do that again," I growl but keep my embrace tender.

"Drake," she whispers and melts into my body. "I have to tell you something."

I step back, but don't let go. I can't. My will to live left me at the thought that she was harmed. There is no way I'll be able to let her out of my reach anytime soon. "What is it?"

"I met with my father," she begins, and my fangs descend at the thought of the man who not only kidnapped my sister but tortured her. "Calm down. He can't get to us right now. But he told me something. Something that changes everything," she tells me.

"What?" I ask, confused. What could he have told her that changes everything?

"He told me that the hunters have a lab where they do experiments in order to make new weapons to fight supernaturals." I can't stop the shock and rage that crosses my face.

"Experiments like what?" I ask.

"He didn't tell me, but I'm sure you've come to the same conclusion as me. They have to be conducting these experiments on supernatural creatures in order to test their weapons. It's the only explanation."

"Where?" Is the only word I'm able to get out of my mouth. My jaw clenched so hard I worry that I may crack my teeth.

"I don't know. He wouldn't tell me. Just that after the hunters win this battle, he plans on bringing me there," she says, and I immediately know what she's thinking.

"No," I tell her. "We will find it another way."

"What other way, Drake? It could take us years to find it without him taking me. Those years will cost countless lives. What if it was Dru who was being held there? Would your answer still be the same?" she asks. I reluctantly release her and begin to pace. She's right. If it were Dru who was being kept there and experimented on like some lab rat, my answer would be different, but it's not. And the thought of her going behind enemy lines scares the shit out of me.

"Let's talk to Alaric and Skarlyt first. See what they think. Chances are it's not only vampires who are being kept there," I say to her once I'm able to get past the lump in my throat, putting trust in my friends that they will help me convince her that it's a bad idea.

"Okay," she agrees and takes my hand, leading me back to the house.

"We need to talk," I growl out, looking at both Skarlyt and Alaric. They look at each other for a moment but nod and follow Rayne and me into the house.

After Rayne tells them her plan, Skarlyt is adamant. "No. Absolutely not."

"Skarlyt's right. There is no way we're sending you in there," Alaric adds.

"But don't you all understand that if I don't, it could be years before we find it?" Rayne pleads. "Imagine the number of shifters, witches, vampires being kept there that will die before we do. Do their lives mean so little to you?"

"It's not that, Rayne. Of course, their lives mean everything to us. But so does yours. Your life is not worth any less than theirs simply because you were not born one of us," Skarlyt says, walking up and placing her hands on Rayne's arms.

"But..." Rayne begins.

"Skarlyt's right, Rayne. You've proven yourself enough. You don't need to sacrifice yourself just to prove to us you're no longer a hunter," Alaric says, and my head snaps up to his. Is that what it was? Does Rayne feel like she needs to prove to us she's no longer on their side?

I watch her head fall and realize the truth. This is because of me. Because of the way I acted when I found out she was a hunter and then my actions every day after. She wants to do this to prove to me that she's not what she was born to be.

"Rayne," I say quietly while walking up to her. "I'm sorry."

Her eyes snap up to mine in question. "I'm sorry if I ever made you feel like you needed to prove to us, to me, that you are on our side. I should never have judged you based on what you were born as, and I'll spend the rest of my days making it up to you. I promise. Please don't do this. You don't need to do this. We will find another way," I tell her.

"What if it's where they're keeping Breanne?" she asks.

"Breanne?" I wrack my brain, trying to think of where I know that name from.

"Where do you think Breanne is?" Dru says from the doorway. Oh, that's where I've heard that name before. Dru's friend who was taken at the same time as her.

"Rayne's father and the other hunters apparently have a facility..." I begin.

"A lab," Rayne interrupts.

"A lab where they do experiments on supernaturals to make new weapons to destroy us," I finish, and Dru's face sinks in sadness before turning red with rage.

"Where?" she growls. I've never seen my sister like this before. Well, not in a long time. She has been so weak since she escaped. I've seen more fire in her the past week than I have in the past decade.

"We don't know," I tell her.

"But my father promised to take me there after the battle. I was going to return to them so we can find the location," Rayne pipes up.

"*Absolutely not*!" Dru screams, rushing over to wrap her in a hug. "Do you think I would ever want to trade one friend for another? We will find this lab together," she pulls Rayne back to look directly into her eyes. "And together we will tear every single one of them apart who dared cross us."

"We're ready," Skarlyt interrupts. "I've got witches set all around the boundary feeding into the barrier, and Alaric has the cages set. If we want to win this before dawn, we need to get moving."

"We will catch up," I tell her as she and Alaric walk outside. I turn back to Rayne. "Promise me," I say to her. She nods, but that's not enough. "You have to say it."

"I promise, Drake," she responds.

"Okay, let's go," I tell her and the three of us walk out of the house. "Wait, Rayne," I call to her as she goes to meet with her assigned group. "Please be safe," I say, before merging my lips with hers. She melts into my body while kissing me back passionately.

"You, too," she responds.

A pang of worry slashes through me as she walks away, and I pray to the goddess that she keeps her promise. I can't lose her. Not again. Not ever.

My team and I head off to the west while the other team goes to the east, and we begin picking off the hunters one by one and dropping them into the cages Alaric designed. At first it feels like we're getting somewhere, but then the hunters just keep coming and coming.

"How many did they say there were?" I ask Colin.

"The jaguar shifter said about five hundred," he responds. I look down at the cage and count close to three hundred inside with more on the way in the arms of my team.

"I think they were wrong," I tell Colin solemnly.

I hear a screech and immediately recognize it as one of the Phoenixes, followed by a very human scream. "*No*!"

Rayne. It has to be her. Without thinking, I leave my task and rush to the center of the battle where there are shifters being shot with tasers and hunters being taken out with magic. I search through the throngs of people and find her. There. In the middle of everyone is Rayne, standing with her arms out in front of an unconscious Phoebe laying in Alaric's arms. I follow Rayne's gaze and it lands on a man who has some similar features to her. As I look back at Rayne, I see a very pale Drusilla staring at the same man. Fuck. This must be Rayne's father. I rush to her side.

"Rayne," I say, pushing her behind me so that I am now in the line of fire.

"Get your hands off my daughter, you monster!" her father screams at me.

"He isn't the monster," Rayne yells, poking her head around me. "You are."

Her father looks taken aback for a moment before his eyes narrow with hatred. The next thing I know, a shot is fired, and I'm knocked to the ground. As I look over, I see Rayne looking down at her chest as blood begins to pool beneath her shirt. She looks back up at her father, blood beginning to drip out of her mouth before collapsing on the ground.

"*No*!" Dru yells, and within seconds is holding the heart of Rayne's father in her hands and is making her way through the hunters, ripping out their hearts, slashing their throats, decimating every single one in her path. There must've been at least one hundred of them and she seems to have no issues. I see my father and mother join her and feel confident that she'll be okay.

I grab Rayne, settling her into my arms while stroking her hair. "No, no, no," I keep repeating over and over.

"Dr..." She tries to talk.

"It's okay. You're going to be okay." I whisper. Her eyes fall closed, and her body goes slack as she loses consciousness.

"Here, try this," Sophia says, coming over to me and handing me a vial. I pour it in her wound and in her mouth using every last drop, but Rayne's breathing still continues to get slower and slower.

"It's not working!" I cry out, tears flowing freely down my cheeks. "Why isn't it working?"

"I don't know," Sophia says, stepping back away from me.

"You have to try to turn her, son," my father says, walking up to us.

"But she doesn't want that," I plead.

"It's either that or she will die. Would you rather have her pissed off at you for the rest of your life or not have her at all?" he asks.

I look over at Dru, where she is completely covered in blood, and she nods. "Tell her it was my choice," she tells me.

I search the faces of our friends, and every single one seems to agree, though all have sullen looks. So, I bring my wrist up to my mouth, biting down hard, drawing blood, and placing it over her mouth. Dru is there within seconds massaging her throat, urging her to swallow while I grasp Rayne's wrist and begin to drink. I need to drain her of as much blood as I can while she drinks from me to force the change.

I suck as hard as I can, wanting to get to the change quicker. When I remove my mouth from her wrist, I note how her breathing has evened out a bit, she's no longer wheezing, but not enough to show that it's working. I search her face, looking over her body, trying to figure out why it's not working fast enough, but the only thing I find is the piece of wood in her chest. After I rip it out, the wound closes, showing that she has gained some of my rapid healing abilities, but as I search her face once more, she shows no signs of waking.

"Why isn't it working?" I ask my dad, who is standing above me.

"I don't know that it isn't, son. Her wounds have healed, and her breathing has evened," he replies.

"Then why isn't she awake?" I scream.

"I don't know," he answers.

"Rayne? Rayne baby? Can you hear me? Come back to me. Please," I cry over her body, pleading with her to come back.

An hour later, I'm still sitting in the same spot surrounded by the same people and Rayne shows no signs of waking. "I don't understand."

"Maybe we should..." my mother begins.

"No," I don't even know what she was going to suggest, but I know that I won't be moving from this spot until she wakes up. "Leave," I tell them all.

"But Drake..." Dru begins.

"*I said leave*!" I scream at them all, unable to contain my emotions. One by one they all back away, leaving me with an unconscious Rayne laying in my arms. I refuse to say she's dead because although her heart no longer beats steadily in the way that a human's does, I can hear her organs moving inside her and know that her body is still working.

"We were supposed to have forever." I tell her, brushing her hair off her face. "Sure, you didn't want to be a vampire, but I had hoped in time I could persuade you or follow you in death when your time came. But not yet. Not right now," I cry over her.

"You hear me?" I scream at the sky. "You give her back to me right now! Whatever gods are listening, you better bring her back to me or so help me, I'll find each and every one of you and rip out your hearts," I promise them. I don't even know if they're here listening to me right now, but either way, a promise is a promise, and I will follow through.

Chapter Twenty-Two

Drake

I sit there for hours. I know that dawn has to be coming soon, but I can't bear the thought of moving. If Rayne is not coming back to me, then I have nothing to live for anymore. I look up at the sky and watch as a light gray replaces the stars.

I hear footsteps through the brush, and I can tell that it's Alaric by the sound of the leaves crunching beneath his feet. For a shifter he's not very light on his feet. Or maybe he's doing it on purpose so I know he's coming.

"Drake," he whispers.

"No," I say to him. I know he's going to tell me that I need to go indoors because the sun is rising.

"But the sun is coming up," he says.

"I know," I sigh. "But if the sun rises and Rayne is not coming back, I have no reason to seek shelter," I tell him.

"You have so much to live for. You have your parents, your sister, your coven," I scoff at him for using the coven as a reason for me to live. "Fine, not the coven, your friends. We don't want to lose you."

I look at him with what I'm sure are my bloodshot eyes. Not

from bloodlust, but from crying. I don't think I've ever cried so much in my life. "Would you be able to go on if you lost Phoebe?"

He doesn't have to answer. I can see it on his face. He wouldn't want to. "I would," he says.

"Liar," I spit.

"I would, if only to ensure that our children are loved," he responds.

"See, that would make sense. That you would want to live to ensure the happiness of your children, but Rayne and I didn't even get to start our lives together, let alone have children. If the only way for us to be together is in the next life, I would rather it start now."

"But what about your sister? Your parents?" He probes once more.

"They will mourn for me I'm sure but what kind of life will I have without her?" I say, looking up at him.

"I don't know." He admits. "But neither do you unless you try. Rayne wouldn't want you to leave Dru unprotected." I know he's right and I wouldn't want that either but a life without Rayne wouldn't be a life. If I wasn't strong enough to protect her, how could I ever expect myself to be strong enough to protect Dru.

"She's better off without me." I say, voicing my self pity.

"Don't say that." Alaric growls. "In the last two weeks, I've seen glimpses of the Drusilla I once knew, before the hunters took her. She will be devastated enough at losing Rayne, but if she lost you, too? I don't know what would happen."

Tears slip out of my eyes at his words. He's right. Dru is becoming the woman she was meant to be, but that has nothing to do with anything I did and everything to do with the unconscious woman laying in my arms. "I don't know how to live without her now. Two weeks ago, I couldn't wait until she was gone, wanted nothing more than for her to go far away from me. But now, at the prospect of never seeing her beautiful brown eyes shine with a challenging stare or hear her evil laugh when she thinks of something diabolical. Hell, I'd give anything right now to have her punch me in the face just one more time."

"I know," he says sadly.

"But you don't. Because your mate is at home right now with your children and the rest of your friends and family. Even if Rayne miraculously pulls through this and transitions, she's going to hate me forever. She didn't want this life, and I took her choice away." I sob.

"She won't hate you."

"Yes, she will. But that's okay. She'll be alive. Even if she doesn't want to bond with me, as long as she's still in this world, I will hold out hope."

"Then don't give up on her," he says and I nod.

"Thank you," I say, looking up at him.

"For what?" He asks, confused.

"For giving me a second chance after I sided with the mages. You had every right to rip my heart out right there and then. I tried to help them take your daughter and instead of vengeance, you offered me forgiveness and friendship." He waves his hand as if it's nothing, but I shake my head and continue, "You don't understand. Even though my father is a brilliant man and even better leader, I grew up thinking I could do better than him. I saw his allying himself with other supernatural factions as a weakness. I couldn't fathom how having shifters as friends could be a benefit. I was an entitled jerk, thinking that vampires were the superior species.

"But after that meeting with you, I saw what my dad had tried to tell me all along. That friendships with other factions aren't weaknesses, but strengths. When I called on you for help, you didn't hesitate, instantly opening up your home. If it weren't for you and your friendship, I'd be sitting here alone."

Alaric clears his throat after a moment. "You don't need to

thank me for my friendship or for my allegiance to you and your coven. We were allies when our fathers ruled, and that is how it was meant to be. We shouldn't be separated into different factions based on species, but as supernaturals as a whole, banding together. Just look at the way the academy is. It works so well. The younger generations are learning from birth that just because I can shift into a wolf and you drink blood, we're not that different. We are all special in our own ways. I, for one, am thankful for the friendship I have with you and with the other supernatural leaders in the area. Without you, Trixie, Axel, and Skarlyt, my pack would've been decimated long ago. We need each other to survive in this world." He says, clasping me on the shoulder and I dip my chin in understanding, looking back down at Rayne.

We sit there in silence until the sky begins turning a slight pink. "What if we just bring her inside? Maybe she will wake up later or tomorrow?" he says, turning to look at me.

I look down at Rayne and back up at him. "I've never heard of this happening before."

"No one else has either. Skarlyt has a theory though," he supplies.

"What theory?"

"She thinks that either because of your tie to the prophecy or her bloodline being tied to the gods, or both, that her transition may be different and take a little longer than normal," he says, his eyes shining with hope. I don't know if that's true or not.

"Promise me. If she doesn't wake in one week, you will let me do what I must?" I bargain with him.

He thinks over my words for a moment before he nods. "Deal."

I gently place Rayne down and allow Alaric to help me up before scooping her body back into my arms. Together, we stroll toward the house, but as we near, I feel a warmth on my body that I've never felt before. I look up and watch, as rays of sunshine through the trees, directly onto Rayne and me.

Hearing that my footsteps have stopped, Alaric turns toward me, and we make eye contact. His eyes go wide at noticing the same. The sun is hitting both Rayne and me in multiple spots on our bodies, and yet I feel nothing but warmth. No fire, no burning. "What is happening?" I ask Alaric. But he looks just as confused as me.

Chapter Twenty-Three

Rayne

I come to with my body jostling about like I'm being carried even though I'm pretty sure I'm supposed to be dead. When I pushed Drake out of the way, I saw the stake go into my chest like it was in slow motion. There is no way I survived that. But as I open my eyes, seeing Drake's angelic face lit up by sunlight, I realize this must be heaven. I reach up and stroke his cheek.

His eyes snap to mine as he nuzzles my hand. "Rayne," he whispers, tears brimming in his eyes. He pulls my body so that I'm tight up against him. "I thought I lost you," he weeps into my hair.

"Drake?" Why would he be saying that if this were heaven?

"Guys. I don't know what is going on right now, but if you want to keep it secret, which I suggest you do, we need to get inside," Alaric says. Wait. Alaric? What is he doing here? Alaric definitely wouldn't be in my idea of heaven. Phoebe? Yes. Skarlyt? Yes. Drusilla? Definitely. But not Alaric.

"Keep what secret? I don't understand," I say, trying to lean back enough to look at both of them.

"You're right," Drake says and uses his vamp speed to rush into the house. He sits down on the couch, pulling me into his lap so I can look around. I watch as Phoebe rushes around the house, securing all the blinds and curtains so that there isn't a speck of sunlight flowing through.

"Okay. Someone tell me what the fuck is going on," I demand.

"Rayne!" Dru rushes over to me from somewhere, wraps her arms around me and pulls me into her. Drake growls loudly, pulling me back against him. The two of them seem to have a game of tug-the-Rayne before both of them win, and I'm tucked securely against them both.

"Okay, seriously. Someone better tell me what the fuck is going on here before I start kicking asses," I demand once again, wiggling easily out of their holds. Holy shit. When did I get so strong?

As I turn my hands over in front of me, trying to inspect them, I note that my vision is better. It was always good to begin with, but I'm able to see almost every single pore on my hands, every raised cuticle. I'm in severe need of a manicure. "What the fuck?"

"Rayne. I think you should sit down," Phoebe says, and I turn to face her so fast my head should be spinning. But it isn't.

"You didn't?" I turn back to look at Drake and Dru. "Please tell me you didn't," I beg, tears brimming in my eyes.

"We didn't have a choice," Dru says while Drake just sits there looking indifferent.

"I made a choice. I'd rather have you hate me for the rest of our long lives than live without you," he spits at me.

"You knew this isn't what I wanted!" I yell at him. "Yet you did it, anyway."

"We all agreed," Dru adds as if that makes any difference.

"So everyone except me got to choose?" I ask her. She shrinks away at my accusation. "I can't believe this," I say and storm to the door, throwing it open and walking outside. I probably should have thought about that before I did it, but rather than burn for my rash actions, I stand out on the front lawn soaking in the sun.

"How?" I ask, spinning to look at the door.

Dru stands there, mouth gaping open, hiding from the sun while Drake walks right out and up to me. "I don't know," he tells me as he reaches out his hands for mine. "It has to be something to do with your blood."

"My blood?" I ask as I take his hands without thought.

"It's the only explanation. Or something to do with the prophecy. Either way. For some reason, we can both be out in the sunlight."

"Oh, good. You two have bonded," Andres surprises us, walking through the trees.

"Bonded?" I ask, looking from him back to Drake with a raised eyebrow. This time he does look ashamed.

"It is one of the side effects of me turning you," he tells me. "It's a perk if I say so myself."

"Drake," I warn, pulling my hands from his but turn back to Andres. "Did you know that we would be able to walk in the sun when we bonded?"

"Not for sure. But I had my suspicions," he responds.

"Great. Just great. More people with their suspicions," I huff and stomp back up the stairs to the house.

"You need to keep this between your trusted allies. No one can find out. Not yet," Andres says before I can go inside.

"Or what?" I challenge turning to face him.

"Well, I would imagine there will be quite a few vampires who would love to be able to walk around in the sun. Just imagine what they would do to get that power," he responds before shifting and flying away.

"Does anyone else feel like he shifts and flies away every time we demand answers?" Phoebe asks.

"Yup," Alaric says in agreement.

"Okay. Get our allies, as Andres put it," I say as I sit in the living room. "I'd rather get it all out at once."

"Who would that be?" Phoebe asks.

I think for a minute. "Drake's parents, for sure. Skarlyt and Lennox, Samara, which means Trevan should be included, too. I don't really know him, but I can't ask her to keep a secret like this from her mate. Skarlyt's brother, what's his name?"

"Sebastyn," Phoebe supplies.

"Yes. Sebastyn and his mate, since he seems to have a lot of knowledge and is also a part of the prophecy. And I suppose your siblings. Unless there's anyone else you can think of?"

"No, that seems like our immediate circle. Other than Charleigh. She can totally be trusted, but I don't think she needs to know quite yet," Phoebe says.

"Might as well bring Charleigh and Ashton up, too. I'd rather not have to tell people more than once," I sink into the couch. Drake tries to come and sit next to me, but after a warning growl and my look of 'don't even think about it', he moves over to the chair. Good boy. Oh, man. I was going to make him beg on his knees until his tongue was too tired to go on, but now, I have to think of so many more things he's going to do in order to atone for this one. Because as mad as I am at not having a choice right now, I know I will forgive him. If the roles were reversed, I'd probably have done the same. But he doesn't need to know that.

They trickle into the room, each of my new friends embracing me and expressing their joy at me being alive, if that's truly what I am. Is a vampire alive? My heart no longer beats, and if you were to ask any scientist, that is a requirement for being 'alive,' though somehow I feel more alive right now than ever. It's as if this is what I was always meant to be. I was born a hunter but meant to be a vampire. How fucked up is that?

"Don't get me wrong. I'm so glad you're alive, Rayne. But why are we all gathered here?" Margaret asks.

"It seems more changed than just my heart ceasing to beat," I supply.

"What do you mean?" Roderick asks.

"I think it will be easier if we just show you." Drake gets up and helps me to my feet.

"Yes. Probably," I agree.

Together, the two of us walk to the front door. "Stop. You'll burn!" Roderick warns.

We don't stop, though; we open the door and walk outside. Gasps can be heard from everyone as the first rays of sun hit us.

"How is this possible?" Skarlyt questions, stepping outside. She circles us, trying to find a reason for our ability to walk in the daylight.

"We don't know," I respond while walking back up the porch and re-securing my spot on the couch. I love Skarlyt, truly I do. But I don't want to be studied. Not when I'm still severely pissed off about the events of last night. Shit.

"What happened to the hunters after I..." I can't seem to finish my sentence.

"Well..." Drake begins with a look at his sister.

"I went a little crazy with bloodlust," Dru supplies.

"Meaning?" I question.

"Meaning after your dad shot you, I slaughtered every last one of them, except for those in the cages," she responds, hanging her head.

"And my dad?"

She peeks back up at me. "I...," she begins through flowing tears, "I killed him."

I look at her in shock, unable to formulate any words. What does someone say to the person that killed their father, even if it was justified?

"I didn't mean to. I just saw him shoot you and rage exploded from me. I couldn't help myself. I promise you I would never hurt anyone on purpose," she falls on her knees in front of me.

"I know you wouldn't," I admit to her not wanting to see her cry.

"Please forgive me," she begs.

"Of course, I forgive you. But I need a few minutes to myself, if you don't mind," I tell her before getting up and going out to the back deck, being very careful not to let any sunlight stream into the house.

Once I'm sitting on the deck, I allow my grief at losing my father to sink in. My dad may not have been the doting, loving father I wanted, but he was mine, nonetheless. I think about my life with him, trying to think of the good times. Unfortunately, the only good times I can remember are him praising me during training, which makes me start laughing. How can I not have any good memories of my father? Normal people would have a lifetime of fond memories to reminisce about at the death of a loved one. Not me. The only time my father showed me any emotion was last night, when he was happy to see me. Not once in my lifetime had he told me that he loved me.

I'm still laughing, with tears falling down my cheeks, when Drake comes outside. "Are you okay?"

"Of course, I am," I tell him. "Why wouldn't I be?"

"Because you just found out that your father is dead? And to top it off, it was your best friend who killed him," he questions.

At him saying it like that, my laughter dies out. "I should be sad. Or mad. Something. Anything. But I'm not." I take a breath while looking into his eyes. "You know I can't remember a time when he ever told me that he loved me. Not once. I was sitting here trying to think about any happy memories I have with him, and you know what I realized?"

"What?" he asks with concern lining his face.

"That I have none. Other than him praising me when I had a good training day, I don't have any."

"That's horrible," he says, crouching down in front of me and rubbing my legs.

"Is it?" I ask. I know he's not going to shed any tears at the death of my father. And why would he? To him and Dru, he is the villain in their story.

"Of course, it is. You should have hundreds of fond memories with your father," he tells me.

"I guess," I admit. "Is it wrong that I'm not as upset about him being gone as I should be?"

"Whatever you feel is exactly right. No one can tell you how to feel." I suppose he's right.

"I think I just need to sleep. I'm so tired," I admit, my eyelids suddenly feeling very heavy.

"Let's get you to bed," he tells me and scoops me up. "I'm going to take Rayne to bed. We can talk more when we wake up," he tells everyone inside.

There is a round of good nights from my friends. But I'm fast asleep before I even feel us reach the bottom of the stairs.

Chapter Twenty-Four

Drake

After getting Rayne tucked into bed in Skarlyt's basement room and climbing in beside her, I have the chance to think about everything. I know she's pissed that I took her choice away, but she can't be that mad at me if she let me carry her down to bed, right?

I brush the hair off her face and place a soft kiss on her head. She's so beautiful. Vampirism definitely becomes her. Her already smooth skin seems to glow, her hair, although dirty with blood caked in it, seems fuller and shinier. Even her eyes—when they were open and rimmed with red—suit her perfectly.

That's the other thing that's weird. When a vampire transitions, they immediately need to feed because they are not able to control their blood lust even amongst friends and family. The fact that she was able to sit and have a conversation with everyone is astounding. There has to be something to Skarlyt's theories. This is definitely not a typical transition. But then Rayne isn't a typical woman, even before as a human.

I pull her small frame into my body, tucking her safely away and fall asleep myself.

When I wake, it's to Drusilla standing above the bed staring down at Rayne like a creeper. "What are you doing?" I ask, and she turns her gaze to me.

"Just making sure you are both alive. You've been sleeping for two days."

I sit up quickly, jostling Rayne accidentally, making her groan. I pull the covers back up over her and slip out of bed, leading Dru out of the room so we can talk. "Two days?"

"Yup. Dad said that you both needed sleep after everything that happened, but I needed to make sure."

I stretch out my muscles. "Obviously, we did. What about the rest of the coven?"

"Dad has taken temporary control to let you and Rayne figure everything out." She looks down. "I kind of had to tell mom and dad some of Rayne's reservations."

I place my hand on her arm. "It's okay. They would've found out sooner rather than later anyway."

"You don't think she's going to be mad at me, do you?"

I chuckle, "No madder than she already is at us for changing her."

"Yeah, I guess. I also got some blood packs in the fridge down here for you. I figured you'd both be thirsty." I nod, creasing my brows in confusion. I should be starving. But I'm not.

"I'll see if Rayne's ready to wake up and meet you upstairs." I know I can trust Dru with this revelation, but as I don't quite understand it myself, I don't share.

"Okay," she responds, heading out the door and up the stairs.

I grab a blood pack and walk back into the bedroom. I sit on the side of the bed and rub Rayne's back. "Rayne, baby. Are you ready to wake up?"

She groans, rolling over and pinning me with the scariest look I've ever seen her make—and she makes some pretty terrifying ones. "No." She says, rolling back over and pulling the covers over her head.

"Come on. We've been asleep for two days."

That has her sitting up as quickly as I did, and I chuckle. "What?"

I cut off my chuckle quickly and ignore her question, knowing I'm going to be in trouble if I continue. "Are you thirsty?" I ask, trying to keep the concerned look off my face. Once again, she shouldn't be able to have this conversation with me without her fangs descending and red rimming her eyes in hunger. As it stands, her eyes are completely back to normal. If I hadn't seen the red rims with my own eyes, I wouldn't believe that she was even a vampire.

"Not really," she says, shaking her head, and I pull out the blood bag.

"You still should have some." I say, pulling the tab off.

She holds her hand up, pushing it away. "Uh. No, thank you."

I set the blood pack down carefully on the bedside table and turn back to her. "Rayne, you have to drink, or we take the chance that you will attack one of our friends."

"I'm not drinking out of a bag," she says, wrinkling her nose.

"We can try and find a live donor, if that's what you prefer."

She shakes her head even harder. "No. No way."

I blow out an exasperated breath. "Well, we need to figure something out."

"Why can't I just feed from you?" She asks, and I pause to think about it. I've heard of mates surviving from drinking only from each other. It could work.

I bring my finger up to my neck, making a small incision with my nail. Her fangs descend instantly, and her eyes widen, her hand coming up to cover her mouth. "It's okay, love. Drink." I gently grab the back of her head and bring it to my neck.

It only takes seconds before her fangs slide in and she begins to drink, a moan slipping from both of us. She moves lightning fast, straddling my lap. Gods. This feels amazing. I've never let anyone drink from me before. But I definitely see the appeal.

She removes her fangs from my neck, licking the blood off her lips, and fuck me if it's not the absolute hottest thing I've ever seen. My cock is in total agreement as it begins pulsing beneath her, and she glances down.

Her lips meet mine hot and heavy, both of our fangs scraping against each other's tongue. I pull her body forward and back so that she's grinding on me, and she pulls away. "I'm still mad at you."

I nod, acknowledging that fact. "Can you be mad at me and fuck me at the same time?" I ask with a smirk.

"Hell yes, I can," she says, merging her mouth with mine once more with a growl. I wrap my arms around her and flip us over so that she's laying underneath me. I rip her shirt in two, not wanting to separate our mouths even for the seconds it would take to remove it gently.

She gasps and does the same to mine, moving her mouth down my neck. She scrapes her teeth back and forth, teasing me but never penetrating and I can't take it anymore. Using my speed, I lower down her body, pulling her pants down as I go. When I reach her center, I consider teasing her like she did me, but all of a sudden, my hunger rears up. I sink my fang into the soft flesh above her clit and begin sucking. She bucks her hips, crying out. I slip two fingers inside her, rubbing the little button inside of her, and she grips them tightly as her release flows through her.

"Drake!" She exclaims, pulling on my head and yanking me up to her mouth. I reach down, unbuttoning my pants, freeing my painfully erect cock and sliding it inside her.

"Oh, gods!" She cries out.

I try to go slow so that I'm making love to her, but my body urges me to go faster. I begin pounding in and out of her with more force than ever. I don't need to worry about breaking her anymore, and it shows with the force that she is meeting me back thrust for thrust.

What seems like only seconds later, I feel her begin to pulse on my cock. I try to hold off my own release, but the way her pussy is gripping me makes me fall over the edge with her.

"Oh, my goddess, that was amazing," she says, and I grunt in agreement, rolling over onto my back. Normally I would've got up and grabbed something to clean her up with but right now it feels like there are no bones in my body. "I'm dead. I think you just killed me." She says dramatically, making me laugh.

"Ditto." I agree. "But we do need to go make an appearance upstairs before Dru comes down to find us again."

She groans but rolls off the bed, picking up the pieces of her shirt as she does. "Did you have to rip the shirt in half?" She asks, looking back at me.

"Yes. It was in my way." I tell her and she smiles, shaking her head and walking to the attached bathroom. I get up and follow her, cleaning myself up in the sink while she hops in the shower. As much as I want to hop in the shower with her and start round two, I think maybe we need to talk about everything that's happened so far. After we go see my sister, that is.

"I'll send Dru down with some new clothes for you," I tell her through the shower.

"That would be great. Thank you," she responds, and I walk upstairs to find Dru.

"Rayne is in the shower; can you bring her some new clothes?" I ask after walking into the kitchen to find her sitting at the table with Alaric, Darren, Phoebe, and Sophia.

"Sure thing," she says, getting up and rushing away.

I grab a seat at the table. "Is she okay?" Phoebe asks, looking concerned.

I nod. "I think so."

Everyone at the table breathes out a sigh of relief, and I smile. It's not just me that Rayne has made an impression on; it seems every single person she has met has come to care for her.

"I have a question," Darren says, looking at me while both Phoebe and Sophia shoot daggers at him.

I smile, knowing that look. I'm also looking forward to having Rayne make the same face at me in the future. "About what?" I respond.

"Well, I was wondering if you think that Rayne would be interested in teaching a class at the academy?" He spits out.

"We told you to wait a few days," Alaric berates him.

"I know, but the new semester starts in less than a month, so classes are still being changed and added. If we can get her in to teach this semester, we don't have to wait another year," Darren argues, looking back at me.

I think about it for a moment, remembering how her eyes lit up when she was training the pack and coven. "What classes are you thinking of?" I ask, rubbing my chin.

"I was thinking of a combat class for the older kids, a self-defence class for the younger ones, and a course on hunters and their practices."

I scratch my chin, thinking about it. "I think you should ask her. I could see her enjoying that," I tell him, and he shoots a triumphant look over at his mate and Phoebe.

"So, other than you guys arguing over whether to ask Rayne if she wants to teach, what else happened while we were asleep?" I ask, looking around the table.

"Not much really. Your dad took the coven back to the compound until the new one is ready. Skarlyt is overseeing construction of the new houses at the academy and the underground bunker for the vampires. And we're trying to figure out how to make the academy for all ages."

"All ages?" I blurt out interrupting Alaric.

He bobs his head. "After all the attacks, a lot of the parents are saying it's not safe to send our children to school in the city. I know your coven has their own classes for the younger kids, but we don't. And short of home schooling them, this is the best plan."

"You think having kindergarten classes in the same building as the high schoolers is a good plan?"

Alaric shrugs. "It's the only option we have right now."

"I wanted to build a smaller school to hold the elementary students and keep the larger one for the older grades. But we couldn't agree on where, so we didn't bring it up," Darren says.

I think about that for a second. The idea definitely has merit, and I know I would feel better if the students were separate. Every pack, pride, coven, sleuth has at least a few bad apples in it, and teachers can't be everywhere all the time. "What if we build a smaller school on the grounds to the right. The buildings would be separate yet look connected, like in an L shape," I supply with a smile.

"That could work if we can get everyone else on board with it," Alaric says, rubbing his chin thoughtfully.

"We have two of the five votes sitting here. All we need is one more to agree, and the majority wins."

"And Skarlyt would agree. I'm sure of it," Phoebe says, rubbing her hands together excitedly. "Maybe we could even have a small day care in the elementary school for teachers with smaller children. That would solve the staffing shortage," She tacks on, looking over at Darren.

"We need to call a board meeting for tonight. That way Axel can get his crew to start building it immediately before the ground freezes," Alaric says, already pulling out his phone and walking into the kitchen. I haven't really had an active role on the board or anything to do with the academy, always delegating to Colin. But I have to admit that it feels really good to be playing a positive role in the future and surprisingly, I'm actually looking forward to seeing what else we can come up with.

"I'll call the older student representatives that were voted in and see if they can attend. I'd really like to hear their take on this as well," Darren says, pulling out his chair and walking out onto the back deck.

"Okay. The meeting is set for eleven o'clock tonight, so two hours from now," Alaric says, coming back to the table.

"Meeting for what?" Rayne calls out, walking through the door from the basement.

"A board meeting for the academy," Phoebe supplies, quickly getting up and grabbing a coffee off the counter and handing it to Rayne. She takes a sip before I can stop her but rather than spitting it out like I thought she would, she moans in delight.

"Perfect as always Phoebe." We all turn and stare at her. "What? Do I have something on my face?" She asks, scrubbing her hand over her face.

"You're drinking coffee," I say, walking up to her.

She looks down at the coffee before looking back up at me with wide eyes. "I am."

"It was another one of Skarlyt's theories," Phoebe says with a smirk, taking a swig of her own coffee.

"What?" Rayne, Dru and I all ask at once.

"Skarlyt's theory is that because Rayne is a descendant of the gods, that her transition into a vampire will be very different from you because she wasn't human to begin with. Think of her more like a hybrid. She will need both blood and human food to survive. At least that's the working theory right now," Phoebe says, and we turn to look at one another.

Rayne shoves the mug into my hands. "Here. You try." She says, and I raise the mug to my nose and take a whiff. Ugh. It doesn't smell very good. I bring the mug up to my lips and dump some of the liquid into my mouth, instantly running over to the sink and spitting it back out, unable to even swallow.

"Nope. I'll stick to blood," I say, wiping my chin. Rayne walks back over to me, taking the mug out of my hands.

"More for me," she says, with a smirk, walking over to the table. "Okay, so you said there's a board meeting for the academy. What's that?"

We all look to Darren to answer since it's his baby and he smiles turning toward her. "It's a school for supernatural children. Obviously, the vampires can't go to normal schools because of the sun, and shifters and witches don't have very good control when they hit puberty with their emotions going all haywire. So, we started a school just for them."

"That's amazing. Can we go see it?" She asks excitedly, looking at me.

"I'm on the board," I tell her with a smile and nod.

"You are? Oh, my goddess, this is the coolest thing ever. I can't wait to see it. Wait. What is the meeting about?" She asks, and Darren fills her in. I just stand against the counter in the kitchen watching her face light up. It seems she's not that upset anymore about being supernatural. After all, she can do both of the things that she didn't want to give up.

"How are we all getting there?" I ask. I immediately groan as the new voice calls out.

"Me," Skarlyt says, walking in from the back deck.

She walks right up to Rayne, embracing her and smiling at the mug of coffee in her hand. "I was right?" She asks, looking to Phoebe for confirmation.

"Yup. Though Drake couldn't," Phoebe supplies, and Skarlyt's eyes snap to mine. For a moment, I think she's going to be serious and not her normal self, but this is Skarlyt I'm talking about.

"That's okay. Drake likes his blood. Don't you? Tell me again, what vein do you prefer to drink from?" She probes as if I had told her at some point before.

I growl at her, and both she and Rayne giggle while Rayne leans over and whispers in her ear. I watch as Skarlyt's eyes go wide and the smile on her face gets bigger. I know exactly what she's telling her.

"Damnit, Rayne," I hiss, though I'm not really upset with her. I can't expect her not to share things with her friends.

"What? She wanted to know," Rayne says with a smirk that tells me she did that on purpose to gain a few spankings and I'm more than prepared to dole them out.

"I'm going to stay home with the kids while you guys go," Phoebe says.

Alaric wraps his arms around her and places a kiss on her head. "We won't be long," he promises.

"Take as long as you need to make this happen," she says.

"Oh, yeah. Perhaps you should tell me what you're planning on discussing before we get there," Skarlyt says, and Darren fills her in. Just like we thought, she instantly agrees, and she, Rayne, and Sophia begin planning the layout straightaway.

Chapter Twenty-Five

Rayne

There's a freaking supernatural academy. My mind is blown! It never even crossed my mind to wonder where they went to school and such. I guess I just assumed they were homeschooled or something. And if that wasn't enough to make this day the best day ever, I can still walk in the sun and consume food. I guess I was worried about turning into a vampire for nothing. I can still do everything I wanted.

"Rayne, before we go, there's something I wanted to ask you," Darren says, walking up to where me and Drake are waiting for Skarlyt to get back from taking Alaric.

"What's up?" I ask, feeling Drake pull me into his body in a possessive manner. I smirk at his tensed jaw. He seems jealous.

"I was wondering if you would be interested in teaching a class or two at the academy?"

He barely gets the words out of his mouth before I open mine. "Hell yes, I do."

I feel Drake's body move as if he's suppressing a laugh and shove my elbow into his ribs. Darren blows out a breath like he was worried I would say *no*. "What classes?" I ask, unable to keep my curiosity at bay.

"We were thinking of adding a course on hunters and the dangers that they could pose, as well as a combat class for the older students and a self-defence class for the younger ones." I nod along with him, loving everything that he's saying.

"As long as the course on hunters is only for the older grades; we don't need to be scaring the little ones just yet," I add, and he agrees.

Next thing you know, Skarlyt is back and grabbing onto my hand, pulling me beside her. "Hold on," she whispers. I cling to her, having never teleported anywhere before. But rather than landing on solid ground, I feel a tingling spread throughout my body, like an awareness or something that is just waking for the first time. I open my eyes and cling to Skarlyt tighter. We're hovering high above the most beautiful school I've ever seen. It looks like a castle with turrets and everything.

"It's so beautiful," I tell her, not able to get enough of looking around. She flies us around the perimeter, so I can see the entire grounds.

"Here's where we're building houses for the more mature students or students with mates. They will have pack houses with others in similar situations." She points out to a secluded area further into the trees.

"What about there?" I ask pointing to a large open area just behind the school. That would be absolutely perfect for a training area.

"That's just the green space," she says, like it's nothing.

"Do you think people would be opposed to me turning it into a training area? I can set up a really good obstacle course and set different stations for weapons and hand-to-hand combat," I begin, my mind buzzing with all the possibilities.

"I think that's a fantastic idea, and I don't think anyone would mind at all. You should bring it up at the board meeting," she says and my smile widens.

She moves us back toward the front of the school. "This is where Drake suggested the new school go," she says, gesturing to a spot in front and to the side of the current building.

"I think that would work," I tell her, and she smiles.

"Me, too," she agrees, lowering me down next to Dru and Alaric before popping away to get the others.

"This place is amazing," I tell Dru, still reeling from everything I saw.

"It is. This is the first time I've seen it, too," she says, with a similar awe-struck look on her face.

"What?" I ask, spinning to look at her.

"Remember that I didn't leave the coven before. Colin showed me pictures, but I have never seen it in person. Hopefully this will stop any stupid teenagers from making the same mistake I did and going out to human parties," she says sullenly, and I dip my chin, holding the same hope in my chest.

"It does. We let the students have a fire here every Friday night so that they can socialize outside of school hours. I guess it will probably happen more frequently once they all move in," Alaric says, and we both turn to him.

"Move in?" I question.

"Oh, I thought Darren would've told you that part. We voted last week. We have dormitories already set up in hopes that students from other areas around the province would send their kids, but no luck yet. So, after the suggestion of one of the teens, we're allowing the students over the age of sixteen to stay on campus."

"Colin said they were trying to push for thirteen," Dru says, confusion lining her face.

"We needed a unanimous vote for that, and your brother didn't agree."

"I didn't agree to what?" Drake calls, walking up to us with Darren, Sophia and Skarlyt.

"Lowering the age to thirteen," Alaric responds.

"Actually, Colin and I spoke about that last week. As long as the parents know the risks and sign a waiver showing that they understand that there will only be a limited number of adults present on weekends and in the evening hours between the day classes and night classes, I'm willing to change my vote," he says, putting his arm around me and pulling me close.

"Really?" Skarlyt asks, sharing a look of excitement with Darren.

Drake nods. "I guess we need to hire more live-in staff or ask some of the seniors to be RA's."

They continue talking logistics, and I tune them out, already thinking of everything that I am going to want to do in my classes and how I'm going to want to build the obstacle course. There's going to need to be different levels for each age group, and I'll need to get some practice weapons, targets for bow and arrows, maybe even figure out how to make a track out there for them to run laps.

Before I know it, we're walking up the stone steps. "You know since we will be running the coven together, we'll share the vote," Drake whispers in my ear, and I spin to him, letting the rest of our group continue.

"You would share that with me?"

"Of course, I will. We're partners. I know we still have things to talk about, to work out between us but..." I cut him off, merging my lips with his. Maybe yesterday, or even this morning, we needed to talk about things. But that was before I found out I'm not giving anything up by being a vampire. If I would've been given the choice, I would never have known this was possible. I would've grown old and died, leaving him alone in this world without ever knowing we could've had forever together.

"I'm sure there'll be bumps in the road Drake, but for right now, everything is absolutely perfect," I whisper as I pull back.

The shock on his face doesn't last long before he's lifting me up and spinning me around. "Let's get in there so we can go home and celebrate," he whispers into my neck, reaching out his tongue and licking it. "Besides I owe you a spanking or two," he says stepping back with a wink making my pussy weep in anticipation.

"I'm holding you to that," I say, swaying my hips a little more than necessary with each step inside. If he can tease me, I can tease him right back.

We walk into a large entryway, and I'm surprised it looks just like you would see in a normal school: the main office to the left, a hallway going left, and right at the end, a hall filled with row upon row of lockers. I want to explore every inch but instead follow our group into a large boardroom beside the office. Inside, a large burly man with a thick beard and a petite blonde woman with large green eyes that remind me of a cat's, await us.

"Axel, Trixie. This is Rayne, my mate," Drake says introducing me.

"The hunter?" The burly man, Axel says, and the boom of his voice has me raising my chin a little more.

"Not anymore," I say before anyone else can jump in, and I flash him my fangs with a hiss. I'm not even sure I knew how to do that. It just happened.

"So, I see. Welcome, Rayne," Trixie says, looking around our group. "Drusilla?" Her gaze lands on Dru and she is up out of her seat, wrapping her arms around her before I can even blink.

"Hey, Trix," Dru says, hugging her back fiercely.

After a moment, Trixie pulls back, looking her up and down. "It's so good to see you. Promise me we can have a girls' night and catch up soon."

Dru nods. "I promise."

"Good." With that done, Trixie returns to her seat, and we all take ours.

"What's on the agenda? Why did we need this emergency meeting?" Axel asks, getting straight to business.

Darren begins, telling him all our plans, with Skarlyt jumping in here or there emphasizing different points. The next hour flies by filled with discussions of how many students we anticipate, what classes, how many teachers we will need. Even the daycare suggestion was accepted with a unanimous vote.

"If that's all..." Axel begins, but Skarlyt interrupts.

"Actually, Rayne had one more thing she wanted to discuss." She gestures to me, and I shoot her a look that says, 'I thought we were friends.' She just smirks so I clear my throat.

"Yes. After talking with Darren about possibly teaching some combat and self-defence classes, Skarlyt took me on an aerial tour of the school grounds. There is a spot just over here," I point to the area on the blueprints laying on the table, "that would be perfect for a training area. I could set up obstacle courses, a range for bow and arrows, a ring for hand-to-hand lessons. There's even room for us to eventually put in a track." Everyone is staring at me as I finish, and I can't figure out if they think it's a good idea or not.

Finally, Axel speaks up. "What about in the winter months?"

My mouth opens and closes like a fish not having thought about that. "Wait. I thought supernaturals didn't feel the cold like humans."

"Vampires don't. Shifters feel the cold, just not as intensely, but witches do," he says, and I can't be sure if he's unhappy that it won't work or unhappy with my suggestions. Or perhaps that's just how his face looks.

"We can put a temporary dome over it until we've finished construction on everything else and have time to build a permanent structure over it." Skarlyt says, and I nod at her in thanks for the support.

"Would you be able to make it last the year? Because between the new dormitories, new school, and our outside projects, that's when we'd be able to get to it," Axel says, looking at her, and I turn to look at her, too. She raises her chin in defiance as if he just offended her.

"The magic will last as long as we need it to," she says with no room for argument in her voice.

Axel dips his chin. "Then I agree. Let's put it to a vote. All in favor?" All the voting members raise their hands, showing another unanimous vote, and I clap my hands in excitement. This is going to be so much fun.

"There is one more thing," Alaric begins. "We need to figure out what to do with the hunters we're currently holding. We can't let them go."

"Let me try and convince them that what they're doing is wrong," I jump in, earning a whole lot of growls from around the table. Drake pulls me back beside him and tries to shove in front of me, but I don't let him. "Listen, I know how you feel. Believe me, I do. But I also know that they don't know any different. Just like all of you, we're born into that life. From the day we are born, it's jammed into our heads that all supernaturals are evil." I get another growl for that but continue. "Obviously, they're wrong. But they don't know that. Let me try and show them," I plead. I don't want all those hunter deaths on me.

"We have over two hundred in cages, double that number killed and the rest took off. If we let them go and regroup, it could mean the end of us," Alaric says, sullenly. I know he doesn't want to kill all those people, but right now he can't see any other way.

"If they don't see reason, we could put them into psychiatric facilities. Scatter them around the country, even, and have people in place to keep an eye on them. They wouldn't be a danger to us then, and even if they try and tell the truth, that they fight supernaturals, it would just make them being in that place more believable," I try and reason. Everyone looks to be thinking about it, but it's Alaric I watch, knowing that whatever he decides, everyone else will agree with. He's like the unofficial leader of the supernaturals in this area.

Alaric inclines his head slightly. "I agree to let you try and reason with them. I also agree to place some in those facilities."

"Thank you," I beam.

"But," he says, pausing to ensure he keeps my attention, "if there are any who we feel are too dangerous to be let go, we will execute them." I suck in a breath at his condition but dip my chin in agreement, knowing that he's only doing what he can to keep his family and pack safe. I'm not going to get a better deal than that.

"Okay," I agree, letting Drake wrap his arms around me and pulling me down into his lap.

Chapter Twenty-Six

Rayne

The last two weeks have been an adjustment, to say the least. If it were just the turning into a vampire thing, I would have been well adjusted by now. But it wasn't. It was another matter altogether: learning that my father had died and, along with that, my lack of emotions about losing him. I guess I'm just more confused than anything. In my brain, I know I should feel something. Anything. Even if it's happiness. But it's almost like I'm numb to it.

Being a vampire is pretty amazing though. If I thought the sex with Drake was mind blowing before, I have no idea what I would call it now. The intensity of my orgasms has increased tenfold. Gods, just thinking about it, I start to get all hot and bothered.

But then I think about the hunters we released from the cages, and my libido simmers back down. I tried to convince them to change their ways, but it seems my becoming a vampire only made their belief in their cause stronger. After shipping half of them off to different psychiatric facilities across the country, we set up a safeguard so if they are ever to be released, we will know. I'm sure we haven't seen the last of them. The other half were deemed too dangerous to be released, even to a psychiatric facility, so after I left, they were executed. I couldn't stay and watch, but I trusted that Alaric, Darren, Drake, Samara, Sebastyn, Axel, and Trixie would make it as quick and painless as possible.

"Are you ready?" Drake asks me, walking into the apartment we built for ourselves in the new compound just outside of pack land. It's a mixture of both of us. I have my very own workout room, fully loaded with all the bells and whistles. Double bag, weights, even a sauna to relax my sore muscles. Not that I get those anymore. In fact, I haven't really enjoyed using it because I don't feel the hot temperature like I used to. Drake warned me that would be the case, but I disagreed. Now I use it just to make sure he doesn't know he was right. It's a matter of principle.

"As ready as I'll ever be," I respond.

"We don't have to do this," he says.

"Yes, we do. We need to find out if he wrote down the location of the lab. Besides, as his next of kin, I have paperwork to sign for the lawyers that they dropped off at the house yesterday," I tell him adamantly. We've put off visiting my family home for this long because I was unable to stomach the thought of going there. I'm sure I'm going to find that my father was even more of a monster than I originally thought.

We drive in silence for the hour-long trip to Orillia. Neither of us seems to want to discuss what we may or may not find. But as we pull up to the house, I'm not sure if I've given myself enough time.

"I don't know if I want to know just how much of a monster he was," I whisper, keeping my eyes trained on the house.

"We can come back if you want. We don't have to do this right now," Drake tells me, rubbing my arm.

"No, we have wasted enough time. We need to find the location of that lab," I steel myself to go into the house. Thinking of the possible supernaturals being experimented on and tortured day after day cements my resolve. I need to get into that house and find any evidence pointing to the location.

"What's the plan?" Drake asks as we make our way up to the door.

"I guess we split up and search different rooms so that we aren't here for too long."

We search the house top-to-bottom, finding nothing. Not even a scrap of evidence that he was a hunter. I never questioned it before, but the only place I've seen any evidence of our profession was in the...

"I guess that's it," Drake interrupts my thoughts.

"Not quite," I begin walking out the back door. "There is one other place we haven't searched yet."

"Where?" he asks, confused, but follows me outside, nonetheless.

"The shed," I explain as we stop in front of the shed. I guess it's not truly a shed, more like a small barn. "I haven't been in here since..." I can't finish my sentence, my emotions clogging my throat.

"Since Dru?" he asks, and I nod.

I take the keys that I found on my father's desk when I was signing the legal papers and unlock each of the locks securing the door. "Drake. I don't know what we will find in here."

"I know," he breathes out heavily. "But whatever we find, we will face it together." He grips my hand, interlocking our fingers, giving me strength.

Emotions rip through me as we pull open the doors. The last time I was in here was when I released Dru. After that day, I refused to enter, not wanting to know, trying to pretend it was all a bad dream and my father wasn't the monster. Now, I'm unable to deny that fact. As I walk in, nothing has changed. The weapons are still hanging on the walls, and the cell is still at the back. But rather than being empty as I thought it would be, it isn't.

"Who are you?" a young girl calls out from between the bars.

I share a look with Drake. What the fuck? "I'm Rayne. This is my mate Drake," I start walking slowly, trying to be nonthreatening.

"Mate?" she asks. "You're not hunters?"

"No, we are supernaturals, but I used to be a hunter." Shifters can smell lies, and since I don't know what type of supernatural she is, I figure the truth is our best bet.

"How are you a supernatural and a hunter?" she questions, tilting her head in the cutest way.

"I was born and raised a hunter, but then I met my mate who, as you can see, is a vampire, so I was turned." As she comes into view, I suck in a breath. Her long hair is dirty and matted, sticking close to her head. Her eyes are the most gorgeous shade of purple that I've ever seen but it's her body I notice the most. The dress she's wearing is hanging off of her, the spaghetti straps looking thick compared to her protruding collar and shoulder bones.

"I know. I must look terrible," she says, wiping her hands down her dress as if she is trying to clean it off.

"It's okay," I tell her, grabbing the keys and placing them in the lock to open the cage. "What's your name?"

"River," she replies.

"That's a beautiful name. How long have you been in here, River?"

"A couple of years now. I woke up after my long sleep and went searching this new world. Gods, you have so many strange ways now. No one seems to care about Mother Earth anymore. Gaia will be turning in her slumber," she responds.

"A couple years? What do you mean by long sleep?" I question.

"My kind tend to go into a long slumber. I couldn't say how

long it was. Just that last time I was awake, humans were still living in houses made of wood and riding on horseback," she tells us.

"And what kind would that be?" Drake asks, reaching out his hand to stop me from turning the lock.

"Dragons," she responds.

"You're a dragon shifter?" I ask.

"Yes. One of the last I suspect, since I haven't felt any others recently, though that could also be due to my lack of strength," she tells us. I turn the key despite Drake's attempts to stop me and open the cage.

"Will you accompany us back to our home? We have a friend who needs to meet you," I ask.

"Friend? What kind of friend?" she asks me in turn.

"A dragon, actually. He's been off searching for more of his kind. But I'm sure he will return soon." as I speak, her eyes light up with excitement.

"Another dragon?"

I chuckle. "Yes. His name is Andres. And he..."

She cuts me off. "Andres?" I bob my head. "Is his dragon gray and looks to be made of stone?"

"Yes..." I respond skeptically.

"Oh, please take me to him right away!" She says as she grabs onto my arm. If I didn't know better, I'd say that she knows him.

"I promise we will. I just need to try and find something in here before we go," I tell her.

"What are you looking for? Perhaps I could help."

"I don't really know. A map or papers pointing to the location of a laboratory of some kind," she goes pale.

"Why would you want to go there? It's an evil, evil place."

"You've been there?" Drake asks.

"Briefly. And I never intend to return," she tells us.

"Would you be able to lead us there?" I question.

At the same time Drake asks, "Are there other supernaturals being held there?"

She nods sullenly. "I can. And yes, there are all kinds. Any kind of supernatural that you could think of is being kept there so they can do these strange things to them. Poking and prodding them. They only kept me there for a short time, and when I refused to shift for them, they sent me here for 'conditioning', as they called it. The man who keeps me here is almost worse than the men in the white coats at the laboratory."

"That man is dead," I inform her.

"Good. I hope he suffered. But I saw him moving that board in the ceiling sometimes, placing things up there. Maybe it is what you are looking for," she points to one of the drop ceiling tiles.

I grab a chair and climb up, moving the tile easily, finding a ledger of some sort with a bunch of loose papers. Among those papers is a letter addressed to me, and I pale. Drake rushes over and notices what I'm looking at.

"We can give you a minute if you want," he offers.

"No. I'm not sure I want to read it. Let's go home and sort through everything later," I tell him, and that's exactly what we do. We drive home in silence, other than River's constant questions about everything: cellphones, cars, airplanes. It seems she is a sponge, wanting to soak in all the information she can. So, I did what every responsible adult would do; I introduced her to Google and YouTube. After providing her with a pair of earbuds, that is.

"Are you okay?" Drake asks me.

"I'm not sure, actually. I mean, I knew he wasn't a good man, but he was still my father, you know? Maybe it was naïve of me to think that he didn't keep anyone else in there after Dru, but that girl has been in there for two years, at least," I spin in my seat and look at River, her eyes wide as she watches something on the phone. "How many times did I walk by that shed and not know?

I'm just as much of a monster as he was, even if it was just because I chose not to see things that were right in front of me."

"You are not responsible for this. And you are most definitely not a monster. No one can blame you for not wanting to return to that shed after all you witnessed with Drusilla," he gives my hand a squeeze.

"You have to say those things as my mate," I chuckle.

"No, I don't. Just like I don't have to tell you that your ass doesn't look fat in those black leggings you love so much," he jokes trying to distract me.

"My black leggings make my ass look fat?" I feign shock.

"Yes, they do. But you knew that already. You also know just how much I love how your ass looks in them. It's why you wear them when you feel particularly frisky," he brings my hand up to his mouth and places a kiss on it.

"You've caught me," I giggle and slide over as close as I can get with the center console in the way and snuggle into him.

As the sun begins to rise on our drive, we decide to head to Alaric and Phoebe's. The coven still doesn't know that Drake and I can walk in the sun, and we are intent on keeping it that way. We have tried some experiments with my blood and Dru to see if drinking it was the key. But even after an entire pint, she wasn't able to withstand any type of UV ray. It has to be something else.

"We are going to a friend's first. Don't worry, you will be safe there," I say to River after patting her knee to get her attention.

"Wait. The sun is up and you two aren't burning," she points out. Drake and I share a quick look.

"You can't tell anyone this. But when Drake and I bonded, and I was turned, we found out that we are able to walk in the daylight. We don't know why or how. But we need to keep it a secret for as long as possible. Okay?" I tell her.

"That is so cool," she responds. Typical teenager. Wait. Is she a teenager? Shit, we should've asked how old she is before giving her unrestricted access to YouTube.

"How old are you?" I ask.

"I suppose to your standards, I would be eleven or twelve. But if you included the years I've been asleep, I would be much older than that." So around the same age as Riley. Maybe she'll be more comfortable staying with Alaric and Phoebe where there are kids her age.

"The friends we are going to visit have a son about your age," I tell her, and she begins to bounce in her seat.

"A child?" she questions.

I chuckle at her once again. "Of course. Weren't there any supernatural children before your slumber?"

"Not really. There weren't very many of us left when we all went to slumber. Uncle Andres convinced my mom and dad to set me to sleep away from them to keep me safe. He said that hunters were after us and that I would be safer sleeping alone," she says solemnly.

"Wait. Did you say Uncle Andres?" I ask.

She nods. "I wondered if you were going to catch that. Andres is my mother's brother."

"Well, shit. I guess the world really is small," I say with a smile. Not that I'm one to keep score or anything. Oh, what am I saying? Of course, I am. But now that I have saved Andres' niece, he owes me one, or a hundred, depending on what she means to him. Seems like Uncle Andres is going to be giving me some information I need about that prophecy he's always so secretive of. It's the least he can do after this.

As suspected, Andres isn't there when we arrive, but Alaric and Phoebe are. We introduce River to the boys and, as quickly as we arrived, they take off to play. While Phoebe rushes around finding clothing and other necessities for River, Alaric and Drake sit and go over the papers found in the shed while I sneak out onto the porch to read the letter from my father.

I sit on the porch swing and steel myself for what I'm about to read. My father was never the type to write letters, so I don't know what to expect.

Rayne,

If you're reading this, it means things didn't go as planned, and I'm dead. I hope that this letter finds its way to you somehow.

I know I wasn't the father you deserved, but I want you to know that although I may not have said it, I love you more than life itself. And because of that, there are some things you should know, things I've kept from you...

I raise my wet eyes from the letter, not knowing how to process what it says. He wrote that he loves me more than life itself, yet I have barely grieved for him. What kind of daughter does that make me? After taking a few shaky breaths and wiping my eyes, I go back to reading.

Your mother was not killed by a vampire. In fact, I have no idea what happened to her. One day she was here, and the next she was gone.

. . .

What? It was all bullshit like I thought. Fury rises in me unlike I've ever known, and I want to crumple the letter in my hands. I force myself to continue.

What you must understand is that in those days, I was much like you: less committed to our cause than I should have been, less on guard.

When I met your mother, it was like the heavens opened and created an angel just for me. She was everything I could have dreamed for, and we were truly happy for a time. Then we had you, and our world was complete. The two of you were everything to me.

But like all good things, it had to come to an end. You see, your mother was keeping a secret from me. A secret that jeopardized my entire belief system. When I found out, I was furious. I didn't understand how I didn't see it before, how I was so blind. I rushed home to confront her but when I got there, she was gone. No trace of her to be found. Except a note telling me that she loved us both and would see us again in this life or the next.

After that day, I recommitted myself to the cause. I found solace in rigorous training and shut myself off emotionally. Even from you. That is my only regret from this life, that I didn't tell you every single day just how much I loved you and how proud you made me.

As for your mother's secret, you'll have to figure that one out on your own. After all, it's not my secret to tell.

She left this note addressed to you before she left. I don't know what it means but I know you will be able to figure it out.

I love you more than there are stars in the sky and fish in the sea.

The light of the moon will set you free.

When you need me, I will be there.

When the time comes, you will know where.

When you find me, you will see.

There is so much more to you, that which comes from me.

Forever your loving father, may we meet in the next life.

Dad.

I re-read the letter over a dozen times. I am having a hard time believing that the same man who raised me also wrote this. How could the cold-hearted father I knew have written something so touching? And what is that riddle at the end from my mother? None of this makes any sense. I'm more confused now than I have ever been.

I fold the letter back up and slip it into my pocket. Maybe eventually I'll be able to figure it out, but right now there are a bunch of supernaturals being experimented on who need my help. I sit at the table while Alaric and Drake fill me in on what they found in the papers.

It turns out that we don't need River to lead us to the facility. My father kept a detailed map and blueprints of the entire lab. Now all we need to do is gather our army and make our plan.

Watch out, hunters. We're coming for you.

Epilogue

Drusilla

When Drake and Rayne didn't return this morning after the trip to her father's, I knew where they would be. Whenever they get caught out in daylight, the first place they go is to the pack. After all, there is a limited amount of people who know their secret.

Just as the sun sets, I am out the door and zooming my way to Alaric and Phoebe's house. As I run through the forest, I reflect. It wasn't that long ago that I would have scoffed at anyone who told me I'd be out running in the forest, alone, if at all. The scars from my time in captivity may have faded, but the emotional damage remains. It's hard to trust again after being betrayed by someone you cared about. Sure, I had only met the boy the night before, but in those brief hours, I thought I found something real. I thought he cared for me the same as I had for him. The notion even crossed my mind that he could have been my mate. I can't believe how wrong I was.

But since Rayne has returned to my life, I can't explain the way she's changed me. I have a renewed interest in life. Not just living for the sake of being alive. But living to experience things.

After all, the chances of us ever reconnecting were slim. If the goddess deemed fit to place us back into one another's lives, it must be for a reason, and I, for one, will not be taking it for granted. The fact that she is now my sister, for all intents and purposes, mated to my brother, is another matter entirely. They say the gods work in mysterious ways, and that was proven right when they mated my hunter-hating brother with the last of the Chasen Hunter bloodline.

I slow my pace and leisurely walk toward the house, taking in the scenery. It's such a beautiful night: clear sky, millions of stars shining with a thumbnail moon. So perfect. The only thing that would make it more perfect is if I found my mate. A pang of loneliness seeps into me, a feeling I'm still trying to get used to again. After locking myself away for so long, I had gotten used to it, but over the last couple of weeks, I became accustomed to being surrounded by friends and family. With the hunter threat over, and Drake and Rayne in their honeymoon phase, I've been alone a lot more than not. But I would never begrudge the happiness they have found in one another.

As I walk through the trees and the house comes into view, I see that large dragon shifter standing on the porch embracing a young girl, and I quickly hide behind one of the trees. I don't know what it is about him that makes the butterflies in my stomach go haywire, but gods above, if he isn't the most handsome man I've ever seen. The feelings he incites in me are both foreign and exciting. And I haven't quite figured out what to do about them yet.

I close my eyes with my back up against the tree, contemplating my next move. Sure, I've been around him before, but never alone or with only one or two people. What would I say?

"Drusilla?" I hear a rumble of a voice say my name from right in front of me. When I open my eyes, he's standing so close I can feel the heat radiating off his body.

"Yes?" my voice squeaks out. What the fuck was that? I sound like a mouse.

"I've been hoping to talk to you alone," he begins.

"You have?" I ask.

"Yes. I wanted to talk to you about us?" he says.

Again, my voice squeaks out. "Us?"

"Yes. And the fact that you're my..." Before he can finish, I rush off. I have a feeling I know what he's going to say. But I'm not ready for that. As much as I would love for him to finish that sentence, scoop me up, and fly off into the night, I know I need to love myself before I can love another, and I'm not quite there yet.

I turn around once I reach the door and see the confusion on his face while he stands by the tree. I vow to be ready soon. Soon I will be able to love another, and if Andres was going to say what I think he was, it will be him.

* * *

Want more from the Westwood Pack?
Of course, you do!
Information on Book 6, Dragon's Destiny here:
https://fdfairauthor.wixsite.com/website

About the Author

F.D. Fair is the author of the Westwood Pack Series. As an avid reader of Paranormal Romance Novels for the past 20 years, she turned her love of everything paranormal into steamy True Mate novels with a twist.

F.D. Fair lives and works in southern Ontario, Canada and

spends her time when she is not working or writing with the loves of her life—Her husband and 3 boys.

She is as weird as they come but is proud of it. Embracing her weirdness makes for some great stories.

Sign up for FD Fair's Newsletter:
https://dashboard.mailerlite.com/forms/76323/58096238431569310/share

Make sure to stalk her...

Instagram:
https://www.instagram.com/f.d.fairauthor
Facebook:
https://www.facebook.com/profile.php?id=100071688648516
Goodreads:
https://www.goodreads.com/author/show/21734156.F_D_Fair
Twitter:
https://twitter.com/FdFair
Bookbub:
https://www.bookbub.com/authors/f-d-fair

More from Foundations

www.FoundationsBooks.net

Spectacle by S.J. Pierce

~Dystopian~

GET IT HERE: https://www.sjpiercebooks.com/full-width-page-2/

International Bestselling Author S.J. Pierce delivers an exciting and refreshingly unique story in the Dystopian genre. Hunger Games and Divergent fans will devour this one...

We might be called Savages, but they're the real monsters.

Miles of open water separate us from New America, a place we once lived before we were exiled.

Welcome to our hell: a nameless island with every terror imaginable.

When my father's secret surfaced - that he was one of many aliens who took refuge on Earth - the humans rebelled against us, and the President saw their abilities as a threat.

My father and human mother paid the ultimate price.

The rest of us were shipped here to fight for our lives against rattlesnakes, boars, and mountain lions. A punishment for our one and only crime - being different.

Now I fight against a bitterness and rage I can barely control...

So when our Elders call a meeting with me and my friends, we know something big is in the works, and we'll all soon have to make a choice: stay here on the island, or sneak back into America and execute a plan for liberation...which could cost us our lives. But when a life of danger and destruction has been all you've ever known, throwing yourself into the fire seems not only natural but necessary.

I want to see the President and his conspirators pay.

Find out what happens when vengeance and dark intentions collide in this "powerful" and "refreshingly unique" Dystopian series. Binge-read today! Complete series available now...

www.ingramcontent.com/pod-product-compliance
Lightning Source LLC
LaVergne TN
LVHW091040080826
845145LV00002B/573
* 9 7 8 1 6 4 5 8 3 1 1 3 6 *